Beyond the Fells

Beyond the fell

Beyond the Fells

Wyn Jackman

Matador
9 Priory Business Park,
Wistow Road, Kibworth Beauchamp,
Leicestershire. LE8 0RX
Tel: 0116 279 2299
Email: books@troubador.co.uk
Web: www.troubador.co.uk/matador
Twitter: @matadorbooks

ISBN 978 1785890 024

British Library Cataloguing in Publication Data.
A catalogue record for this book is available from the British Library.

Printed and bound in the UK by TJ International, Padstow, Cornwall
Typeset in 11pt Aldine401 BT by Troubador Publishing Ltd, Leicester, UK

Matador is an imprint of Troubador Publishing Ltd

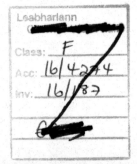

MIX
Paper from
responsible sources
FSC
www.fsc.org
FSC® C013056

For my family

Chapter 1

Appleby, March 1839

'To be transported beyond the seas – seven years.' The judge's gravelly voice echoed round the court at the Spring Assizes. A barely audible intake of breath sighed through the courtroom, like a summer breeze whispering through the cotton grass on the fells; but within seconds quiet resignation had settled on the faces of those gathered in support of their neighbours. This was a characteristic response from this breed of dignified, taciturn men as they struggled to make sense of this harsh sentence. Tom glanced sideways at his young companion and watched the colour drain from his cheeks.

Outside the light was fading on a bitter March morning. Icy rain bombarded the windows of the courthouse, and a horse-drawn cart clattered along the wet cobbles. The clock on St Lawrence's Church chimed the hour as the judge busied himself gathering his documents. The jury, an unrepresentative collection of landowners, successful farmers and a parish priest or two, shuffled to their feet mumbling approval at the sentence.

The prisoner, sandy-haired and stubbled, with a ragged scarf knotted round his neck, dropped his eyes to the ground. A jagged white scar, high on his cheek, caught the light of the

1

lantern on the judge's table and a tracery of lines, etched by the sun and bitter winds, was evident on his forehead. He wiped away cold sweat with the back of his hand as he was ushered from the dock. On reaching the door he raised his shoulders, turned his slim frame towards the gallery and fixed troubled blue eyes on his son – a long, enigmatic stare. Transferring his gaze to Tom, he raised a clenched fist, cleared his throat and bellowed:

'Ee leave my wife and lad alone, ee sly bugger. There's nowt for you at Highburn and never has been. I hope ee rot in hell.' Two constables wrestled him to the ground and applied handcuffs. Tom pushed a strand of brown shoulder-length hair behind his ear, and slid a calming arm round Edward's shoulders. The boy withdrew from his touch, instinctively as though from a flickering flame on a mountain fire. A fire he and his father had shared through many a long night as they supported their meagre flock through the rigours of lambing.

'I'll be back afore ee know it and put all of ee out of business,' was the prisoner's parting shot to the small dishevelled group now assembled on the highway outside the courthouse.

Tom Shaw had been away from his county of birth for five years, serving as a curate in an East Lancashire mill town. Here he shared a background with many of his flock who were from rural stock similar to his own. His temporary return to Westmorland came about when he received a subpoena to attend the trial of Joseph Teasdale from Shap, in the county of Westmorland. Jos stood indicted upon a charge of having, during the month of June 1838, stolen three sheep; the property of his neighbour Jacob Armstrong.

Tom had been unable to shake off the sense of foreboding which came with this summons. He had slept badly, struggling in a twilight world between full and part consciousness in which negative thoughts spun in ever-decreasing circles. He had a long history with both families and was in anguish over doing the right thing.

The case for the prosecution opened with the testimony of Jacob Armstrong, a bent septuagenarian with abundant white whiskers.

'I'm a small farmer, struggling as we all are. Last summer I brought down my sheep from the fells and I counted them when they were washed. There is sometimes a mistake in counting sheep, but I can swear I made no mistake on this occasion as nummers are now very low. I had forty-six ewes and three wethers,' he mumbled in a state of mild confusion. 'I counted them again in the sheepfold at the last clipping and I only had forty-three ewes – I was missing four… no, no, three. I'll swear I had that nummer.' Good-natured merriment rippled through the chilly room. 'There are a good many potholes on the fells and I searched them with my son for a full day, looking in bogs and crevices for any dead sheep. I was looking for sheep with my ear smit and a blue mark on the wool. But I couldna find a trace. What we did come across were three shorn sheep. Three li'l ewes with part of the ear removed, running on the heaf with Jos Teasdale's flock. I went straight away to call on Teasdale, and 'ave it out with him.' He paused and looked defiantly at Jos.

'Ee shouted at me, waved a stick – a stick, at an old man like me – and told me to get off his land. So I called again later with my son when I knew he was up at the slate quarry, and we were able to look over the fleeces rolled up in his barn. There were thirty-nine, and three, I swear, were of a lighter colour than the others. The fleeces of my sheep are pale because of the salving I use – my great-grandfather's Scottish recipe. I can recognise my fleeces anywhere. I know they came from my sheep.'

A murmur of low conversation reverberated round the court as Jacob Armstrong sat back on the bench, and looked about him with an air of self-satisfaction. The chatter subsided and the deposition was handed to the prisoner for his response. Jos took the document and raised it in an apparent attempt to catch the light from the easterly windows.

'I can read the writing sir, certainly I can, but I can't see it very well. I can perhaps with spectacles.'

Quiet, ironic laughter spread through the court and a pair of spectacles was handed over. Tom watched Edward drop his eyes to the floor and dig his grimy nails into his hands to maintain his composure. His heart went out to his boyhood friend who, despite his circumstances, was still trying to keep up appearances.

Jos studied the papers with exaggerated concentration as he combed his fingers through his lank hair, and stroked the light stubble on his cheeks. He replied in his soft dale voice, choosing his words carefully.

'When I brought down my sheep for salving there were thirty-nine, and on that occasion the priest, Thomas Shaw from Halesden, was with me and can confirm the number. I was pleased to find, sir, that I still had the same number when my son and I brought them down from the tops for the annual clipping.'

The defence called upon the Reverend Shaw for a character reference. Tom's heart thumped wildly as he stood before the judge and took the oath. He drew a deep breath. His voice, now devoid of the vernacular or any local twang, carried authority and filled the hushed room.

'My family have worked and socialised with the Teasdales for many years. Joseph and I were inseparable boyhood companions. Circumstances have meant we have seen little of each other in recent times, but from my past knowledge of the plaintiff he is a good man who participated at a high level as a wrestler and sportsman, activities in which honesty is paramount. He has always worked diligently and unfailingly on behalf of his family.'

'And were you with the plaintiff on the day of the salving?'

'Yes sir, I was on a visit to see my family.'

'And did you witness the counting of the sheep?'

There was a discernible pause before Tom gave his reply with grinding weariness. 'No sir – when I left the sheep had been herded into the intake furthest from the farm towards Western Beacon. Jos and I didn't leave the yard during my visit.'

The case rumbled on for another ten minutes, with the prosecution calling witnesses from neighbouring farmers to provide evidence. Some became confused under cross-examination as accusations were made of damaged ear smits, and suspected tampering with the identifying marks on the animals' fleeces. Each witness repeated the same sorry tale of straitened circumstances, hardship and suspicion amongst a community that had previously always pulled together.

The judge, in passing sentence, emphasised that had the plaintiff been able to supply a witness to confirm his story he might not have been in this sorry state.

'The evidence is stacked against you,' he declared. 'For plundering a neighbour's property I have no alternative but to find you guilty.'

Tom rested his head in his hands while the sentence was read out.

Chapter 2

'He didna, he didna do it,' Edward repeated as he and Tom braced themselves against the northerly wind for the trek home across the fells.

'Aye lad, that's what you think…' Tom didn't finish his sentence, but bent down to pick up his drawstring bag. They lingered, some feet apart, until Jacob Armstrong and his supporters, some astride their ponies, melted into the cloud cover. Once the occasional guffaw could no longer be heard they set off.

The desolation of the landscape mirrored Edward's despair, and flurries of hail stung his face like the grit scattered from the farm-carts trundling along the Carlisle road. He pulled down his hat and lowered his head against the onslaught for the twenty-five-mile hike which stretched ahead. In the space of an hour his life had been turned upside down. His father was to be sent to the penal colony of Australia and now he and his mother would have to cope alone. He shivered uncontrollably, although whether from the cold or the anger which welled up inside he couldn't be sure.

Edward had always liked his Uncle Tom, and looked forward to his visits for the insights they provided into life beyond his circumscribed world. As a small boy he had listened eagerly to Tom's tales of Robin Hood in Sherwood Forest. In more recent times, his knowledge of the discoveries being made by British scientists and explorers had been the main focus of their conversation.

Edward was also aware that Tom made his mam happy. She would coax her hair into place and straighten her clothes when she saw him approaching, laugh merrily at any small witticism, and blush when he complimented her on her cooking. Knowing what store she set by the church and the Bible, Edward had always assumed this special affinity had developed because of Tom's calling as a priest. Until today his father had seemed indifferent to these small attentions, so Tom had been stunned by his outburst in court. For the first time he had cause to question the relationship between his parents and Tom. Moreover, having heard the evidence, there now dwelt a doubt in his mind as to his father's innocence. He struggled to control the emotion in his voice.

'Da used to tell me you and he were like brothers. I thought brothers trusted each other, supported each other, did right by each other. Why didn't ee give him his alibi?'

Finally, the question Tom had been dreading. He knew he had abandoned Jos to his fate and Edward deserved an explanation, but he struggled to find the words.

'I'd sworn on the Bible to tell the truth,' he said defensively.

'That's a bloody weak excuse,' Edward lashed out. Succumbing to suppressed anger, he shouted and beat his fists against Tom's chest, tears of frustration shining in his dark eyes. 'Are priests always so feeble?' He attempted a punch and Tom staggered backwards. 'How do ee think Mam is going to manage now?'

Tom, still a physically strong man, overpowered his

young assailant and held him in an armlock until he had quieted down. 'I was as shocked as you by the sentence,' he said. 'I would never wish you or your family any harm. You must know that.'

'Ee was my da, and you were his friend,' Edward responded sulkily.

They tramped on over familiar territory, giving Tom plenty of time to revisit the intervening years and analyse how they had reached this crisis. Every twist in the lane, every dry stone wall and hollow oak held memories of his carefree childhood. As the track dropped down, following the margins of the river, his mind drifted back to a time when he and Jos were ten years old. It was spring and the riverbank was spangled with wild daffodils, their pale heads moving in rhythm with the soft breeze. His sister Lucy was with them and, as always, Jos was on the lookout for a free meal.

'Luk at that beauty.' Jos motioned to his companions to keep quiet. They stepped back into the shadows as a large brown trout glided serenely upstream. Jos flashed them a grin as he rolled up his sleeve, revealing a grubby, freckled arm. They watched him lie down on his stomach and slip his hands into the water. A quick flick of his wrist, and the unsuspecting creature took cover under the overhang of the bank where Jos lay in wait.

'Gently, little fella,' he murmured as he located the bemused fish. With a deft and delicate stroke of its underbelly he tightened his hands round the gills, and with a shout of triumph threw the trout onto the bank.

'Congratulations, Jos!' said Lucy. 'Ee can do that better than anyone else I know.'

Not to be outdone, Tom had shouted, 'Run for it! I can see the bailiff up beyond the spinney.'

Jos had slapped the fish on a stone and slipped it, wet and slimy, inside his jacket. He was about to take to his heels when Tom laughed. 'Caught yer! Your mam will be asking what the bad smell is when ee tek that jacket off.'

Jos raised his hands like the horns of a bull and charged at Tom. They wrestled good-naturedly on the grassy bank and Lucy wandered off to pick some daffodils. When she returned, clutching a large bunch, Jos had a puzzled look on his face.

'Why did ee pick those?' he asked.

'They're for Mam, she likes us t'bring her flowers. Why don't you gather some for your mother?'

'Nah,' he replied, selecting a stone and spinning it across the water.

They were about to head away from the river when Jos hesitated, crouched down and started picking. Slowly and carefully, so as not to break any of the delicate heads, he amassed an armful of golden daffodils. He raised his eyes to Lucy and a wide smile spread across his face. With their bouquets, and the trout safely stowed away, they set off home.

On reaching Ravendale Lucy ran ahead. 'Look what I've brought you, Mam.' She thrust the flowers at her mother. Their mother's kind eyes glistened with pleasure as she hugged her daughter and patted Tom's shoulder.

'Daffodils for Easter, how lovely.' She poured water into a stone pot and carefully arranged the top-heavy stems. 'The beginning of a new year. Let's hope it'll be good for all of us.' She included Jos in her smile as he stood shyly in the doorway. Tom remembered so clearly the questioning look on his face as his eyes moved uncomprehendingly from Lucy to Mam.

Lucy had stayed back at the farm when the two

boys struck off across the stepping-stones at Kirk Gate towards Jos's home. As they climbed the land became increasingly ill-drained, and the lack of tree cover offered little protection from the winds that blew from the north and east. A flock of rooks and jackdaws dipped and called overhead, disturbed by their arrival. As if in answer, Nell, the Teasdales' sheepdog, came bounding out to meet them. Jos fondled her ears as they crouched to enter the homestead.

Tom remembered being struck by the chill and yawning bareness of the place; no rag rugs on the hard earth floor, no pictures on the blackened walls. Edmond and Martha Teasdale sat wheezing in semi-darkness, either side of a smoky peat fire, each clutching a mug of warm ale. A sour smell of unwashed wool and damp dogs hung in the air. Jos stepped forward hesitantly, suppressed excitement lighting up his face.

'I picked these for ee, Mam.' He laid the flowers on her lap. Martha Teasdale scowled.

'What the 'ell do ee expect me to do with these?'

'The lad's goin' soft on us like 'is brother,' said his father scornfully as he swept the daffodils to the ground. Tom saw his friend's lip tremble.

'Ee can both go to hell,' Jos shouted, slapping the fish on the table and pushing past Tom. With Nell at his side he stormed off.

The incident had never been mentioned since that day, and Tom struggled now to remove the image of the situation he had been forced to confront.

A break in the cloud let a thin shaft of sunlight play on the trunks of the trees, and a robin fluttered ahead of them on the path. Darting from left to right, he seemed to be enjoying their company and was a welcome distraction. Edward eventually broke the silence.

'Mam won't even be able to say goodbye.' He gave Tom a cautious glance, as if unsure of his reaction to his outburst.

'She will... you both will.' Tom's response was matter-of-fact. 'It'll be a while before your da is allocated a ship. You'll have a chance to visit while he's in the lockup in Carlisle.'

'Won't they send him straight to a port? Whitehaven, mebbe. We could p'raps get to see him there.'

'He'll be bound for Australia so London's more likely – somewhere on the Thames.' Having re-established communication Tom was anxious to keep the conversation going. 'The husband of one of my parishioners in Halesden was deported to Van Diemen's Land. He sailed out from Woolwich.'

'What did ee do?'

'He was one of a gang who pulled the plugs on the boilers at a local mill; letting out the steam and bringing the machinery to a standstill.'

'That's criminal damage. Ee deserved a long sentence.'

'He didn't see it that way. For generations his family had been handloom weavers and he thought he was doing the right thing, protecting his job so he could support his wife and children.'

'How long did ee get?'

'Seven years, the same as your da.'

They fell silent again as they scrambled past a shallow waterfall on the river. With the sound of gushing water Tom was once again transported to another time, when he was a young man lazing with Jos and Lucy on the springy turf by Ravendale Force. The mist from the falls was bouncing on their faces, and the caressing sun building a tan on Lucy's slender legs.

Tom had been reading to them from a book the poet William Wordsworth had given to their brother Jonathon. Inside, used as a marker, was a tattered piece of parchment on which was written the last stanza of a poem. The final line flashed into his mind.

'Would plant thee where yet thou might'st blossom again.'[1]

It buzzed, repeatedly, in his head. Could this simple sentence be a turning point for the Teasdales? Suddenly elated, he sensed something positive he could share with Edward and Hannah. Maybe, as the iron door on the prison closed behind Jos, it would open another on the far side of the world, in a new land of opportunity.

Edward broke into his thoughts. 'How long will the voyage tek?'

'Around three and a half months, on a good run. It depends on the wind and tides, and how long they stop to take on provisions. The weather can be tricky in the southern straits.' Tom stooped to retie his bootlace. He lightened his voice as he continued. 'The sooner he gets there the sooner he can return home… or you could both join him in a few years' time' once he has earned his freedom. It could be a God-given chance to start a new life.'

Tom sensed a wistful tone in Edward's reply. 'Mam will never leave the dale, except by the Corpse Road.'

'In that case we must hope he is allocated a passage as speedily as possible.'

'Ee'll want his fiddle. It's the most important thing in the world to him.'

'Of course he will, and they're sure to let him take it. A musician on board will be an asset for the captain; someone to entertain those below deck.'

'Even if ee plays hymns?' Tom was forced to smile.

'Especially if he plays hymns.'

They were now close to home, and their way led across a bridge to a gravelled road, running parallel to the River Lowther. A family of Herdwicks meandered towards them chased along by a pedlar, his bag of wares slung across his back and a tartan cap perched jauntily on his head.

'Ye breed some mighty queer mutton round here, maister,' he addressed them good-naturedly. 'Are these scrawny creatures sheep or mountain goats?'

Edward gave a spirited response. 'Ee can mock, but ee'll never taste sweeter meat. You should try my mam's mutton pies.'

'Sounds like a gud offer to me, lad. Where d'ye live?'

'Highburn, t'other side of the beck.'

'I ken it well. Tell your mammy Jimmy McDonald will be calling on her next time he passes this way; but it might not be for a few years.' He laughed heartily. 'I'll barter a few ribbons for a good mutton pie any day.'

Following this brief exchange of banter with the itinerant Edward's spirits lifted, and he was encouraged to look around. On high ground, almost obliterated by the mist, the towering turrets and crenellations of a castle loomed. As a small boy he had imagined that this fairytale building must be the home of a prince, or even a king. Now he knew it was the country home of the earls of Lonsdale, built with the riches amassed by the family from their ownership of coal and iron mines, and the port of Whitehaven from where the cargo was shipped. His father, and most of the farmers in the district, leased their land from the earl, and his Uncle Simeon was employed in the stables.

The clatter of a horse's hooves, approaching at a lively trot, caused them to step back off the carriageway to let a stranger pass. The horse's coat was polished like wet coal and the brass attachments on its bridle shone gold in the murky light. The rider reined down to a walking pace and called out as he drew near.

'Edward... is it Edward Teasdale?'

'Who's asking?' Edward winced at the hard elbow in his side as Tom answered on his behalf.

'Yes sir, this is Edward Teasdale.'

A middle-aged man pulled up and addressed Edward. 'How did your father fare in court today?'

Edward looked wonderingly at the man's pale muffler before dropping his eyes to his immaculate gloves and soft leather riding boots. He took a moment before mumbling, 'They're sending him to Australia.'

'Oh, I'm so sorry,' replied the rider. That will be a wrench for you and your mother.'

'We'll manage, thank ee sir.' Edward stared at the ground.

'I'll let Simeon know.' He turned his mount. 'Come up to the estate office if you need work, I'm sure we can find something for you at the castle.' Without acknowledging Tom he set off at a canter, retracing his path towards the bridge. Edward watched, bemused, as the heir to the estate receded into the enveloping gloom.

'It'll be down to you now Edward, to make your mam's life easier and plan for the future.' Tom looked meaningfully at his young companion. With the dark shadow on his upper lip and his broad shoulders, he already had the appearance of a grown man. He waited for a response, but as it was not forthcoming he held his counsel.

Through the mist the moorland farmhouse, with its few acres of boggy wetland, came into view. Jos's forbears had occupied the same property for generations, shepherding their sheep which roamed the common land. Now his son spent most of his waking hours working alongside him on the fells.

Edward put his fingers to his lips and gave a long, low whistle. Out of the gloom came a collie, limping towards them on three legs, furiously wagging her wet tail. Edward bent down, inspected her paw and scraped away a thorn.

'You take Meg and check the sheepfolds while I find your mam and explain what's happened,' said Tom.

Ducking to enter the homestead, he found Hannah sitting at her wheel in front of the window, treadling away in the fading light. The single room was sparse but tidy. Bunches of dried lavender and rosemary hung from the bar above the fire, and a sweet smell of smouldering peat filled the air. She had worked hard to turn the ramshackle building into a welcoming home. Tom joined her on the window seat and broke the news of the trial. Hannah listened attentively, absorbing the information, but her demeanour revealed nothing. No surprise. No anger. No sadness. She continued rhythmically working the pedal and twisting the wool.

'You'll be staying over?' was her only comment.

Tom hesitated. He could think of nothing more tempting, but Jos's words, spoken directly to him as he sat in court, erupted in his brain. 'D'you want me to?'

'That's a question you surely don't need to ask.'

'How d'you think Edward will react?'

'I doubt he'll be back.' She seemed unconcerned as she directed him to the clap bread and malt whisky laid out on the table. After a long day, which had been both physically and emotionally draining, Tom welcomed the food and strong liquor.

'This is a lovely spread. Tell me, Hannah, were you expecting Jos back?'

'I thought it might be a prison sentence, but not transportation,' she replied, evading the direct question.

As the daylight faded he recounted the conversation he had had with Edward on the way home. 'D'you want me to go and look for him? It's a miserable night out there.'

'Ee'll be best left on his own to think things through,' Hannah replied. 'Ee's like his da in many ways – ee just shuts down. If ee comes back ee'll sleep in the hay barn with the dogs. Ee always does that when out late, so as not to disturb Jos and me.'

She took Tom's hand and extinguished the taper. Unfaltering, she pulled off his jacket and unbuttoned his braces, letting his trousers fall to the ground. She slipped out of her own outer garments and pulled back the patchwork coverlet, inviting him into the only bed in the homestead. To succumb to an intimacy he had been denied for many years; to submit to the sensation of having a woman's naked flesh so close to his; to once again feel Hannah slide her cool fingers down the length of his spine…

'I'll tek the floor, lass,' he said, giving her hand a gentle squeeze.

The following morning Hannah rose early. The wind had turned to the south-west and there was the first hint of spring in the damp air. She busied herself feeding the hens, collecting the eggs and carting a basket of peat turfs from the stack to feed the fire. Weary from the weight, she rested on a tree stump overlooking the stepping-stones Jos and Edward had laid the previous summer, across a marshy stretch of footpath. It had been a gruelling task, and taken them many hours to complete. She felt confident that Jos had taught Edward everything he needed to know about running the farm. They could manage – so long as her son chose to stay in the dale.

A raven took flight from the edge of a crag, and flew eastwards down the valley towards her. An inky silhouette against the dove-grey sky, it circled and called overhead. Tom stepped up behind her and pecked her on the cheek. His beard tickled her lips in passing and made her giggle.

'Luk, there goes the devil's bird,' she said, pushing back her untamed mass of flaxen curls. 'There's many of them hereabouts. I canna help wondering what future that wicked crow can see fer us all.' She shielded her eyes against the rising sun as she looked skywards. 'It's nesting again on a ledge halfway up Black Crag. Jos thinks it may already have young.'

'He's probably right.' Tom settled himself beside her. 'They're usually the first.' He gave her an encouraging smile. 'And don't you worry about the ravens, Hannah. What bird did Noah send out from the ark to look for dry land?'

'Of course, yer reet,' she said with a quiet chuckle. 'And it's a chatty old bird – like others I know.'

From high above the crags the raven dropped like a vulture. She watched with dismay as it set about attacking a newly dead ewe, lying in the shadow of a boulder. It was one of the Teasdale flock. Again and again the raven swooped, pecking at the creature's eyes and pulling at the flesh.

'One less t'lamb this season.' She laid a plump hand over Tom's. 'How did it come to this, Tom?'

'You do understand I couldn't lie for him,' Tom said.

Hannah let his comment hang in the air as a clatter of loose stones from towards Black Crag made them look up. It was Edward and Meg slinking off in the direction of Harter Fell.

'Mebbe he's going to climb up to the nest, to destroy the young. That's what you and Jos would have done when you were young. You were always collecting bird's eggs, stones for catapults or sticks for bows and arrows.' She let her eyes glaze over as a second raven floated down to join its partner. Together the birds strutted, croaked and shook their shaggy throat feathers.

'Do you blame me?' Tom persisted, breaking into her thoughts. 'Your son does.'

'Nah, I can nivver blame you. Jos and I both knew our days here were numbered. Edward's young. Ee never said, but I think mebbe he had plans to move away. Now ee must be feeling trapped.'

'Things may work out better than you expect,' said Tom. 'It is said there are good opportunities for fit, industrious men in Australia. If Jos keeps his head down, which I'm sure he will, it'll only be a few years before he gets his freedom.'

'Jos is certainly a hard worker, and strong for his age,' Hannah agreed.

'Would you join him if he sent for you and Edward?'

She gave him no answer, but rose to her feet, brushed her apron down with her hands, and returned to the cottage.

Chapter 3

Ravendale, 1814

Tom Shaw was on the threshold of adult life and his spirits soared in anticipation of an exhilarating day of sport. The hunt was one of the highlights of the farming calendar, a test of stamina and resistance for the local men. Today he and his friends were eager to prove their physical ability to keep up with the field.

Misty, his Lakeland terrier, bounded at his side, her hindquarters quivering with restless excitement as a pale golden glow emerged from the mysterious darkness, the grey fells floating on a lake of mist. As the cloud rolled away a hidden world came into view: rabbits and sheep grazed together, and early birdsong filled the air.

Indistinguishable shapes morphed into the outlines of the huntsman and his hounds as the pack came into view. Gaining momentum, the dogs tacked from side to side across the short-cropped grassland bordering the beck, their noses bent close to the ground searching for a scent. Tom was watching for Tess, the hound his family had kennelled throughout the summer. Pale in colour, she was easy to identify.

Glancing ahead a distinct track snaked, like a black line drawn by a charcoal pencil, through the dew-soaked grass.

There was little doubt this was the trail created by some animal, and it may well be that of a mountain fox returning to his kennel somewhere high up among the heather and rocks. If so, the scent should still be strong.

A lass, sauntering along the path below, caught his eye. Her tousled blonde hair was blowing across her face, and her loose-weave gathered skirt clung to her buttocks, blown from behind by the westerly wind. It was Hannah. He watched, until she disappeared up the path which led to her cottage at the foot of the valley. There was something about her that he had failed to notice before. The thoughts she released in his head took him by surprise.

The last few hundred feet brought him to a flat plateau where Jos Teasdale, Luke Yarker and Richard Green sat on the sparse grass. 'You've taken yer time,' said Richard, with a knowing look. Tom grinned sheepishly.

'They've struck a good drag, we reckon they'll be making for Mossdale,' Jos added. Turning up their collars against the biting wind circulating at this higher level they headed off along the edge of a ridge, which teetered precariously over a steep drop. This was the quickest way to get ahead of the action.

'Stop!' Luke motioned with his hand. Fifty feet below, on a conveniently positioned bink, a vixen perched, warily surveying the valley below. They froze, until she sped off across the scree. Burnished and beautiful, her brush held high, she dodged from left to right, taunting her followers.

'There's a free spirit if ever I saw one,' said Luke in awe. 'She's going t'enjoy the chase as much as the hounds.'

The approaching pack was now in full cry and making for an overhanging outcrop of rock. Beyond, a gill gushed down, feeding the beck below. The troupe flew straight over the water, like a well-disciplined army – all but one wily, independent hound.

'Tess has broken off from the main pack!' shouted Tom. 'She must've lost the scent.'

'There she goes,' called out Richard. 'She's jumped the beck and turned upstream.' Their heads spun round. 'Luk, she's got the fox in her sight, she's scaling the gully.'

Mesmerised, they watched in admiration as fox and hound scrambled up the steep ascent, the overhanging foliage of juniper bushes and rowans providing cover. With her light body the vixen was more sure-footed than Tess, and used her strong claws to jump from ledge to ledge, avoiding the cascading water. As the lads clambered higher they hit the remains of the icy, crusted snow, locked in the crevices and protected from the sun.

'Come on Tess, show us what yer made of.' They roared their encouragement as the combatants scrabbled for footholds. Tom knew he could stand back no longer.

'I'm going after her.'

Breathing heavily, and with aching calves, he set about the perilous climb up the slimy wet rocks so as not to lose sight of the pair. He arrived just in time to see Tess sink her teeth into the loose flesh beneath the vixen's throat. The two animals rolled over and slid unceremoniously into a shallow pool at the side of the gill. Here they scuffled, limbs and water flailing in all directions, and then fell silent. Tess released her grip, and shaking herself vigorously hurtled towards Tom with a few eager barks before the herd instinct propelled her back to the pack. Meanwhile, the quarry lay wet and bedraggled, her head cradled on a mossy pillow of rock, a small jagged wound seeping blood from her neck.

Tom squeezed the water from his jacket sleeves. He

knew he had a story to tell. He had been the only one to witness the demise of the vixen.

'It's a kill,' he shouted from halfway up the gully to a rousing cheer from the bystanders.

'Well done, lad,' said the master of the hunt. 'One less to bother your lambs this year.'

The followers milled around and Anthony Wilder, the old Ravendale priest, held court while they waited for the carcase to be brought down. Anthony had hunted all his life. Now in his seventies, he was a fund of knowledge on the stamina and pace of different hounds. But all were in agreement that today's prize for a good nose and individual initiative should go to Tess.

The master delved inside his waistcoat. 'I've a letter here which needs delivering to Shap. There's fourpence for one of you to get it there by tomorrow morning,' he said, directing his comment towards the young men.

'I'll tek it,' Jos volunteered immediately. The sealed envelope and coins were handed over, and Jos slipped them into his jacket pocket.

'Have ee heard?' said Richard's father, Dick Green. 'Alfred Baxter is moving his family from Fellside to Manchester.'

Anthony shook his head in dismay. 'I knew they were having a hard time with such a large family to feed. No doubt he hopes the girls will be able to contribute by getting jobs in the mills.'

'They're going to tek the old man with them. It'll break his heart to leave the dale, but what else can they do?'

Tom, who had been following the conversation to this point, strolled off to see if there was any sign of his sister coming up from the valley.

Jos wandered over to join Tom. 'What are ee thinking aboot? How yer'll be the toast of the evening?'

'Nah, I won't be taking part in the festivities. Lucy will be coming along soon and we'll carry on to Ambleside. Jonathon needs our help to bring down his ewes for lambing.' Tom gave Jos a brotherly slap on the back. 'You can have my quota of ale.'

'That I will, and tek all the credit for Tess.' They both laughed as they stood side by side, surveying the barren spine of High Street.

'You can see for miles today,' said Tom. 'Just try to imagine, Jos, how it must've been for our ancestors as they crouched here amongst these crags, and watched the invading Roman centurions striding along that ridge. Horses silhouetted against a pale sky, shields glinting in the sunlight.'

Jos gave his friend a questioning look. 'They must've been scared witless,' he said. 'Just wondering who the strangers in uniform were and what was going t' happen next.'

'Life is different for every generation,' said Tom. 'I wonder what you and I will have to face?'

Jos stood quietly, fingering the envelope in his pocket, recognising that his friend was in a reflective mood. Finally he withdrew it, and asked casually, 'Tom, can ee help me? The ink seems to have smudged on this letter and I can't quite read the address. Can ee make out the name of the farm?'

Tom glanced over his shoulder. 'Thornthwaite. Thornthwaite Farm.'

'Aye, that's it.' He slipped it back in his jacket. 'Luk,' he said enthusiastically. 'Here come the girls.'

A high-spirited laugh and a holler from below announced the arrival of Alice Watkins and Lucy, their cheeks pink with the exertion of the climb. Both wore thick grey capes, under which Lucy carried a basket slung across her body.

Alice was not from these parts. With her strawberry-blonde hair, freckled arms and confident, teasing personality she was a source of intrigue to the local lads. Beguiling and promiscuous, she spoke with a Welsh lilt, and when her family were present chatted away in an unfamiliar language, much to the frustration of the natives.

Mining had expanded rapidly in the district, and many itinerant single men had been drawn to the area from as far afield as Wales and Cornwall. The Watkins boys, Dai and Bryn, had learned their trade as lead miners at Beddgelert, and moved north to the Mossdale slate quarry a couple of years back. When their mother and sister joined them, the family established roots by building a stone cottage on the open common. Alice had quickly integrated with the local youngsters, and bounced up to plant flirtatious kisses on the cheeks of the young men standing nearby.

Lucy, meanwhile, stopped by to chat with the Reverend Wilder, who knew all the youngsters from the dale and outlying farms, having combined teaching at the village school with the office of curate. Anthony had spent his entire life within twenty miles of where he was born; yet he was a well-read and educated man, able to converse on most of the topics of the day. His son, Stephen, now held the living at Ravendale.

'Tom and I are off t' Ambleside,' Lucy said, her eyes sparkling. 'It's the first time I've been so far from home.'

'You should have a good journey.' He smiled. 'The weather's set fair. You may also meet some interesting visitors when you get closer to Windermere. Give my best wishes to Jonathon. He was an excellent scholar and I'm proud he's making his way so successfully in the world.'

'Aye, I will.' She moved away to rejoin Alice and Jos, who had been hovering nearby, when Jos sidled over to the priest and once again pulled out the envelope.

'I've been given this t'deliver,' he said. 'I can see it's for Thornthwaite Farm, that's obvious, but I canna quite make out the name – the writing's not too clear.' He passed the letter to Anthony.

'It's addressed to the Lightwaters,' he said. 'Peter Lightwater.' Smoothing the surface, he handed it back.

'Aye of course, I can see it now.'

Alice let out a peal of laughter. 'No you can't, Jos, no use pretending. You haven't the schooling.'

Jos turned on her, his pupils dilated. 'Shut up,' he growled, 'and mind yer own fuckin' business.'

Those standing nearby stood speechless at his outburst; but Alice merely shrugged her shoulders and flounced away.

A long note from the huntsman's horn refocused their attention back to the hounds. The quarry was now a grey dog fox. The excitement intensified as the pack gained ground – until the fox dived, unexpectedly, into a well-known borran near the top of Harter Fell.

'The bugger's gone t'ground,' grumbled one of the followers. 'We'll have t'flush him out.'

Lucy joined those nearby as they hammered on the rocks with their sticks, and made a great hullabaloo. When this proved unsuccessful they released the terriers, who had been barking wildly and straining at their leashes. The game little dogs fought and tumbled over each other like boisterous puppies in their eagerness to get into the borran. Now the onlookers could do little except shout encouragement.

The men paced about as suppressed squeaks and barks echoed through the chambers, and the occasional rattle could be heard as a stone dislodged deep within the mountain. A fight underground could mean the end of the fox, or one of his pursuers. Many a good dog had died in the dark passages below the rocks.

'Ee's free!' went up an excited cry. The quarry, closely pursued by Star and a battalion of terriers, charged out of a low vent and struck off across the open moorland.

Tom looked round fearfully. 'Where's Misty? Where's my dog?' She was nowhere to be seen. A chill swept through his body. He called and whistled, but to no avail. Seeing the dilemma his companions held back as he crawled a short way into the crevice where the dogs had exited. With his ear to the ground, he caught a quiet whimper.

'Misty, is that you, ol' girl?' A miserable whine was confirmation. He wriggled onto his back, but with his bulky frame was unable to squeeze much beyond the entrance.

'You can get a crowbar from our cottage,' volunteered Alice, who was close by.

'I'm small, let me try first.' Lucy sank down on her knees, and ducked her head to enter the tunnel.

"Ang on, I'll go in.' With a grin Jos pulled at her shoulder to clear the way. 'I'm skinnier than the rest of ee, and we can't let a lass get soaked. I can manage just grand.' Lying on his stomach, he wriggled himself through the entrance until his boots disappeared from view.

'Nowt we can do now but wait,' said Luke as he crouched down on his haunches. Alice and Richard joined him, but Tom noticed Lucy was unable to settle. Her usually calm face looked strained as she paced around, her boots flicking the loose gravel in her path. As children, he and Jos had often played imaginary games in these subterranean tunnels and had no fears, but now he was sharing Lucy's concern. He sensed the weight of the rocks above, the cold, wet earth on his knees, the jagged edges of the rocks, and most of all the claustrophobic darkness.

Stones could be heard rattling deep inside the mountain, and the occasional swearing from Jos as he squirmed and twisted his way deeper through the fissures. Then it came. A heavy, deep-throated rumble, rapidly followed by a crash like thunder; the rush and clatter of collapsing rocks; a slow trickle of settling stones; muffled echoes and a chilling silence. Even the birds seemed to hold their breath.

'Dear God, what was that?' Richard exclaimed. Tom turned towards Lucy. Her eyes were open wide, her cheeks pallid.

Chapter 4

Lucy pulled off her cape, and waved it like a flag to attract the attention of the hunting party who were unaware of the drama unfolding back at the borran. She was dimly conscious of the blast of the huntsman's horn recalling the hounds, and the returning figures coming into view as they scrambled back to the top of the fell; but her anguished thoughts were with Jos. She imagined him lying injured, or worse, pinioned beneath a rock fall in the impenetrable darkness, enveloped like a shroud. She tried to control her shaking hands as she bent down to put Star on a lead.

'What's up?' the master called out as he approached. 'We felt the rumbling. We thought they must be blasting over at the quarry.'

Tom pointed to the narrow tunnel. 'Jos Teasdale crawled in there t'rescue my terrier. A boulder must have dislodged and caused a slippage, and now we can't make contact with him.'

Lucy dropped onto one knee at the entrance. Desperately she called and whistled, but there was no response from inside the mountain. She was on the point of giving up when the lead was dragged through her hand as Star pulled away with a frenzied bark.

'Can I be of any help?' a cheeky voice called out from the other side of the borran. Alice let out a shriek of joy, and

Lucy caught Tom's eye as they both exhaled a deep breath of relief to see Jos clamber up the incline towards them, Misty tucked inside his coat. His trousers were soaked, streaked with mud, the skin scraped raw through the holes in the knees. A savage gash across his cheek dripped dark blood onto his grubby shirt. Lucy noticed how tenderly he handled the little dog, and how the terrier showed no inclination to struggle. She had seen him adopt the same technique with a newborn lamb being encouraged to feed.

'What happened?' they all clamoured to know.

'I found Misty easily enough by following her whines.' He wiped his nose on his sleeve. 'She was in a frantic state, poor thing, because her front paw was jammed between two jagged rocks. 'Twas lucky she didn't do more damage trying t'wrench herself free. I was able to release her leg, and then made for the nearest shaft of daylight, which was on the north side. 'Twas while I was wriggling through a narrow stretch that I must've disturbed some loose stones behind me, and that brought down a load more. Such a racket, it sounded like an avalanche in there. I thought t' mountain was going to collapse.'

'And so did we,' said Luke, puffing out his cheeks. 'We thought it might have buried you both for evermore.'

Jos set the little dog down on the scree. Limping and bedraggled, she bounced over to Tom, who scooped her up in his arms and bedded his face in her rough coat. Lucy could see it was to hide the tears welling up in his eyes. Once he had regained control he raised his head towards Jos. 'Thank you, pal. Thanks for saving her.'

'Nah, it's nowt,' said Jos, pacing about and watching the pair as the group stood round in a silent protective circle.

Lucy stepped forward and started unknotting the grubby rag Jos was using as a necktie.

'What yer doin'?' His hand shot up to stop her.

Falteringly she replied, 'I was going to dip it in some water and clean up that cut. It looks deep.'

'I'm fine,' he said, backing away. She felt herself blush uncomfortably, and to avert attention turned towards her brother who patted her shoulder.

'We'll need to be getting on our way if we're to reach Ambleside before darkness sets in,' he said. With the shivering dog in his arms he strode over to Richard Green. 'Could ee tek her home for us? I don't think she'll manage the long trek ahead.'

Richard nestled her in his coat while Lucy replaced her cloak and basket in readiness for several hours of walking. Tom turned to Jos and held out his hand.

'Have a safe journey,' said Jos. 'The clouds are high. That's a good sign.'

Jos followed in the wake of the field as they retraced their steps back towards the lake and inn. Hearing laughter drift past on the westerly wind he glanced over his shoulder to see brother and sister, walking hand in hand, towards the rock shelter at the head of Nan Bield Pass. Their intimacy triggered a subliminal feeling of envy. He simply did not know how to react to the gentle touch of a woman, and now regretted how he had distanced himself from Lucy's concern when she had shown him sympathy.

Down at the inn the numbers were augmented by the old men no longer able to follow the hunt – all waiting to hear an account of the kill, and the rescue of the terrier. A log fire roared in the hearth, and tankards of ale littered the tables when Jos arrived to a rowdy welcome.

'I wish I'd put a wager on that Tess,' said one old man, sipping his ale noisily.

'How did ee know yer way out of the borran?' asked another.

'I roughly remembered where the passages led, from the days when Tom and I used to squirm through the tunnels as small boys.' Jos replied. 'A gud game we used to have up there.'

'And all he suffered was a cut on the cheek,' added Luke with a mischievous wink, 'and Lucy offered to tek care of that.'

Jos willed himself to smile before swinging his leg over the bench where Tom's father, James, was sitting hunched forward in conversation with the priest. Like Tom and Jos they had been good friends since childhood.

'I had a long chat with your Lucy today,' said Anthony. 'She's a fine lass.'

James nodded.

'Why don't you let her go back to school? She's a bright girl with an interest in the wider world – unusual for her sex.'

'Schooling wouldna do anything for her except make her hanker for what's out of reach. What's the gud of that?

'But Lucy has talent, just like her brothers,' Anthony persisted. 'She could move out of the dale and find herself a husband who earns a good living.'

'She's a'reet as she is.' James puffed deeply on his pipe.

'But times are changing, Jas. The Lowthers could get her a post in service, perhaps in London like her aunt.'

'Yer reet, Anthony – she has a gud heed on her, but there's nowt she needs she can't get here in Westmorland.'

The priest smiled wearily.

Lucy surveyed her surroundings with an inner glow of delight. The view from the top of Nan Bield was expansive, with the clouds and snow-topped mountains uniting, undulating and rolling into the distance, like the waves on the Atlantic Ocean beyond the Cumberland shoreline. She had never crossed these mountains before, but was completely at ease with the peace and sense of awe created by the solitude. She shielded her eyes against the sun as a pair of peregrine falcons circled overhead.

'Listen,' said Tom. 'Can you hear anything?'

She stood rock-still, and concentrated. A breeze fanned her hot cheeks, and a single ewe called once, from somewhere far, far away.

'Nah,' she said, 'nothing except the gentle wind… it's eerily quiet.'

'Exactly. The birds have fallen silent and the animals have fled to their burrows. Where are the skylarks we heard earlier?' Tom's eyes turned skywards and he pointed a finger. 'They're all wary of those two deadly arrows hovering overhead, re-establishing their territory from last year.' As he spoke one of the birds dived earthwards at tremendous speed, missed its target and rose again to join its partner. The local wildlife remained hushed and vigilant.

Tom idly picked up a stone and added it to the cairn where the paths met. 'Now let me tell you all the details of our hound's prowess at the kill.'

Lucy listened intently, remembering how a few years earlier she had sneaked out in the evenings to watch a family of fox cubs, somersaulting and playing like puppies; and how she had kept their habitat secret from the adults, knowing they would be hunted or shot. 'I think it's sad we have t'destroy such an intelligent animal,' she said. 'They have a right to share the land too.'

'Aye, but surely better this way than dying from starvation caught in a trap.'

Evening was well advanced by the time they passed the Kirk Stone and started the steep, winding descent from the top. Protected from the wind, the resultant warmth quickened their speed, and with their first glimpse of Brothers Water Lucy felt so happy she started to sing.

In the middle distance a couple came into view, walking in their direction along the track. The man, in a deerstalker and cloak, appeared to be forging ahead while his companion, a slight woman, scuttled along to keep up with his lengthy strides. As they gained ground to overtake them the man stepped aside to let them pass.

'Good day to you,' he said. 'I thought the nightingale had come early this year.' He addressed Lucy, coaxing a smile. 'Have you much further to travel?'

'No,' Tom replied, 'we're bound for Ambleside.'

'Have you come far?'

'From the east side of Harter Fell.'

'That's a fair distance,' said the stranger. 'I hope you have somewhere to sleep tonight?'

'Yes, sir, with my brother. He's the village schoolmaster.'

The stranger nodded enthusiastically. 'Ah, Jonathon Shaw – I know him well. He's a good man and well thought of in our village.'

The woman, whom Lucy had been quietly observing, stood with her arms crossed over her chest with what appeared to be a notebook in her hand. She raised her head quite abruptly at the mention of Jonathon, as though something had caught her interest. But she didn't enter into the conversation.

With nightfall the path became more difficult to follow, and Lucy was reassured when the market cross came into view. On one side of the square stood a three-storey, double-fronted whitewashed building, which she thought might be the home of some southern gentleman. Alongside were wood-framed houses with animal feed and farm equipment stored beneath, and hens roosting on the beams. The school, church and a row of cottages, all built of the same blue-black stone, snuggled together opposite. The smell of dung hung in the damp air as half a dozen cows lazed contentedly on the dusty road.

Jonathon stood waiting for them at the door of his lodgings, puffing a clay pipe. He was the second son in the Shaw family, and had left home when Lucy was a small child. He now acted as a mentor to his younger siblings. Lucy stood on tiptoe to kiss him before handing over the contents of her basket: knitted socks, oatcakes and some raw mutton – all presents from their mam. Hidden away at the bottom she had secreted some rum butter, to be relished once Lent had passed.

Jonathon was eager to hear news from home, and being a keen huntsman himself was particularly interested in the events of the day, and Misty's misadventure in the borran.

Having exhausted the gossip from Ravendale, Lucy wanted to find out about the families who used the school, and the wealthy town-dwellers who were making summer pilgrimages to the lakes. She mentioned their chance meeting with the odd couple on Kirkstone and Jonathon was able to enlighten her.

'That would have been Mr Wordsworth and Miss Dorothy. William's a local poet who finds wandering about in the countryside an inspiration. His sister often accompanies him and takes down notes. The locals think they are a bit mad and they certainly behave like an eccentric couple. There have been rumours…'

'What d'you mean, rumours?' Lucy asked.

'Nothing of consequence, just local gossip. Perhaps you have already heard of William Wordsworth?'

'Nah, I canna say I have.'

'He's establishing himself as quite a celebrity in the area since he came to live at Rydal Mount.'

'You speak as though you know him,' said Tom.

'I do, he often calls by for a crack and to bring me old copies of the London newspapers. He enjoys a spirited discussion, and getting the angle of local people on national events. He's also keen on education and a great supporter of our little school.'

'His own sons and daughters attended a village school before coming here.' Jonathon got up from his chair and threw a log on the fire. 'The story goes that the family lived very frugally in a small cottage in Grasmere, and it was here they entertained their literary friends. Pretty cramped it must have been, with Miss Dorothy doing most of the cooking and housework.'

'Does he make a living from his writing?' Lucy asked.

'I doubt it, though I'm sure that would be his choice. Thanks to Lord Lonsdale he was recently given the post of a government tax inspector. That must have improved the family's financial standing. Not long after he moved here he gave me a signed copy of his book of poetry, *The Lyrical Ballads*.' Jonathon leant over to lift the seat of the settle and brought out a small oblong package, wrapped in butter muslin. He handed it to Lucy. 'Open that.'

She carefully laid back the folds of cloth to reveal a leather box, open on one edge. Inside nestled a book bound in maroon leather. She fingered the gilt edging and delicately turned the flimsy pages – she had never seen anything so fine. A torn sheet of parchment, used as a bookmark, fluttered to the floor. She replaced it and handed the book back to Jonathon.

'I'll read to you later,' he said. 'He tells a good yarn. I sometimes recite the poems to my pupils and get them to copy out verses; the ideas and rich imagery strike a chord. It makes a pleasant change from the classical literature I'm obliged to teach most of the time.' He laid the eating irons down on the table. 'I think you'll both be surprised. Now it's time for us to eat.'

Lucy found staying in the centre of a village an exhilarating experience. Through the windows she could see the candles and rushlights fluttering in the neighbouring cottages, and when the church clock struck the hour the vibrations penetrated the walls. She drew a patchwork rug tightly round her shoulders as Jonathon laid the open book on his lap and began.

> '*Upon the forest-side in Grasmere Vale*
> *There dwelt a Shepherd, Michael was his name;*
> *An old man, stout of heart, and strong of limb…*'[2]

The tale continued. Michael married Isobel late in life and they raised one beloved son, Luke. When Luke was seventeen Michael, through no fault of his own, was in danger of losing his land, and he and Isobel agreed that Luke should go away to work for a relative to earn the necessary money to pay off the debts on the farm. Before he left, Michael took his son to lay the first stone of a sheepfold that he undertook to complete in readiness for his return. But once away from home, Luke fell into bad ways, and was forced to find a hiding place overseas. This broke Michael's heart.

> 'There, by the Sheepfold, sometimes was he seen
> Sitting alone, or with his faithful Dog,
> Then old, beside him, lying at his feet.
> ...and the remains
> Of the unfinished Sheepfold may be seen
> Beside the boisterous brook of Greenhead Ghyll.'[3]

The poem took an hour in the telling. Lucy's eyes filled with tears as it drew to a close. She felt a connection, something she had never experienced with such intensity before. Something deep inside told her this could be a defining moment in her life. She looked towards Tom, who leant across and squeezed her hand.

Chapter 5

Jonathon was elated to see how much his young brother and sister enjoyed the reading. 'Do you agree, he has the common touch?' he asked.

Tom stared into the fire as a rogue flame flickered into life. 'Aye. He has such insight in the way he describes everything... the people, the landscape.' He turned to his sister. 'What d'you think, Lucy?'

A dreamy expression spread across her face. 'It's as if ee sees and hears... even feels as I do. I can follow everything ee's saying.'

'That's exactly my point,' said Jonathon. 'I have to read Homer and Virgil with my pupils, sometimes Shakespeare. With so many classical references there's nothing for them to connect with – the context is unfamiliar and the meaning obscure.' Jonathon closed the book.

A note of disbelief crept into Tom's voice. 'But do the scholars in London really think his writing has merit?'

'It seems so. They're visiting Ambleside in their droves, all of them wanting to meet the great philosophical poet. They refer to him as the master of modern writing.'

'I suppose it's only right poetry should change and adapt in the same way as language,' said Tom. 'I wonder if Latin and Greek will always divide those with and without an education?'

Jonathon laughed. 'That's a philosophical thought too, brother.' He stood up, gave the fire a final rake, and doused the tapers.

The following day Jonathon and Tom were up at first light to prepare for the children's arrival at school. For once Lucy had time alone. She brushed the dry mud from her skirts and heated up some water to wash her hair. Next she busied herself bringing in wood and preparing a large hotpot with the mutton brought from home for their midday meal.

Sitting eating at the break, the family were interrupted by a friendly shout from the lane outside.

'I expect that's one of the fathers bringing me fuel for the schoolroom fire.' Jonathon raised his voice. 'Come in.' Bending his head, there entered the man in the deerstalker whom they had met out on the Pass. Stunned, Lucy glanced at her brother – could this really be the author of *Michael*?

'This is my sister Lucy and brother Tom,' said Jonathon, introducing his family. 'They are staying with me for a couple of days.'

The visitor smiled and nodded. 'Yes, we met briefly last night, out on the Pass.' He shook their hands warmly before turning to Jonathon. 'I've brought you some back copies of *The Times* so you can discuss the progress of the Peninsular War with your pupils – and share them with Tom and Lucy here. As we know, the news trickles through slowly to this part of the world, but what you'll find in these papers is still current. One of them describes Wellington's success at the Battle of Orthez, on the way to the capital, and that was just two weeks ago. I'm sure you'll find them interesting.' As if as an afterthought he added, 'I hope you can read, Lucy.'

'Just a little, sir,' she said, trying to disguise a defiant edge in her voice. She listened intently as Jonathon and their visitor continued to debate the progress of the long-overdue end to the wars with France.

'You were all too young to have been aware of the dangers we were in at the start of the hostilities,' said Mr Wordsworth, 'but the fear of invasion was very real. You may have seen some of our soldiers trying to make their way back home to Scotland over the mountains; half-blind, limbs missing, clothes in tatters. It's very sad.'

'One stopped off at the school just yesterday, begging for food,' said Jonathon. 'He'd lost a hand and his face was disfigured with scars.'

'We'll win through,' said Mr Wordsworth confidently. 'Napoleon might have the military power, but with our manufacturing industries doing so well we have the economic edge.'

'I hear tell the ships plying back and forth from Whitehaven to the Americas are doing tremendous business,' agreed Jonathon. 'Not to mention filling the coffers of the Lowthers,' he added with a meaningful look at his visitor. 'Thank you for these.' He spread the newspapers neatly on the window ledge. 'Now will you join us for a drink and bite to eat?'

'I'll take a jug of water, but nothing more.' Mr Wordsworth perched himself at the oak table and Lucy poured a tankard from the iron kettle.

'I've been telling Tom and Lucy about the recent influx of visitors from Manchester and the south,' said Jonathon.

'And have you told them about the yacht races and regattas they will be holding on Lake Windermere this summer? That should appeal to you young people.'

Lucy, who had been sitting quietly observing, found this turn in the conversation interesting. 'Surely it can't be reet, foreign folks with fancy ideas intruding into our way of life?'

'Regretfully, you can't stop progress,' said Mr Wordsworth. 'With travel getting easier the rest of England was bound to discover what we have always known – the Lake District has a lot to offer.'

'The visitors bring benefits too,' mused Jonathon. 'They buy our goods, provide work for our craftsmen and domestic jobs for the women and girls. William's right, we have to change with the times. I was the first of my family to move beyond our dale and I expect you, brother, will do the same. Cotton is king, so they tell us, and our parents' sheep farm won't sustain a family of our size in the future.'

Lucy laid down her fork in a gesture of frustration. 'It seems there'll just be the mills for the likes of me.'

'You never met Aunt Mary,' said Jonathon, addressing Lucy. 'She went up to London in service to one of the earl's family. It must be nearly twenty years ago, but she recognised change was coming even then. She is the same age as brother James and regularly came to stay at Ravendale when I was young.'

Lucy's eyes lit up. 'I know who she is.' She nodded her head enthusiastically. 'She sent us a parcel a few years back, a couple of fine wool dresses for Mam and some lace-trimmed linen handkerchiefs. Mam gave me one, and said I was t'look after it as it was very delicate. I keep it wrapped up in my box.'

Jonathon smiled at his sister. 'As I recall she was a spirited youngster with chestnut hair – just like yours. They say she made a good marriage.'

Their visitor's pulse began to race, and he was aware of a sweat breaking out on his brow as an incident he had suppressed for many years resurfaced. He was once again a young man, back in a steamy coffeehouse in the heart of fashionable London; intoxicated by stimulating conversation and pretty serving girls. He got up from the table and stood looking out of the stable door with his back to the family. The cool air steadied his nerve.

'I'm familiar with London. Where did she live?' he asked in a casual tone.

Jonathon tapped his fingers on the table as he tried to recall. 'She started with the earl at Carlton Terrace, but she moved out of private service and acquired a position somewhere near Euston – Somers Town if I remember rightly.'

Mr Wordsworth sucked in his breath inaudibly before replying. 'I know that district well. I lived there for a few months in the nineties after I returned from France. I was inspired in those days by the political scene and had hoped to find a position writing for one of the more radical newspapers. We used to spend hours in coffee shops, discussing and plotting... many of us supported the idea of an English revolution. Looking back, it was a volatile and exciting time.' As he turned a shaft of sunlight through the open door lit up Lucy's glossy mane. Controlling his voice, he continued calmly. 'And that's why it's important for young people to be exposed to the wider world. It raises their aspirations, and it's the reason I hand on these newspapers to you, Jonathon, for your young students.' He included them all in his smile, but his eyes rested on Lucy.

'Do ee think you need ambition to be happy, sir?' she asked. The question took him by surprise, and he noticed Jonathon and Tom exchange glances.

'Not necessarily, Lucy,' he replied good-naturedly.

'What matters to me now can be found in the simple country way I live; the symbiotic relationship with the land and elements. But we all benefit from increasing our knowledge; it helps us to reach decisions.'

Lucy ran her tongue over her lips as though digesting his words, before slipping past him to retrieve the collie who was barking ferociously at a peddler calling out his wares on the dusty road.

'She's a bonny lass,' he remarked in an aside to the brothers.

'Aye, and has a waywardness about her that hasn't yet been tamed.' Jonathon winked at Tom.

'I'm glad of that – deference can make dull company. I hope no one ever tries to clip her wings.'

A crescendo of chatter was heard coming from the schoolroom as the children gathered in readiness for the afternoon session.

'I must ring the school bell,' said Jonathon, getting to his feet.

'And I must be on my way,' said their visitor, slipping on his tweed cape and battered hat. 'I've so enjoyed meeting your family.'

'Jonathon read us one of your poems last night,' Lucy said as he ducked his head to go out into the street.

'I hope you enjoyed it,' he said. 'I find some of my poetry appeals to young people. Perhaps we will meet again and you can give me your opinion.' With that he bid them good day, and with head bent low set off along the road to the Mount.

Lucy was overjoyed to find Ambleside teeming with activity when they set off to collect Jonathon's ewes. Thin trails of smoke curled upwards from the cottage chimneys, and steam rose from the slate roofs as the sun penetrated the thin layer of ice. Tradesmen, farmers and children jostled along the main street and called out greetings to Jonathon. The wild daffodils were in bud and celandines flowering in abundance on the margins of the intake fields as spring rolled up from the south. She revelled in the bright sunshine, and as they climbed higher she heard a single church bell tolling in the direction of Windermere.

Within the hour they had located all Jonathon's sheep, which were grazing on common land near Troutbeck. 'That one's pawing the ground already,' said Tom to his brother. 'She's ready t'drop.'

'Then let's get them down as quickly as possible. I could do with some healthy lambs to sell.'

Tom and Lucy's visit was short as their father expected them to be home for the Easter service. Jonathon packed Lucy's basket with haver bread and sheep's cheese for the journey and, as an afterthought, tucked the carefully protected *Lyrical Ballards* under the picnic. 'You may borrow this until the next time I come over to Ravendale,' he said. 'I trust you to take very good care of it.'

'Aye, we certainly will,' said Lucy excitedly.

They left as the dawn chorus filled the air. Spurred on by the springtime music from the thrushes, blackbirds, robins and chaffinches, they made good progress during the first hour. But, as so often happens in the fells, the day which had started with such promise began to cloud over. A light mist drifted soundlessly over the mountaintops and as they climbed the air grew noticeably colder. Lucy stopped to flick the moisture from her hair before pulling up her hood. As she did so she glanced back towards the village and was aware of a movement among the larch trees below the track. Judging by his attire she was fairly sure it was Mr Wordsworth, part-hidden from view in the copse. She wondered whether to give him a wave, but as he made no acknowledging movement she wrapped her cloak tightly round her body and quickened her pace to catch up with Tom.

'I think we should stop and wait for the clouds t'shift,' said Tom. 'I can't be sure we're on the right track. We don't want to go sailing over the top of a crag; we aren't eagles,' he added in an attempt at jollity.

Lucy laid her head against Tom's arm as they perched on a boulder, sheltered from the easterly wind by a pinnacle of rock. Although it was now midday the light was impenetrable, the familiar sounds muffled by the grey blanket. She could hear an occasional bleat, but there were few sheep out on the fells at this time of year. She trusted Tom, but in this claustrophobic, damp landscape she had to fight hard to control a rising panic.

It was the cold that finally drove them on. They strained their eyes for anything which would show that the way ahead was safe. If only Misty had been with them Lucy would have felt more confident. Soaked through, her hands and feet were numb, her ears stung and her eyes watered endlessly. Neither spoke as they trudged along in single file, each concentrating on the step ahead.

Lucy's reactions were slow, and a broad stretch of scree caused her to slither and slide as she struggled to regain her footing. Once back in control she lifted her head – the level of light had changed, revealing a welcome sight.

'Luk, Tom, luk! I can see the tarn!'

Ahead, bathed in a narrow shaft of sunlight, gleamed a patch of water. It was as though a door had been left ajar into a darkened room. Many times she had witnessed this sudden rolling away of the mist, but never had it made the impression that it did today. She slipped her arm through Tom's as warm tears streaked her icy cheeks. She knew they were now on the right track and it was an easy drop from here into the valley.

Protected from the wind, the warmth of the late afternoon sun began to spread through every vein in their bodies. Lucy's concerns quickly dissipated as their farmhouse, with its moss-coated walls and protective circle of sycamore trees, came into view. She even imagined she could smell the woodsmoke rising in a thin column from the chimney. She knew the situation in which they had found themselves was not uncommon, and was miffed with herself at having displayed her frailty.

Beyond their farm gate a well-groomed mare was tied to a sycamore tree, pawing the ground as though impatient to be off.

'I think Da must have a visitor,' said Lucy. 'That horse shows all the signs of having come from t'castle.'

Tom chuckled. 'Wherever that mare's come from she looks mighty uncomfortable with the company she's keeping now.'

They removed their muddy boots and wet outer garments before going into the kitchen. Here Sir William's bailiff was sitting at the table, a glass of whisky in his hand, absorbed in conversation with their father and brother Matthew. Lucy heard her da say, 'It's a generous offer, sir, but while I can manage the fees for schooling at Bampton I want my sons t'tek advantage of the excellent teaching available there. I expect' – he emphasised the word – 'Matthew to follow his brother. I think he will be well suited to the church one day.'

The bailiff stroked his clean-shaven chin. 'I can see you have your mind made up, Mr Shaw.'

'May I ask why you particularly wanted Matthew when my son Thomas is probably the more robust?'

The bailiff hesitated before answering. 'The young master thought Matthew's disposition would be better suited to caring for the horses.'

Lucy's father nodded and rose to his feet. 'Well thank ee for calling, sir. Now we mustn't take up any more of your time.'

Peggy leaned on the farm gate as she waited for her family to join her in the short walk to the chapel. The rooks which nested in the nearby trees circled overhead, creating fast-moving shadows on the sunlit grass. At her feet a black cockerel and his harem clucked around, rustling the dried leaves as they scratched about. In the nearby field there were now a dozen or more newborn lambs; some tottering, some bouncing like marionettes in their haste to get to their mother's udders. Although it was something Peggy had witnessed for nearly fifty years' their antics still made her laugh out loud. She felt the promise of a good season ahead. If the weather was kind they should raise three hundred or more lambs.

In recent years the congregation from the dale had joined the worshippers at Shap for the Easter service. But this year Priest Wilder had permission to hold a service in Ravendale. Peggy was pleased. She loved the unpretentious little chapel with its plain font and faded frescoes. She glanced up to the fells opposite, where the dry stone walls marked out the parson's fields. Here Stephen, like his father before him, planted oats and raised a few sheep to supplement his salary. She knew the living was poor by any standards at around fifty pounds a year.

'Come on,' she called out impatiently, 'can't ee hear the bell ringing? The priest is cumin, we munna be late.'

Her family tumbled out into the lane, laughing, James and the boys handsome in clean shirts, their hair neatly brushed. Her three daughters flaunted straw hats decorated with fresh flowers; the sweet tang of rosewater wafting about them as they swished past. Four of her children were now missing. James, the eldest, was farming a few miles distant; Jonathon was in Ambleside and Adam away teaching near Appleby. Elizabeth would be attending her husband's church at Bampton.

The Sunday service was the main social event of the week, and afterwards provided the residents with an opportunity to air their grievances and discuss the politics of the valley – attendance was usually high. Today Stephen waited in his white vestments ready to lead the procession into church, and Peggy was happy to see Jos walk towards the altar brandishing his fiddle. With musical accompaniment it promised to be an uplifting celebration.

The prayers and readings were familiar to them all as Stephen focused his address on the traditional Easter story.

'Now let us be upstanding for our final hymn, *When I Survey the Wondrous Cross.*'

Jos lifted his bow and played an introductory bar. The congregation joined in with exuberance, but slowly dropped off, one by one, as each became aware of a single sweet voice, hitting the notes with perfect intonation. A round of spontaneous applause rose as the final verse ended... followed by an angry shout from the churchyard.

'Where's that son of mine? Jos! Come 'ere, yer bugger,

and stop wasting yer time in that place. We've a ewe in trouble.' With this hostile interruption the mood was lost.

'That was quite a performance,' Jos whispered to Lucy as he ran past to do his father's bidding.

Peggy was equally baffled by her daughter's unexpected extrovert behaviour. 'Where did that come from, lass?' she asked, not sure whether to be embarrassed or proud.

'I'm not sure.' There was a restless edge to Lucy's reply. 'I just felt an urge to raise my voice. I wanted to be heard. I think mebbe it was because of something Mr Wordsworth said.'

Chapter 6

The sheep had been returned to their heafs, and the grain was not yet ready to harvest. This lull in the round of seasonal farm activities allowed brother and sister the time to wander up to their favourite retreat. Lucy gathered together some pieces of charcoal, a precious sheet of paper and a thin flat slate into a canvas bag. Tom slipped the book of poems Jonathon had lent them deep into a pocket.

The air was alive with the whirr and buzz as myriads of insects hopped, flitted or droned their way amongst the grasses and wildflowers. A light breeze fluttered Lucy's skirt as they weaved their way between the drumlins. She relished the coolness as it spread up to her bare legs. They paused to watch a school of young lambs playing chase and defending their castles amongst the mysterious humps.

'D'you remember how Simeon and the older boys used t'tell us they were the homes of slumbering trolls?' she chuckled. 'And when there was a full moon they would slink around, stalking anyone caught out alone on the moors?'

Tom laughed. 'Aye, but ee didna believe them?'

'Well… mebbe sometimes, and so did Hannah,' she said defensively.

The path from the farmhouse led to a flat bank perched alongside Ravendale Force. Here, after rain, the beck frothed and foamed before leaping over a precipice to splash into the pool below. The pool was a regular haunt of the local children, and on hot summer days they paddled and splashed naked in its icy waters.

Idling their way along the sheep walk, the gentle hum was broken by a shrill whistle coming from the crags. The call which followed was easily recognisable; it was Jos signalling to his dog. As the cloud rolled away a dark figure came into view, and the outline of a black and white collie. They stopped to watch as Nell set about rounding up a pair of Herdwicks, crag-bound on a plateau partway up the mountainside.

'They must be a pair of stragglers ee's returning to the heaf before bringing them all down together,' said Tom. Lucy watched, fascinated, as a barely audible whistle sent Nell charging down the mountainside a hundred feet below. From there she barked ferociously and the ewes, frightened by this unexpected aggression, scrambled up the steep gradient away from the dog to the safety of the level ground above. Within less than a minute Nell had spun round the edge of the escarpment and was lying quietly behind them, her nose between her paws and her ears cocked for any new instruction from her master.

'There's no one better with a dog on these fells,' said Tom in admiration.

'They're a good team,' Lucy agreed. 'But I sometimes wonder how much Nell does under instruction and how much using her own initiative.'

'It's an understanding bred through the generations. I expect Nell's family has been linked with the dale as long as the Teasdales,' laughed Tom.

'At least ee has a loyal companion,' Lucy mused. 'I'm glad of that.'

'If only it was as easy with people,' Tom said before cupping his hands over his mouth and delivering a distinctive holler. An acknowledging wave came from halfway up the mountainside.

Lucy seated herself on a cushion of springy grass, her back supported by the warm rocks. Every sound was magnified. The occasional bleat, the call of the skylarks high up in the atmosphere, and the gentle gush of the beck as its waters splashed rhythmically over the polished stones. She was looking about, deciding what to sketch, when her deliberations were brought to a halt. A thunderous boom blasted out, reverberated round the mountain range and echoed through the passes. The dogs jumped up in alarm before emitting low, grumbling barks. A flock of crows took flight, and the lambs which had been playing on the drumlins scampered off to the safety of their mothers as a shiver of panic concertinaed through the animal kingdom.

Ravendale Force was a hundred yards from the track, used by the men going to and from the quarry on Mossdale Common. Here tunnels were being forged into the face of the mountain, and the green slate they extracted carried by sledge and hurdles back to Shap. Before daylight Lucy would hear the local men, shepherds and farmers' sons, plodding past their farm heading for this alternative form of employment. She often wondered how they adjusted to replacing a life of birdsong and fresh air with the noise and dust of the mine.

'Let's hope that's all the blasting we'll have to suffer today,' she said as she set about sketching the rowan tree overhanging the gill.

Tom looked up from the page he had been reading. 'Here comes Jos.'

Nell bounded up the track, her master in close pursuit.

'We've been watching you both. That was a tidy recovery you made from Black Crag.'

'Aye, she's a clever ol' girl,' said Jos, slapping Nell's rump. 'And what are ee up to?'

'I've been reading to Lucy here... some poetry written by William Wordsworth.'

A look of comical disbelief crossed Jos's face.

'Come and join us,' Lucy said. 'Ee might be surprised.'

'Nah,' Jos scoffed. 'That sounds too clever for the likes of me.'

Tom tapped the ground beside him with his index finger. 'You can close your eyes, tek a nap. I'll read you a poem that tells a story.' His work-worn hands turned the fragile pages with great care until he found the narrative poem, *The Brothers*. He started to explain: 'This is a tale of two young boys, brought up by their grandfather amongst the fells. When they fall on hard times, Leonard, the older boy, goes to sea hoping to earn enough money to eventually return and rejoin his brother in running the farm. Much of the poem is a conversation between Leonard and the old priest he meets when he returns twelve years later to look for his brother.'

'Tek heed,' Lucy warned, 'it has a sad ending.'

'Apart from that, it could be our story,' said Tom. 'D' you want to hear it or not?'

Jos shifted uneasily. 'If yer like.' He lay back on the grass and pulled his hat over his eyes. As they listened Lucy's gaze was drawn to his hands; the long fingers, the dirty half-moon nails tapping out a rhythm on the ground. She wondered what was going on in his head.

'What d'you think?' Tom asked when he had finished.

Jos supported himself on one elbow. 'Yer reet. It's not what I was expecting.'

53

'But did you enjoy it?'

'Aye, aye, I did. It relates to a life I recognise. I thought poetry was all aboot Roman battles and Greek tragedies, but this is different. Who is this fellow Wordsworth?'

'We met him when we were staying over at Ambleside,' said Tom. 'Jonathon told us he's one of a group of modern poets who have put down roots in the Lake District. I think he's quite famous.'

'Ee was born in Cumberland, and seemed a homely sort of gentleman to me,' Lucy added. 'And ee's a good friend of our brother – ee gave him this book.'

There was a mocking tone in Jos's voice when he said, 'Fancy ee mixing in such company.'

Jos continued to bask in the midday sun, lost in thought. 'That bit about the deer and ravens, he cud have been talking about us. Read it again, Tom.'

Tom returned to the page.

> *'Leonard and James! I warrant, every corner*
> *Among these rocks, and every hollow place*
> *That venturous foot could reach, to one or both*
> *Was known as well as to the flowers that grow there.*
> *Like roe-bucks they went bounding o'er the hills;*
> *They played like two young ravens on the crags:*
> *Then they could write, aye, and speak too, as well*
> *As many of their betters…'*[4]

'Stop there!' cried Jos. 'That ruins it.' He pulled himself up on his elbow. 'I'd like t'have the chance to see what life can offer beyond the fells; t'be like Leonard; to really make it our story.'

'But what could yer do?' asked Lucy.

54

'I don't know. The mills are the obvious choice but that sounds t'me like swapping freedom for slavery.'

'There's always the militia,' Tom suggested, 'though I'm not sure you'd take to the discipline,' he added with a quizzical look.

'I canna leave my parents. Anyway the war's nearly over, there isn't the need.'

'Don't you believe it – there'll always be confrontations. If not overseas, the army are needed to subdue local rebellions, like those we hear about among the farm labourers down in the south.'

Lucy laid down her charcoal. 'Sometimes I feel so shut in by these mountains, like a squirrel caught in a cage. I'd like to escape too.'

Jos was somewhat taken aback by her remark. 'Ee've got food on the table and peat for the fire. One day you'll likely have yer own home and children. What more does a woman want?'

Lucy sighed. 'There must be summat more. The chance t'learn, t'experience new things, t'visit London, t'travel overseas.'

'You don't even know what the sea looks like,' scoffed her brother. 'None of us do, although we live less than thirty miles from the coast.'

'I've seen rough weather on Hallswater, the waves lashing the banks and the fishing boats struggling to land.'

'Aye, but that's nothing. They say there are seas in the Southern Ocean as high as the old yew at Lowther. The sailing boats carrying the convicts can bob on top of the waves like small birds, then slide into the deep troughs never t'be seen again.' He looked from one to the other, seeking a reaction.

Lucy patted his arm. 'You're the one most likely to

escape, Tom. When you become a priest, or a teacher, you'll be away to Manchester.'

'If I do take holy orders I'm not sure I'd want t'be cooped up in an industrial town.' Tom frowned. 'A country living in the south, somewhere with thatched roofs and a village green sounds more appealing.' He laughed. 'But wherever I end up you can always join me as my housekeeper.'

Lucy turned to face her brother. 'Ee'll have no need of me, Tom. You'll find a wife soon enough.'

'There'll always be room for you – if that's what you want.'

'Aye, of course I do.' Lucy's eyes danced with excitement at his suggestion, and Jos could see how at ease brother and sister were with each other as Tom gave her shoulders a squeeze. 'If you really mean it I'll need t'show I've had an education too,' Lucy said. 'I'll start by copying out some of these poems, before you return the book to Jonathon.'

'Ee canna write,' scoffed Jos.

'I can. Not verra well, but I can copy and learn to form the letters.'

Jos let her comment pass.

'There're several short poems in here about a young girl called Lucy I'm sure Jos would like to hear.' Tom winked at his sister. 'I'll read you one.'

Lucy joined in, having memorised the words, and her brother let her take over as they listened to her crisp young voice.

> 'Strange fits of passion have I known:
> And I will dare to tell
> But in the Lover's ear alone
> What once to me befell.

56

When she I loved looked every day
Fresh as a rose in June
I to her cottage bent my way,
Beneath an evening-moon…' [5]

Jos was unnerved by the way the words touched him. 'I wonder who Lucy was?' he said when the final verse came to an end. 'P'raps someone from his childhood?'

Lucy looked up from her sketching. 'Ee mean someone he grew up with. Like you and me?'

Tom sucked the end of a blade of grass. 'Aye, mebbe. It certainly sounds as if she was his muse at the time.'

'Which poem shall I start writing out first?' Lucy asked.

'*The Brothers*,' said Tom, punching Jos playfully in the stomach.

'Nah,' Jos cut in, 'start with a Lucy poem – they're shorter.' He pulled himself to his feet, and looking over Lucy's shoulder, scrutinised her drawing. Even using the limited palette of charcoal, it seemed alive. The rowan, its bark wrapped in fine tentacles of silver lichen, was bent, as though seeking healing in the cascading water. The distant mountains stood out stark, angular and menacing.

'She's good,' he said. Giving a nod to Tom, he strode over to the water's edge, and bent down to scoop some fresh water from the pool beneath the waterfall. He immediately gagged and spat it out. 'That's foul.' He wiped his mouth on the back of his hand. 'There must be summat wrong upstream.'

Tom jumped up and held out his hand to catch the water directly from under the fall. 'You're reet, the water's brackish. Let's see if we can find the problem.'

They didn't have far to climb. Floating in a rock pool was a bloated sheep which had presumably stumbled into

57

the water, and with the weight of its saturated coat been unable to regain the bank. They waded in and hauled it out onto the bank. Jos withdrew his knife from its sheath, and slowly and carefully removed the coat.

'Let the ravens do the rest,' he laughed as he squeezed as much moisture as he could from the fleece before rolling it up.

'Mebbe we should check the marks to see who it belonged to,' said Tom.

'Too late!' Jos swung the dripping fleece onto his back, ready to set off homewards.

'We'd better be getting along too.' Tom offered Lucy his hand.

'I'll wander on a bit,' said Lucy. 'Tell Mam I'll be back within the hour.'

Jos drank in the air, sweet with the scents of midsummer and newly mown hay. The fleece had been a bonus at the end of what should have been a perfect afternoon, yet he felt dispirited. Not for the first time he had been forced to acknowledge that the dale was on the cusp of change. Even Lucy was talking of moving on.

His family had always been fiercely independent, but his father had been sinking yearly into deeper and deeper despair. He likened it to the tunnels being excavated at the slate quarry, where the blackness ahead meant you could see no way out. Their few acres were heavily mortgaged, and his da's comfort was the home-brewed ale and malt whisky which did little for his temper. Step by step he and Martha had divorced themselves from the community support which bound the inhabitants of the dale. Simeon, his only brother, had gone into service when he was twelve, so Jos often had to manage the livestock on his own. He knew he had gained in survival skills and had an affinity with nature, but he had lost out on the schooling which could open the door to other opportunities.

He shouted at Nell, who dropped her tail and slunk along at his side.

Lucy scrambled up between the sparse thorn bushes in search of sphagnum moss for her monthly menses. Having time alone allowed her to reflect on the afternoon's discussion. Her meeting with Mr Wordsworth had sown a seed, a desire for a more fulfilling life. Until today she'd never given Jos's situation much thought. Now she could see they were both trapped.

She paused to regain her breath. Glancing eastwards, something white caught her eye. Shielding her eyes from the bright sunlight she recognised the pale blonde hair of Jos's brother Simeon, his arm resting across the bare buttocks of his companion. The two men were lying on their bellies with heads raised, as though intent upon some animal in the distance. She crouched down, partly so as not to disturb their target, but mainly because her instinct told her she might be interrupting something private.

'He's away!' she heard Simeon call in a hoarse whisper. A splendid stag, in full regalia, bound off to take cover in a copse lower down the valley.

'S' long,' called his companion, rising and belting his trousers round his waist. Swinging his stick, he set off towards the wood, and as he turned to give a last salute Lucy thought she recognised William, the eldest son from the castle. She watched and waited while Simeon pulled on his shirt before walking down to join him.

'Hello,' he said, securing his scarf round his neck. 'Where've you sprung from?' Lucy noticed the familial long fingers as he adjusted his clothes; but unlike his brother's his hands were smooth, with clean, well-trimmed nails.

'I've just climbed up via Sheep's Crag. Was that the earl's son I saw in the distance?'

'Aye, he's off in search of that stag we keep hearing about it. Did you see it? What a splendid creature. We hadn't expected to get a sight of it at this time of day.' Lucy sensed Simeon's eyes appraising her body; he bit his lower lip. 'Our horses are tethered down by your farm,' he said hastily. 'I must be on my way too.'

Lucy sat down and waited, hoping the stag might return. The summer haze had turned the mountains into a characterless backcloth, but skylarks soared overhead and a grey wagtail bobbed along the margins of the beck. She now understood why Simeon, a humble groom, received special treatment from the earl. He was a handsome man.

Chapter 7

It was the first week in July, and the weather warm enough for the ewes and hoggs to be stripped of their winter coats. It was the local custom to start at the foot and work to the head of each dale, the neighbours helping out with the shearing at each farm as they progressed. No money was exchanged, but at each farmstead the womenfolk supplied the food and a quantity of ale. It was thirsty, back-breaking work.

On the morning before the shearing was due at Ravendale Peggy watched her sons set off in opposite directions, to bring down their flock from the high fells. Later, when the sun had sunk behind Harter Fell, she sat with her husband on the bench outside their porch to wait for their return. James puffed his pipe and she clacked her knitting needles, both alert to any activity above the crags. With her eyes scanning the fells to the west, Peggy was the first to identify movement.

'Here they come.' She elbowed James in the side.

He shielded his eyes, looking towards Shap. 'And I can see the crocodile coming over from t'other direction.'

Two distinct lines of ewes and lambs appeared on the horizon simultaneously. Like legions of soldiers they could be seen winding their way down from the tops, following the contours of the land to converge in the intake fields below the farm. When united there would be upward of six hundred animals waiting in readiness for the hectic activity ahead. Once down in the valley they would savour the lushness of the lowland grass, and pass the night in trusting resignation.

In the cool of the early morning the clip began. James, his sons and neighbours sat on stools under the shade of the sycamore trees, each man with a sheep tucked underneath his arm. The shearing would continue until the daylight faded.

Peggy, her hair knotted back with a handkerchief, bustled up to Tom with a pitcher of water. Perspiration ran down his face and his shirt clung wet to his broad shoulders.

'How many so far, son?'

'We've managed around thirty apiece, Mam, so we're on target to finish before nightfall.'

A grey fleece, complete and pale on the underside, fell to the ground. Releasing the animal's head, he gave her rump a sharp slap to send her on her way to be corralled in a temporary enclosure. Here Matthew and his team were carrying out the marking, and smitting of the ears of the lambs.

Lucy, her sisters and the other women from the dale were kept busy in the barn tying the fleeces in readiness for the packhorse train, bound for the Kendal wool market. The girls sang as they worked, their hands soft from the lanolin in the wool.

Out in the open the eerie silence of the previous night had been replaced with a loud, persistent bleating as the ewes and lambs milled round in a dazed state, until at length they were reunited, the lambs' tails trembling with delight as they latched onto their mothers' comforting udders.

The frenzied activity of the clip was always followed by a holiday – a time for the youngsters to gather and celebrate. Lucy rose early. She craved a quick dip to refresh her body, and she needed to do this before her companions arrived. The chosen bathing pool was a volcanic tarn, set in a hollow in the mountain, with a shingle shore and pure, sparkling water which tasted divine on a hot summer's day. As a child she had learned to swim with her brothers in the pools of the Lowther, and from the shores of Hallswater. The tarn was exceptionally deep, and it was only the boys and Lucy who had the confidence to plunge into its dark depths.

Tom, soon to be joined by Jos, also set off ahead of the gang. After the heavy labour of the previous day he welcomed the sun on his aching back. As they ambled up the fell side towards the pool a young woman could be seen standing on the edge of the water, pulling her dirndl skirt up to her neck, and using it as cover as she slipped off her flax blouse and undergarments. It was Lucy. Unaware of their presence she dived from the bank in one fluid movement; her slight, androgynous body alabaster white, a dark shadow between her thighs. Like an eel she entered the water with barely a ripple shattering the glaze as she disappeared into the dark chasm. An involuntary tingle spread through Tom's body as she broke the surface. With the ripples rolling rhythmically towards the shore she raked back her hair, and swam to the opposite bank.

Tom had seen her dive in naked many times before, but this time his reaction was different. He noticed that she was beautiful. This unexpected arousal shook him. From now on he needed to remember she was his sister. He glanced furtively at Jos, and wondered what might be going through his mind.

Lucy saw them and waved. 'Let me get dressed and then you can come on in,' she called out. 'The water's as silky as milk.'

'Later,' Tom shouted back. 'I just wanna check whether there are any deer about.' He strode on in an attempt to show disinterest. 'Are you coming?' he called over his shoulder to Jos.

'Nah, I'll stroll over yonder and see if t'others are on their way.'

When Tom returned Lucy was sitting on the shore alone, her skirt drawn up to her knees and rubbing her hair dry with her petticoat, which she then spread out in the sun to dry. Her downy, tanned arms and legs glowed pink with the exhilaration of her swim.

Laughter and squeals from Alice announced her imminent arrival with Luke and Richard, Tom's brother Matthew, and Jacob Armstrong, the Teasdales' neighbour. Twenty yards behind dawdled Hannah Jackson with Sally, the Shaws' hired help. Alice plumped herself down on the grass and pulled her chemise off her shoulders, displaying a generous cleavage. Sally and Hannah squatted a little way apart on the edge of the group. Scattered about, the newly shorn Herdwicks and their lambs munched contentedly.

The six lads stripped off their dusty clothes and plunged into the water. All were competent swimmers, and once they had adjusted to the screaming iciness of the water organised races across the width of the tarn, to the steep crag side on the opposite bank. On their return they shook themselves dry, causing an uproar amongst the girls as the freezing droplets landed on their exposed skin. Stretching out on the warm heath they draped their shirts across their bodies, with chests bared to the sun. A leather bottle of home brew was passed round and the conversation turned to the clip.

'I love t'watch as each newly shorn sheep is returned to join its friends,' said Hannah, turning shyly to Tom.

'Aye, they look mighty unsteady and confused,' Tom agreed.

'And the way t'others greet them, they seem to be saying, "Stop worrying... we all look just as silly."' She gave a nervous giggle.

'That ole ewe you sheared near the end was a handful,' said Matthew, addressing his brother. 'I thought you were never going t'bring it down. We were all doubled up with laughter as you struggled to get a grip.'

'And when ee tripped over the bucket with the dye in I really cracked up,' added Luke. 'But your da didn't seem to see the joke.'

They all joined in, laughing over the memory, which seemed funnier than the actual incident.

The sun was now high in the sky and the shadows foreshortened, opening up the valley below. Tom scanned the view, immersed in drowsy contentment. 'We've been lucky this year to have had no rain. It's been a good clip.'

The others nodded in agreement.

'Who had the highest score?' asked Alice.

'I reckon 'twas Richard's da,' said Jos. 'Ee's really fast.'

Richard looked pleased at the recognition. 'Let's have some more fun with the ewes,' he said, getting to his feet and holding a hand out to Jacob. 'Remember how we used to mimic their bleating and lead them off their heaf?'

'Jos did that on our way back from Shap Fair,' giggled Alice. 'Hilarious, it was. He led Mr Armstrong's flock, like the Pied Piper, all the way over to Locks Bottom. Then he stopped calling. A well-dressed couple from Manchester were visiting the ruins of the abbey at the time, and Jos told them the leader had been trained to take the flock to the abbey for evening prayers… he said it was bred in them!' She gave Jacob a wary glance. 'Luckily your father was still celebrating at the fair.'

Jacob looked ready to remonstrate when Jos intervened.

'Nah, leave the sheep alone, they had enough stress yesterday. We'd be better off teasing the girls.'

The moment passed, but the banter, bragging and sexual innuendo continued, and Alice, who always strove to be the centre of attention, pulled up her skirts, displaying soft pink thighs.

'I so love the feel of flesh against flesh when I cross my legs,' she purred in her soft Welsh lilt. The lads sniggered, and encouraged her flirtatious talk. She dropped to her knees beside Tom and laid a freckled hand on his thigh, stroking the dark hairs against the line of growth towards his groin. He was unable to control his reaction, and Alice shrieked with laughter. The others joined in and Tom gave a wry smile as he rolled her over in a clumsy fumble; mildly repulsed by the alcohol on her breath. As he sprawled on top of Alice he watched Jos's shadow fall across Lucy. He saw him cup her face in his hands and kiss her – a kiss which lingered too long. He noticed her blushing cheeks, and felt unexplainably possessive towards her. As a distraction he jumped to his feet and challenged Jos to a wrestling match.

The shadows began to lengthen and Tom was aware that the consumption of alcohol was changing the dynamics of the group, creating tensions. Jos kept lashing out at Alice, and Hannah and Sarah exchanged uneasy glances.

'I'm going t'be on my way,' said Hannah, picking up her shawl. 'It's getting chilly and it'll be dark by the time I get home.'

'*Nos da*,' called out Alice mockingly. Jos struggled to his feet and threw a restraining arm round Alice's neck. He pulled her head backwards and kissed her roughly. She wriggled free, and slapped him on the face.

'I'll come with you,' said Richard and Jacob in unison as they followed Hannah. Without comment Matthew, Luke and Sally got to their feet and tailed the retreating group, their silhouettes growing smaller and smaller as they trekked back towards the valley floor. Lucy looked unsure, but hung back.

'What now?' asked Jos, with a lecherous eye on Alice.

'Shut your eyes and count to two hundred; then see if you can find us,' she said, dragging Lucy by the hand. The two girls ran off together, before parting to follow separate paths.

Once the lads reached two hundred they rose unsteadily to their feet. 'Summat moved over there, by that gully,' Jos said. Tom followed as he stumbled off over the uneven moorland, shouting as he went.

'I can only see one lass,' said Tom as a shadowy form, jumping from one mound to the next, wove a path a hundred yards ahead.

'That'll be Alice,' said Jos. 'That's the way she goes home.'

'Let's leave her be,' Tom responded uncertainly.

'Nah, she's like a bitch on heat, and she's not really one of us,' Jos replied.

'I dunno,' Tom slurred.

'Come on, I tell ee she's up for it. We should be able t'bring her down by Miner's Hollow,' he exclaimed, as though she was an escaping deer. Jos cracked on, the excitement mounting as the grog fuelled his confidence and lust. 'Come on Tom, you can't let me down now,' he said, charging ahead up the sheep path.

Tom was reeling on his feet. Somehow he lost sight of Jos but continued to track Alice, who was moving surprisingly nimbly over the uneven surface. He was finding it difficult to make up the ground. 'Damn this weak moon,' he grumbled to himself as it slipped behind a bank of cloud. He heard what sounded like a sharp cry immediately ahead, and the shape he had been following disappeared from view. Twenty yards further on he slumped into her, a crumpled pile of clothes lying motionless on the soft earth. Alice had tripped.

He caught a faint fragrance of lavender mingled with sweet, damp peat as desire overtook him. He tasted the stickiness of blood on his lips and damp hair in his face as he cupped a hand over a small white breast. A battle of arms and legs; fresh, laboured breath; cheeks wet with tears followed. With his guts wrenching he heaved himself up, fumbled for his breeches and staggered off. Far away a barn owl screeched, and as blackness overwhelmed him he sunk into oblivion on the soft grass.

Daylight was approaching when he regained consciousness. Disorientated, shivering and retching, he retraced his steps of the previous night. He cursed, utterly ashamed of what little he could remember of his animal passion. She had asked for it, he kept telling himself. He knew Jos had taken advantage of her charms on more than one occasion; she was a whore. But was she conscious? He suspected she had been drinking as much as the lads. And there was something else about the encounter, something which, even in his confused state, filled him with dread.

He found the flattened grass where his knees had straddled her, and a smear of blood on the rock nearby, but no trace of Alice. Thank God, she must have made her way home.

Chapter 8

With a pitching stomach and throbbing head Tom stumbled and lurched his way downhill towards home. On the final leg of his journey he was hailed by Jos making his way up to check his flock. 'What happened to ee last night?' he called out cheerfully. 'I came back with Alice… we had a reet good time.'

Tom's heart beat like a Highland drum in his chest. 'Yer lying,' he mumbled.

'Nah, why would I?'

Tom swayed and thought he might pass out. He concentrated on slowing his breathing. 'What happened to Lucy?' he finally managed to ask.

'I dunno. We thought you must've caught up with her, and you'd gone home together.'

Tom tried to focus his eyes on Jos, his giddy thoughts spiralling out of control. 'I don't remember much after we started t'follow the girls. Guess I just had too much grog. I woke up out on the fell, about an hour ago.'

'Looks like you're still half-cut,' laughed Jos, as he sauntered off up the path towards the quarry.

'Yer bastard. I'll knock the hell out of ee one of these days,' Tom spluttered as he stomped off. Glancing back over his shoulder he saw Jos had stopped in his tracks and was watching him; hands on hips and with a mystified expression on his face.

Arriving home, he kicked the mud from his boots against the farmhouse wall, before going into the dairy where his mam was preparing cheese for market. She and Lucy had been hand-milking a few of the sheep since the lambs were weaned, and finding it a profitable source of extra money.

Peggy pushed aside a wisp of greying hair with the back of her hand as she watched her son fumble with the latch. A mischievous smile played on her lips as she called out, 'Ee look like ee had a good night, son, pity yer have t'pay for it this morning.'

He ignored her comment. 'Is Lucy about?' He hoped his tone sounded casual.

'She's in the living room with yer sisters and some of the strays who helped out wi' the shearing. She took a tumble on her way home last night, but seems to be fine this morning.'

Tom gripped the wooden draining board. 'Did she say how or where she'd fallen? We lost sight of her and Alice when they went off to hide.'

'Nah, she nivver said,' his mother replied, wiping her hands on her apron. 'Now you look as if you're in need of a good wash and change of shirt; there's blood on your sleeve.'

Tom had to walk the length of the farmhouse living room which was thronged with family and neighbours, still celebrating the end of the clip. A nauseating smell of smoke rose from the clay pipes of the old men, and the usually scrubbed table was awash with beer stains, pots and pewter mugs. He knew instinctively where Lucy was seated, but avoided looking in her direction. He nodded a brief acknowledgement to the assembled group as he edged through to the wooden doorway leading to the upper rooms where they slept. A ripple of laughter followed in his wake as he climbed the newel staircase.

Alone, in the safety of the loft room, he threw himself down on the straw mattress he shared with Matthew. With his mind in tumult he lay on his back and counted, then recounted, the rafters on the sloping roof. A jackdaw thumped around on the slates above and a spider scuttled between the joists before dropping on a thread towards his face. Utterly miserable, he drew the knitted blanket over his head, and relived the events of the previous night.

He had been tracking Alice, he was quite sure of that, but if… if what Jos said was true, why hadn't she shouted or beaten him off? Had she lost consciousness? Did she have any idea who had raped her? The details of the encounter were so hazy, but the desperate feeling of shame was all-consuming. How could he have taken advantage of any young woman lying injured, possibly unconscious? He searched for some memory, something, anything that might connect him to Alice.

Recall came in a blinding flash – it was the fresh, sweet smell of his victim's breath. Tom now knew for certain it had been Lucy he had abused. Lucy, his dearest sister who had shared his secrets and ambitions, comforted him when he was sick or unhappy. What had he done? She was his flesh and blood, someone he should never touch, except in the most brotherly way. He screwed the blanket in his hands, his nails biting into the palms, and screamed silently into the straw pillow, 'I'm sorry, I'm so, so sorry.'

The summer drifted on with the usual round of farm activities, interspersed with country festivals and entertainment. For Tom they were dark days and he remained withdrawn, eaten up with self-loathing. He searched constantly for reasons to transfer the blame, and each time his twisted thoughts returned to Jos. It was Jos who had manipulated the situation. Jos who had precipitated his downfall.

He worked from dawn till dusk shepherding the sheep. He cut peat, repaired walls and filled in the potholes in the road leading to the farm. He would stumble in late at night coughing and covered with oat dust from threshing in the barn, and leave the house again at sunrise. By tiring himself out he knew the chances were good for a long, dreamless sleep. But his troubled thoughts remained his constant companion out on the hills. He watched Lucy from afar. She gave no sign of anything untoward having happened, and there were times when he began to doubt his own memory. Maybe it was all an alcoholic nightmare; or maybe she had no recollection of being violated.

Lucy was in a similar turmoil. She was despairing, knowing her relationship with her brother, the one with whom she had always had a special bond, could never be on the same footing again. Although she had been teetering on unconsciousness she knew well enough who had raped her; but was it rape? Maybe it was her fault. She knew she hadn't put up much of a fight; but was that because she had been knocked senseless by the fall? She couldn't be sure. They had spent many hours together in the last few weeks, and she was aware her feelings towards him were changing, in an unsettling way. Did Tom feel the same or had he, in his drunken stupor, mistaken her for Alice? Did he even know what he had done? So many questions, and no one with whom she could share her anxieties. From childhood she had been steeped in the teachings of the church, and her innocence, lost in a moment, could never be regained.

They had both sinned, and she now thanked God for saving her from any physical consequences from the encounter.

She mused long and hard as to how to handle their changed relationship. Desperate to reach out to him she couldn't resolve how to approach the subject, so took the easier option of pretending it had never happened. She maintained a cheerful demeanour when they were in each other's company, though they rarely communicated beyond everyday formalities.

What Lucy missed most was the quiet times, at their waterfall rendezvous. Her solace became the *Lyrical Ballads*. She bought a commonplace book at Shap Fair, and whenever she could steal away for a couple of hours headed off into the fells, alone. Her writing began to flow. No longer did she have to follow the words letter by letter; she could read a phrase, remember, and write it down. She added sketches to enhance the text. On one page an eagle, wings spread as it landed on its eyrie; on another two boys in pursuit of a red deer. Below one of the Lucy poems a young girl bent over a spinning wheel, her skirt hitched above her knees.

On her return she would slip into the stone barn furthest away from the house. Here she found a ledge, just beneath the roof, where she kept her book. She sewed together an oilskin bag, and this she placed between two large slates so it lay flat and protected from the weather. Lucy knew she was being secretive, but was driven by the fear that her family would laugh at such a futile activity in a woman destined to become the wife and helper of some local farm labourer.

When alone she would leaf through the other books stored in the settle. The Bible, *Pilgrim's Progress*, *Grimm's Fairytales*. More practical offerings were *Kearsley's Annual*

Ten-Penny Tax Tables and an absorbing leather-bound pocket book with a metal clasp and handwritten receipts relating to rents and stock. Her favourite was a cloth-bound *Atlas of the World in 1805*. Beyond the tiny blob she identified as Westmorland stretched Europe, the Ottoman Empire, India, the great continents of America and Africa and, most mysterious of all, a large unchartered island, many times the size of Great Britain and bordered by the Southern Ocean: New Holland.

'What are ee up to?' her mother said sharply. 'There's nothing in there for you t'bother with.'

Lucy jumped; her heart fluttered like a bird trapped in a small room. Completely absorbed by the maps, her imagination had drifted to another place. She was perched on a leather sofa reading to two young children who sat drawing exotic foreign animals with their coloured chalks. The nursery was spacious, fitted with oriental carpets and silk drapes, and a rocking horse stood in the bay window which overlooked a park. Beyond rose a skyline of towers, spires and domes.

At night her wildest dreams took flight. Kindled by the meeting with the poet in Ambleside; fuelled by her subsequent obsession with learning and fanned by the loss of Tom as her mentor, it all fell into place. She needed a job to earn her own money and to travel. Excited by the idea, she started to piece together a plan. She would to write to her aunt in London, the aunt Jonathon had spoken of. She would ask her about finding a position in the city described by William Wordsworth as he stood on Westminster Bridge:

> '*Ships, towers, domes, theatres and temples lie*
> *Open unto the fields, and to the sky.*'[6]

Chapter 9

Jos was also missing Tom's companionship, confused as to why he had been distant and even antagonistic towards him over recent weeks. 'Why has Tom gone to ground?' he kept asking around their friends, but no one seemed to know. The annual Grasmere Fair was scheduled for the coming weekend, and he hoped that in competition in the wrestling bouts and time spent together on the journey they would regain their easygoing relationship.

Jos, Tom and Luke were to stay overnight with Jonathon in Ambleside, and he had heard that Lucy might be joining them. The prospect added an extra frisson to the event.

He rose at first light to complete the morning tasks for his parents and then set off alone. On passing the borran his mind turned to the rescue of Misty, and how Lucy had showed her concern. Since that day she had often invaded his thoughts. He didn't catch up with the others until he arrived at Ambleside and spied them amongst the crowds thronging the sideshows. Approaching, he noticed Lucy was standing away from the others in deep conversation with Jonathon. He hung back to listen.

'Mr Wordsworth often asks after your welfare,' he overheard Jonathon say.

'Ee certainly made me stop and think what it is I want out of life,' Lucy replied, rubbing her hands together. 'I've decided I need to move away, probably to London. I was going to ask if you have an address for the Aunt Mary you spoke of when we stayed with you in the spring.'

Jonathon bit his lip before answering. 'Have you discussed your plans with Da?'

'Nah, I want t'have all the arrangements in place before I approach him. I'm expecting opposition.'

'I'm sure you are,' her brother said. 'And no, I don't have an address.' He touched Lucy lightly on the shoulder. 'I seriously think it would be better to forget the whole idea, Lucy. Wait until Tom is settled somewhere, then you can spread your wings and support him at the same time; without upsetting Father.'

Lucy shook her head decisively. 'That cud tek years. I canna wait that long, Jonathon. I need to get going while I'm still young.'

A cloud passed across the sun as Jos stepped back into the crowd.

The wrestling contests rounded off the day, and took place amidst a frenzy of drinking and betting. This was the first time Tom and Jos, who had both gained a certain reputation locally, were competing as seniors, and this was a considerably bigger competition. They won their opening bouts and were drawn against each other in round two.

Lucy was seated between Jonathon and Luke. She nudged them to listen as two old farmers sitting behind discussed the new contenders.

'The dark one's a stone heavier than t'other. Ee must have the advantage.'

'Aye but look at t'shoulders on the blonde fellow. Ee has a body like an arrow,' said his companion.

'But not t'chest... yer need a broad chest. Where are they from anyway?'

'Ower t'wards Shap. One of them's a Shaw... related to the schoolmaster at Ambleside. They say he has other brothers who have done well in wrestling over Bampton way.' The two old men nodded sagely. 'They breed 'em well in the Eastern Fells.'

Jonathon gave her a wink. 'Prize cattle?'

'Hold!' The umpire raised his voice. Avoiding eye contact, Tom laid his chin on Jos's right shoulder. Jos followed suit. With heart beating against heart, they gritted their teeth and set about the task of unbalancing each other to achieve a fall. Lucy watched with a mix of excitement and apprehension. Her feelings ran deep for both combatants as she watched them battle like stags at the autumn rut.

Tom won the first throw and Jos the second, which left the third to establish the winner. The crowd shouted their approval as they clung together, challenging each other with their physical strength and persistence. Pressure from Jos's shoulder caused Tom's foot to slip – he raised his leg in an attempt to regain his balance. Jos retaliated instinctively by raising his foot in what looked like a deliberate foul. The umpire brought down a hand firmly on each of their shoulders.

'Both contestants disqualified!' he called out in dismissive tones. 'For turning the contest into a brawl.' The spectators jumped to their feet shouting their disapproval of his decision – and Tom stormed out of the ring.

Her brother had not returned by the time Lucy bedded down for the night, and had left the following morning before she rose.

'I saw him through the window heading for Troutbeck,'

Jonathon said. 'He must be taking the eastern route home.'

'I'll see Lucy gets back safely,' Jos assured Jonathon as they relaxed over a late breakfast. 'Tom's narked ower something. Ee seems to have a grudge against me and I don't know why. It's ever since that evening at the pool.'

'He did get verra drunk that night,' ventured Luke. 'You both did.'

'Aye, but summat else must have happened. I didn't think ee was that smitten with Alice. Did you see him after the girls went off t'hide?'

'I followed t'others as soon as you started the count,' said Luke. 'I cud see I was in danger of playing gooseberry.' He turned to Lucy. 'How did you get back?'

Lucy focused her eyes on the worn toes of her boots. 'I wasn't far behind you all,' she replied.

'It's just a mystery,' said Jos, running his fingers through his hair in obvious frustration.

Exhilarated by the freshness of the morning, Jos strode up the stony track with Lucy and Luke in his wake. The sun laid short shadows across their path, and all eyes drifted skywards as the mystic mewing of a curlew floated down from the crags. After a couple of hours they reached a welcome resting place, overlooking the mountains in the direction of the Solway Firth.

'Let's stop here for a breather,' said Jos.

'I need t'keep going,' Luke replied. 'My da is having trouble with his lumbago so there'll be a lot t'catch up with when I get home.'

Lucy sat down on the springy turf and spread her skirts about her. Jos smiled tenderly as she wiped her forehead with the back of her hand, her skin glowing from the exertion of the climb. Despite the distraction of having

Lucy to himself he was unable to let his concerns over Tom go. He dropped down beside her.

'I miss Tom,' he said. 'I always thought we trusted each other, but ee won't even talk t'me.'

'He won't talk t'me either,' she said. 'Ee just buries himself in work, but neither of you seem to disclose what really goes on in yer heads.' She plucked at the grass, disturbing a colony of ants which darted in all directions. 'Yer both the same, outgoing and withdrawn by turns. It must be because you spend so much time with only the sheep for company.'

'Yer probably reet,' said Jos distractedly before changing the subject. 'Just look at the berries on that rowan, Lucy. What a splash of colour. Your Mr Wordsworth would know how t'describe that.'

'He isn't my Mr Wordsworth,' Lucy laughed.

Jos blew out his cheeks in a gesture of frustration. 'I wish I could read and write.'

'I could teach you – now I'm getting better. Tom's no longer interested in what I'm doing so I'm keeping my handiwork in the long stone barn. I made a sketch of the mountain ash that hangs over our waterfall, like the one over there... I'll show you one day.'

'The barn at the end of yer lane? That's a strange place. Are you trying t'hide them?'

'Mebbe, for the time being.' She gave him a shy, embarrassed look. 'Jos, d'you mind if I ask you something, something I doubt you've ever discussed with Tom? How did your sister die?'

'You're reet, it was not the kind of thing we would talk about, but I think he understood all the same.'

'Well, tell me aboot it. It must have been truly horrible for you.'

Jos gave a deep sigh. He picked up a stone and started to draw patterns on the dry earth. Without looking in her direction, he began to talk. The words flowed, like a gushing brook. Sometimes his eyes studied the ground, sometimes they strayed towards the distant hills. Lucy sensed he was reliving every minute, seeing and feeling what had happened that day – the day little Becky had perished.

'It was 'er birthday – she was born at Candlemas – and she was still wearing her nightclothes. She was two and she'd been made up with a doll Mam had knitted for her. She sat on her little stool dressing and undressing it, talking to it like 'twas a real baby. I told 'er not to be so daft, it was only a bit of wool. Tilly came in – this one's mother.' He laid his hand on Nell's silky head. 'She was only a pup and very playful. Becky started showing her the doll and teasing her with it. Tilly thought it was a game and seized the doll, so Becky jumped up and started chasing her. We knew we weren't allowed near the fire but she forgot in her excitement, and when Tilly bounded past she toddled after her. I yelled, but it was too late… she tripped and fell face first into the smouldering embers. 'Er nightdress shot into flames like it was tinder. I pulled her out by her feet but I didn't know what to do next. She was screaming… I was only five.

'I dashed outside and yelled for Mam, who was feeding the hens. She came running but it took a time. I knew water put out fire but it was frozen in the pails, and 'twould have taken me ages to collect fresh from the beck. I just stood helpless until the flames died down. It all happened so quickly, just a couple of minutes. I went t'stroke her, t'calm her down, but my fingers stuck t'her skin… it came away on my hands, it stuck t'my fingers. The smell of burning flesh overwhelmed me. I didna know what to do.' His shoulders shook as he clenched his fists. Lucy remained quite still. 'It's that smell, I nivver, nivver want to experience that again.'

'Then what happened?'

Jos took a deep breath. 'Mam came in and all hell broke out. I was sent to fetch our neighbour Jacob Armstrong. I ran back home as fast as I could, but when I got back the house was silent – Becky wasn't whimpering anymore. I picked up the doll, wet with Tilly's saliva, and was about to tell them how it had happened. Mam snatched it away from me, and threw it on the fire. She just stood as if transfixed as it burst into flames. I kept sneaking a look at her face... she was crying. It's a terrible thing when you're a child, to see yer Mam cry. I crept up and took her hand, but she just pushed me away. They nivver let me explain. They just didna want to know.'

Lucy laid her hand on his. Jos sat, his eyes tightly closed.

When he opened them a solitary tear ran down his cheek. As if in an attempt to explain himself he added, 'Much as I'd like t'move on and see the world I canna leave them, they couldn't cope. I owe them that.'

He turned to face Lucy, and without warning took her head in his hands and pressed his lips down onto hers. His cheeks were rough but his breath fresh as he searched her mouth with his tongue. He started to wrestle her, just horseplay, but she thumped his chest in an attempt to push him away. He responded instantly, as if noting the change in her mood.

'Sorry,' he said. 'I didna mean to hurt you.' He held out a hand to pull her to her feet.

'I'm fine.' She smiled as she dusted down the back of her skirt with her hand. They walked on in silence, a shadow having slipped between their easy intimacy. The tension lifted when Jos sighted a golden eagle, soaring high on the thermals.

'Look, Lucy!' He gripped her arm. 'Did ee ever see such strength and beauty? The way it hangs motionless in the sky, it's as though it's dangling on an invisible thread above the clouds. It's probably come from Riggindale – several pairs nest over that way each year. Have you ever been to Hugh's Cave?'

'No.'

'I'll tek you there. There's nothing so inspiring hereabouts. To watch them circling in pairs with the sun glinting on their backs...' He shook his head, as if unable to find the right words.

'I can see why they call them the king of the skies,' said Lucy. 'I'd like to go. Mebbe in the spring when they're nesting.'

'Nah, we should go before the winter sets in. It'll only tek us a few hours.'

On descending the last escarpment they noticed a thin column of smoke rising from the fire of a local shepherd.

'I wonder if that's my da?' said Jos. 'His sights not t'good, but I wonder what he'll make of it if he sees me with you.' Laughing, he took her by the hand.

Approaching the threshing barn Lucy heard a low whine and, she thought, Tom's voice. She stood quietly in the doorway, concealed by a pile of straw, before edging forward. In the far corner Tom sat cross-legged in front of a bed of soft bracken; a lantern by his side. Remy was having her first litter. She watched the first pup arrive before slipping out unseen. An hour later she was in the kitchen washing dishes when Tom came in.

'Remy has given birth to five pups,' he said with a broad grin. 'Four bitches and a dog. I'll tek you to see them in the morning.' It was the first time he had addressed her directly since the night at the pool.

Elated, she stepped out into the kitchen garden to collect some mint. From far down the dale the lilting music of a fiddle wafted on the still evening air. A seductive Scottish tune echoed amongst the crags, like the call of a siren across a Grecian sea. Lucy smiled to herself. Jos had some winning ways.

The sledge cut a swathe through the dying bracken. Once bright green and waist-high, it was now bronze and bent to the ground. Tom, his father and brother worked rhythmically, loading and dragging with a harmony established over the years. It was back-breaking work, and James stopped to mop his brow before addressing his son.

'Ee realise, Tom, you'll nivver be able t'make a go of hill farming.'

Tom raised his shoulders, and methodically started to unbutton the shirt that was sticking to his back with the exertion. 'Aye, Da, I've known that for a long while.'

James continued. 'We heard yesterday that Matthew is to officiate at the little church at Troutbeck. Although it will be hard t'find the fees I've decided that now yer brother has found worthwhile employment you can tek his place at the grammar school.'

Tom turned to watch his brother swing the scythe with the body of someone used to physical labour. He tried to imagine him standing in a pulpit and addressing a congregation. He grinned with familial pride. 'Congratulations, Matt,' he called out. His brother responded with an upturned thumb.

'Yer a smart lad too,' said his father. 'With the benefit of a classical education you can do equally well. Luke Yarker will be starting with you, and while you're there you can both live with Elizabeth at Knipe. Ee can pay for yer keep by helping out on their farm at weekends.'

Chapter 10

Because of the high altitude and short summers, oats were the only successful cereal crop grown by the dalesmen. Their harvest was one of the last landmarks in the farming calendar, and the whole family pitched in. It was an exhilarating sight on a bright autumn day to see men, women and children working and singing together, as they followed in the wake of the scythes.

The Shaw family were reaping in the field adjacent to their farmhouse when Jos passed by on his way to work. Standing quietly under a sycamore tree, his eyes settled on Lucy – spellbound by the sway of her skirt and the toss of her hair beneath her scarf, like the tail of a sprightly pony. He was utterly unfamiliar with the emotion she aroused in him; but it was powerful. Having had a foretaste on the way home from Grasmere he ached to once again touch her silky skin, and press his lips to hers. More than anything he wished for her to reciprocate his feelings, and having eavesdropped on her conversation with Jonathan there was now a sense of urgency. Lucy had the potential to transform his future; but he was conscious any impetuous behaviour on his part could be destructive.

The team working the scythes turned in his direction and he beckoned. Lucy skipped across, a welcoming smile on her dusty face.

'It seems likely there's a few days of good weather ahead. How aboot coming over t'Riggindale with me – t'watch the eagles?'

Lucy dropped her eyes. 'Let's wait till the spring.'

'Now would be a gud time,' he encouraged. 'It cud be a bit of an adventure. If I tek my da's gun I might even be able to get a rabbit or two before the eagle has them. No one will hear the shot.'

She gave a half-smile. 'I'll have to get the approval of my da,' she faltered.

Jos took that as submission, and was confident her father would give his permission. 'I'll ask him. I could pick ee up mid-morning after I've finished with the sheep. It should only tek a couple of hours to get there. We'll be back long before nightfall.' He gently lifted a lock of hair which fell across her cheek, and pushed it behind her ear before striding across the field to speak to James.

Lucy had mixed emotions at the prospect of the excursion. She was conscious of a mutual attraction and there was much she admired about Jos: his work ethic, knowledge of nature and innate intelligence. He had the makings of a long term companion, maybe a husband. Three months earlier she might have set off without a backward glance, but now she had serious reservations. She didn't want to jeopardise her secret plans.

Jos collected her as arranged, his father's gun slung over his shoulder. Remy, on her first outing since the birth of her pups, trotted at her side. The skylarks weaved and trilled overhead and the conversation turned to Hannah Jackson after they saw her in the distance, bent over and pulling something from the ground.

'What's she up to?' Jos asked.

'The earth's damp over there, I think she's gathering moss… their neighbour has a new baby.'

'Yer probably reet,' said Jos. 'That's Hannah for you, always caring for other people. Out on the fells I have plenty of time t' think. I only know what I see around me, and I sometimes compare you lasses to different birds. Hannah is like these skylarks flying overhead, content and happy t'stay near home; as sure of Jesus, and a life beyond the grave, as she is that the sun will rise and set.'

> *'With a soul as strong as a mountain river*
> *Pouring out praise to the almighty Giver.'*[7]

Jos gave her a questioning look and Lucy giggled. 'That's how Mr Wordsworth described the skylark. I think it fits Hannah too.'

'Now yer showing off,' Jos mocked.

Lucy disregarded his comment and ploughed on. 'I think Hannah would make someone a fine wife.'

'If they'd no greater ambition,' he said in a dismissive tone, before returning to his bird allegories. 'Now when I think of you, Lucy, I imagine the arrival of summer and the return of the swallows; graceful, carefree, yet surrounded by mystery. They come back t'nest in our old barn at Highburn every year, but where do they go in the winter?' His voice softened. 'I held an injured swallow once. It was so small and light, the colours so bright. T'think it may have travelled hundreds, even thousands of miles in search of our warm weather and insects… it just didn't seem possible. Ee canna help but be charmed.' He shook his head as though unable to grasp the idea. 'Aye, swallows are special.'

Lucy thought about his comments, savouring the

aptness of the imagery. Warming to the idea, she asked, 'And which bird would you choose t'describe Alice?'

'That's easy – Alice has to be a dunnock.'

Lucy laughed merrily.

'D'you think you'll tek to the wing, fly away like the swallows at the end of summer?' Jos quizzed her.

'Ee know that's what I hope for; one day.' A silence fell between them until Lucy asked, 'And what bird are you, Jos?'

'I don't like t'think too much about that. I'll settle for the golden eagle we're hoping to see today, and then I'll be the undisputed king of our dale.' His laughter turned to a frown, as though another thought had struck him. 'Or mebbe you and I could just be a couple of doves, like that pair I can hear in the woods, down by the river.'

Lucy lowered her head, and busied herself retying the scarf that held her hair in place.

They crossed the undulating, featureless common, and followed the steep, zigzag descent into the next dale. With the advancing of the year the sun had lost much of its heat but the view never failed to warm Lucy's heart. Stretched ahead was the lake, ringed round by tumbling fells displaying their autumnal patchwork of colours; the green and gold of the grasses interspersed with the rust of the dying bracken and soft grey of the rocks.

'It's all so beautiful,' she said with a sigh.

Jos drew her towards him; 'and so are you.' His manner was caring and relaxed.

Crossing the floor of the valley they passed the church, shielded by a ring of old yews, and the inn where the hunt regularly met. Climbing towards High Street the sense of isolation returned. A solitary raven croaked overhead, and intermittent bleating could be heard from the Herdwicks dotted around the crags. The barren terrain, broken only by stony outcrops and the occasional gnarled hawthorn covered with ruby berries, unrolled for as far as the eye could see. This was new territory for Lucy. Apart from occasional outings to Shap, to her sister Elizabeth at Knipe, and her recent visits to Ambleside, she rarely left the confines of her home. Jos helped her negotiate the boggy patches and slippery rocks. She felt comfortable with his attention as he took her hand.

There had been no farm buildings in sight for nearly an hour when they reached the high, remote corrie where the cave was located. A deep-set cavity, carved into the granite and roofed by fallen rocks, it was now a shelter used by the occasional traveller, or a hide for viewing the young eagles. Evidence of recent occupation was a thick lining of soft dried moss. Lucy found this secret dark chamber troubling.

'Tell me the history of this cave,' Jos said. Lucy's family had, for generations, been friends of the Holmes' and she had often heard them recounting the story of their origins with considerable pride.

'I'm sure you know it quite as well as I do.' She chuckled.

'Mebbe, but I like t'hear your voice,' he teased.

With a good-humoured sigh, she repeated the story of the Swedish fugitive Hugh Holmes, who had sought refuge in this very cave. 'And t'think that was five hundred years ago, and his descendants are still here today,' she concluded with a shake of her head.

'It's a romantic story,' Jos mused. 'I wonder if anyone from our dale will match it? T'found a new dynasty in a new land, that really would be something.' He pulled out a leather bottle of whisky and offered it to Lucy. She refused, and watched him sink a long draught. 'Here they come!' he whispered, pointing skywards.

Flying directly towards them, were a pair of the most majestic birds Lucy could imagine. She dropped to her knees and watched as they circled, overawed by the iridescence of their plumage and arresting behaviour.

'It's just as you promised – what beautiful creatures,' she murmured in awe. 'Oh, t'have their wings.'

Jos encircled an arm round her shoulders. 'Wasn't that worth the trek? Yer see that ledge on Eagle Crag? They nest there every year. Can yer see the sticks? Inside it'll be lined with moss just like our nest here.' She felt a shudder of excitement pulsate through his body as the birds swooped and performed in the clear blue sky. Beyond, she noticed a bank of cloud blowing up from the sea.

Jos pulled a pocketknife out of his jacket and began scratching something on a rock at the mouth of the cave.

'What are yer doing?'

'Carving our initials.'

She watched as he struggled to form the letters, resisting the temptation to help.

'JT, LS. Now that's our commitment, like the eagles. I wonder if they'll still be there in five hundred years?' He looked her straight in the eye. His expression was inscrutable, and she sensed a change in his mood. She had been happy, and she wanted to please him, but she was far from home and under a threatening sky.

'It looks like a storm's cumin,' said Jos. 'We'd better shelter in the cave.' He pushed her playfully onto the mossy floor. 'Burrow down.'

Jos was gentle. He stroked her hair and kissed her tenderly, but now fully focused on a different future, she wasn't ready for any commitment. The smell of whisky on his breath alarmed her and the muscles tightened in her stomach as he slipped his hand inside her loose blouse.

'Please, Jos, no!'

She began to panic as his rough hands explored her womanly form. His body felt hard and tense and the laughter had faded from his eyes. She grasped his fingers, pushed his hand away and wriggled in an attempt to resist his attentions. A silent scream rose in her throat, but there was no one to hear. She felt his long fingers pressing against her neck, and his weight bearing down on her chest, constricting her breathing. Within a moment he had straddled her slight form, spread her legs, and it was too late.

She lay quite still, frozen into inactivity, until a nudge in the face from Remy roused her spirits. Summoning up all her strength she rolled out from beneath him to lie curled up in a ball, the cold air blowing against her bare buttocks. She shot him an outraged look before her anger dissolved into tears. His voice softened as he looked down with dismay at her reaction.

'I nivver meant t'do this to you. This is not what I meant t'happen at all. I'm sorry, Lucy, I'm so sorry.' His voice was faint and flat. 'I thought you wanted me.' He picked up his gun and turned on his heels. Lucy watched him over her shoulder; every movement of his lean body seemed to demonstrate his displeasure at her response. She could hear him muttering profanities, until all went silent. Staggering to her feet, she brushed the dried moss from her skirt and stockings and drew her cloak round her shivering body.

As so often happens in the mountains the squall passed as speedily as it had arisen, but the sun was sinking fast and it would be dark long before she reached home. She knew if she lost her way she could be in considerable danger from the peat bogs.

Her breathing was shallow as she set off, relying on Remy to memorise the track. Using her stick she made steady progress down from the dale head, guided by the sound of rushing water in the beck. During this part of her journey the terrain was open, and apart from the crags there was little cover in which Jos could hide.

On reaching the lake she stooped to pat the collie. 'Which way, ol' girl?' With a knowing swish of her tail Remy led her towards a wall bordering an overgrown track. Here blackberry trails crossed her path and snatched at her skirt and ankles. When she trod on a fallen branch it rocked, pitching her forward. An overhanging blackthorn gored her face. She rubbed her cheek, feeling stickiness on her fingers. A fox wailed nearby, echoing her unease.

She moved as quietly as she could, just the chafing of her skirts and Remy's claws pattering on the stones breaking the silence. Was she walking in Jos's footsteps, or had he branched off in another direction? How much whisky had he consumed? Was he still angry with her? Sometimes she strained her eyes, thinking she could see his outline ahead. Sometimes she stopped, immobile, thinking she could hear his boots crunching on the gravel track behind. Once, when she dared to turn round, she found a friendly ewe following in her wake.

In the moonlight, the trees cast moving shadows across the lane, and the mountains seemed to loom ever larger in the darkness. A sharp incline to the high plateau slowed her progress. Her legs ached and she tried desperately to silence the breathing that pounded in her ears. Finally she reached familiar territory, and lit by a haloed moon crossed the desolate moorland back into her own dale where her home squatted in the darkness in welcome.

Although chilled and tired, she went straight to the

water butt. She had an overwhelming need to wash. She pulled off her boots and stockings, and then, raising her skirts, splashed herself repeatedly with the icy water. Consumed by the cold and self-pity, her body shook with sobbing.

Jos reeled, his heart and guts sickened as his anger turned in on himself for losing control. Despite all his good intentions to woo her slowly, to make it a pleasure, he could not deal with his arousal. Tormented with desire, he had behaved as though he was with Alice. He picked up his gun and cursed when his head hit the roof of the cave. After traversing a few hundred yards he slumped down behind a pinnacle of rock, out of sight of the cave, and swallowed the remaining whisky in his flask. He sat, head in hands, waiting for the alcohol to obliterate the humiliation raging in his brain. He had wanted so desperately to make her his own. He felt for her in a way he had never experienced before; there had been so much at stake, and now he had confirmed he wasn't worthy of her.

When Lucy struck off for home he followed – but at a distance. Once she reached Ravendale Head he slipped quietly past, hidden by the farm wall, and carried on to Highburn.

Chapter 11

Tom tugged at his collar, and attempted to brush the mud from his trousers. From all quarters students, ranging from small boys to young men, could be seen approaching the school. Some rode on ponies, some walked from the outlying farms, and some ambled across from the headmaster's house where they were boarding.

The standing of this educational establishment, on the banks of the Lowther, was unexpected in such a remote area. The credit lay with the headmaster, Mr Baxter, a teacher with over forty years' experience. Thanks to his reputation, the school attracted pupils from all levels of society, with small hill farmers' sons sharing the benches with those of wealthy landowners, merchants and professionals. His methods had withstood the test of time, providing many young men with a crucial stepping-stone into the wider world. A favourite saying in the district was that Mr Baxter's boys ploughed in Latin and harvested in Greek.

With such a wide age range a flexible approach was needed. This the headmaster achieved by motivating his academically able pupils to instruct the younger ones, whilst he concentrated on the senior boys. Books were in plentiful supply, both in the headmaster's study and at the public library which had been set up a century earlier, and now boasted more than eight hundred volumes.

Tom and Luke were enrolling as young adults, but both had had a good grounding at the little school in Ravendale, where the priest-cum-master had himself been one of Baxter's pupils.

As they approached the bridge Tom's attention was drawn to a well-dressed young blade of similar age, mounted on a thoroughbred mare. He immediately recognised him as George Bland, the eldest son of the Blands from Steele Hall. Although a wealthy local family they were, like so many in the area, in the pay of the Lowthers, with George Senior working for Sir William, advising on finance and investments. Tom sensed he was being appraised when the young man's eyes engaged his, before drifting slowly down to hover on his muddy boots.

'*Salve*! I haven't seen you here before,' he said, addressing Tom in particular.

'I'm Tom, Matthew Shaw's brother.' It was now Tom's turn to inspect the young man with the obvious pedigree, who was looking down on him. 'Have you been a student here for long?' he asked.

'Forever, it seems. I can't go up to Oxford until I'm eighteen. In the meantime I should be able to teach you a thing or two. How are your wrestling skills?' he asked with a not unfriendly smile.

'Tom's quite useful,' interrupted Luke. 'This year he took part as a senior at the Grasmere Sports.'

George raised an eyebrow. 'Did he? That's splendid, we should have some challenging bouts. I find there's not a lot of competition here.' With that he dismounted, and walked his horse round to the back of the school, tethering it beneath a copse of oak trees. Tom and Luke paused to watch a pair of red squirrels chase each other through the trees in the churchyard, before joining the rest of the students for their first day.

At school Tom and Luke had to adapt to the humiliation of being taught by boys several years their junior. This acted as a spur for Tom. He enjoyed the discipline of study, and within a few weeks had caught up with his peer group, was receiving instruction directly from the headmaster, and was studying alongside George Bland. George stimulated Tom's competitive spirit, both in work and on the sports field. His manner of speaking adapted to empathise with that of his colleague, and the use of the Latin tongue began to slip easily into his conversation. He speedily established a following among the younger students because of his prowess at wrestling, and exhibited a confidence that Luke warned him would not be well received back in the dale.

Living away from home gave Tom the time and space to re-examine his past friendship with Jos, and he was now anxious to rebuild their relationship. The annual shepherds' meet, scheduled for the second Saturday in November, would have given him this opportunity, but he was committed to helping out his brother-in-law.

Free on the Sunday, he left early, well muffled against the bitter weather, to join in with the ongoing celebrations. A week of heavy frost had masked the still waters of the ponds with several inches of ice, and even the edges of the fast-flowing beck had hard, jagged edges. The birds had returned to the protection of the valleys in search of food, and now perched, feathers puffed up, on the bare branches of the trees.

Raucous laughter echoed down from the heights as he approached the foot of Meredale; its source a group of

97

revellers. With the changes in wind direction came snatches of a favourite chorus as their sled pitched and swayed down the snaking path.

'*Away, away,*
Away, me lads, away.'

Tom hailed the group, but they failed to acknowledge him. He carried on to the inn where his father sat supping ale with a group of shepherds and farmers from the district. They looked up as he approached.

'How did the racing and wrestling go?' he asked by way of greeting.

''Twas verra cold up there, and slippery. Even the small tarn is under a thick sheet of ice,' said James. 'Some of the runners took falls, but luckily no bones broken.'

'Jos won the fleece for his class in the wrestling,' said Matthew. 'That's what all the noise is about. They've been celebrating ever since.'

''Twas a pity you missed the dancing and entertainment,' Luke joined in. 'Simeon came over so both Teasdales performed – they can play anything. The whole valley throbbed with the beat of the music. 'Twas such a great night.'

Tom felt despondent as he turned to greet Jos and his friends, who had now reached the inn with the sledge. Alice jumped off and threw herself upon him, but Jos barely acknowledged his presence as he forged ahead with his companions, none of whom Tom recognised.

Noticing the puzzled look on Tom's face, Matthew explained. 'They've taken on more men up at the quarry… not from around here. Jos has started working up there regularly and seems to have taken over as their leader.'

'I suppose he has the local knowledge,' said Tom.

'Mebbe, but I'm not sure they're a good influence,' said

James. 'There's talk of an illicit still, and cock fighting with heavy betting. I doubt he's making good use of any extra money he's earning. We haven't seen him up at Ravendale since you left.'

Jos swaggered past, a broad grin on his face, and a spurred cockerel stuffed under his arm. 'S'what are yer learning up at that grammar school?' He addressed Tom and Luke with a knowing smirk. 'Virgil, Shakespeare?' His followers roared with mirth.

Irritated, Tom responded without thinking, '*Scientia est potential.*' His pompous comment elicited a string of abusive words, and he knew there would be no chance of ironing out his differences with Jos this weekend. 'I'll be off home to see Mam and the girls,' he said to his da. 'They should be back from church, and I should be just in time for some dinner.'

Striding out over the common, the heaviness of the cloud cover looked ominous. He lifted the heavy latch to be suffused by the warmth of the peat fire, and the welcome from his mam.

'Yer looking well,' said Lucy, pushing her hair back behind her ears and tiptoeing to kiss his frozen cheek.

'Come on, I need more than that after all this time away.' He held her close. She laughed but her body remained rigid, her hands by her side. Looking over her shoulder he saw Hannah, her profile caught in the low sunlight, stirring a cooking pot. The smell of smoking bacon tantalised his nostrils.

'My da and the boys are up at the meet,' she said.

Tom nodded. 'There's snow on the way.' He opened the door briefly. 'Listen, you can hear the sheep calling.' A distant chorus of bleating could be heard as the ewes and lambs started their steady journey down from the tops.

Like the birds, they knew when it was time to gather in the lowlands, and were on the march as the first few flecks of snow blew in on the wind.

Within the hour a succession of shepherds, farmers and quarrymen were exchanging farewell greetings as they tramped along the track making for their homes. In the intake fields several hundred Herdwick stood motionless, a sea of white faces gathered together for protection.

Tom's father and brother Matthew called in briefly.

'We're on our way t'collect any stragglers we can find,' said Da, shaking the snow from his coat. 'Are you lads cumin?' Robert jumped up to collect his boots which were warming by the fire.

'I'll follow as soon as I've seen Hannah safely home,' Tom assured him.

Hannah had cooked and cared for her father and two younger brothers since she was little more than a child herself. They had lost their mother in childbirth, and Hannah had accepted the situation and her responsibilities without question. But she had missed out on being a child herself. There had been no time to join in with the other youngsters in the dale, and she was ill at ease in ribald company. Her solace was the Sunday service. Her idol, the local priest.

Today she was dressed in her Sunday clothes and knew she looked her best. She tried to conceal her pleasure that Tom had chosen to take her home before joining the rescue party. He unhooked her cloak from the peg where it had been warming in the inglenook, and placed it round her shoulders. She sensed something different about him, a confidence and maturity of manner. It must be this new school.

'Take my arm,' said Tom. 'We don't want you having a fall.'

Shyly, she slipped her arm through his.

'I assume there weren't many folks in church today,' he said.

She giggled. 'Nah, just the women, some small children and Harry.'

'Any dogs?'

'Just ol' Bob with Harry – he snored his way through t'sermon as usual.'

'Bob?'

'Both of them!'

Tom laughed. 'Poor Stephen, he must have begrudged having to spend time in church when there was so much going on in the next dale.'

'It's his duty to carry out t'Lord's work, that's what he would want to do.'

'I expect you're right. What biblical text did he choose?'

''Twas all about the evils of alcohol,' she replied with a serious nod of her head. 'The priest quoted from Proverbs. He said, *in the end it bites like a snake.*'

'Did he? That sounds frightening.' She noticed Tom turn away, as if suppressing a smile.

Large snowflakes were now falling fast and the icy flurries stung Hannah's cheeks. 'I hope the revellers all get home safely,' she said.

'They're familiar with the territory so I doubt there'll be a problem. But the weather is certainly deteriorating, and it will be worse on the tops.'

Hannah stamped her feet to improve the circulation. 'Luk, I can see our house from here and there are flickers of flame rising from the chimney. Da and the boys must be home. Ee'd best get back t'help your da.'

'You're so caring of your family,' said Tom. 'You've been a rock since your mam died.'

Hannah felt her face flush with pleasure at the compliment.

'Look after yourself.' He patted her hand as he turned to leave. 'Let's hope we aren't snowed-up for long. I need to get back to school.'

Hannah sneaked a look, as he disappeared into the white oblivion. It had been a long time since she had felt so happy.

Passing Ravendale Head, Tom called in to pick up a flask before setting off in pursuit of the others. Their footprints had long gone, but progress wasn't too difficult as the reflection from the snow generated its own light. He whistled at intervals to locate his father and brothers, and within the hour received a reassuring response. He eventually met up with them on their downward path towards home; led by white-muzzled collies and accompanied by thirty or more sheep they had tracked down on the higher fells.

''Twas too dangerous to carry on,' explained James. 'There's so much frozen water under the snow. We'll have another go as soon as it gets light.'

'Have you seen or heard anyone else out there?'

'We were overtaken by Jos earlier. He was making for the moorland beyond Artle Crag. ''Tis a long way off.'

'Was he alone?'

'I think so, I only saw Nell.'

Tom hesitated. 'I'll just give him a few whistles before I follow you back. Can I take one of the young dogs with me?'

'Aye, tek Rock. He's a bit excitable, but sure-footed and

has a good nose. Don't stay out on your own too long. This is turning into a blizzard,' his father warned.

Tom trudged on with head bent. Now on open moorland the wind was driving the snow and reducing visibility to a few yards. The freezing air stung his lungs, and where the snow had drifted, it was now over his knees. He gave Rock his head, and kept whistling and shouting Jos's name. When a dark shape loomed ahead, he was disconcerted to recognise it as Harter Fell. He hadn't realised he had wandered so far to the west.

Straining for any sound in this muffled world, he thought he heard a voice coming from below the ridge. Tom knew he couldn't be far from the tarn where they used to bathe. Surely, Jos wouldn't have strayed so close to such an expanse of deep water. He wondered how clear his mind was after forty hours of drinking.

With a sudden spring and a flurry of snow, Rock bounded off, having picked up the smell of Jos and Nell. Try as he might Tom could not get his attention as the young dog plunged on downwards. From below echoed frantic warning shouts from Jos. At the bottom Tom could see a wide sheet of smooth snow, like a welcoming circular field in the middle of the mountains, and gathered in one corner, under the shelter of the black-faced cliff, were a score or more sheep, huddled together in a tight circle. Beneath this smooth, inviting plain lay fathoms of ice-cold water.

Tom part-clambered, part-fell down the mountainside. Driven by adrenaline the blood pounded in his head as he slid on ice-covered rocks, bumped against boulders and ripped his clothes on rocky outcrops.

Jos, usually so in control in difficult situations on the fells, stood motionless, paralysed with fright and indecision.

Tom struggled to regain the breath that had rushed from his body and delivered a long, low whistle. Rock slunk slowly back to his side.

'I canna lose them, I've gotta get them back,' Jos hissed. He stepped onto the snow field.

'No!' Tom ran forward. 'No, Jos, you canna take the risk.' He summoned all his remaining strength to pull his friend back onto firm ground. 'Let them settle.' Jos struggled as Tom grasped him in an armlock. 'If we call them quietly from below the tarn we may encourage them to move slowly forwards, down towards the lake. Trust me, Jos,' he said in a hoarse whisper.

Then it came; a heart-stopping moment. The crack they had both feared rang out like the boom of a rifle. They watched in silent terror as the whole flock smashed through the ice into the dark waters.

Chapter 12

Stunned, Tom squatted with his hand on Rock's collar, and watched a sickening scene unfold in the diffused light reflected by the snow. The muffled stillness reverberated with the frantic bleating of the ewes, and he could hear Nell whining as she nuzzled against her master's legs.

Jos remained transfixed; his hands over his ears, his eyes glued to the far side of the tarn. There the water was whipped into foam as the animals thrashed about, struggling to keep their heads above the surface until slowly, one by one, the woolly faces slipped from view, dragged down by their waterlogged fleeces. The last air bubbles rose and dispersed. A gaping black hole remained in the snow field and an eerie silence returned to the tarn. It was as though the horror had never happened. Tom pressed his palms hard into his eyes, in a vain attempt to eradicate what he had just witnessed.

'Trust 'ee! I'll brek yer neck for this.' Jos's chilling voice shouted in Tom's ear. He was beside himself with anger as he struck out. Tom took up the brace position as fists were thrown at his face and body, parrying the blows until Jos's rage was spent. A final thump with a left hook caught him unawares and split the skin above his eyebrow. When he regained his senses, Jos was nowhere to be seen.

He struggled unsteadily to his feet, unsure how long he had been lying face down in the snow. A red stain, and splattered drops of blood, spread across the white blanket where he had lain. With Rock at his heels, he staggered off on the long journey home.

It was several hours later before he stumbled through the door. The claustrophobic atmosphere, in a room laden with humidity from the wet clothes hung above the fire, made him dizzy. Matthew caught him as he stumbled and manhandled him into a chair, his face ashen and streaked with dried blood.

'Half the Teasdale flock have been lost in the tarn,' he blurted out. The family exchanged concerned glances.

'Did yer find Jos? Is ee safe?' asked Lucy.

'I dunno, I expect he's home by now. He set off before I did.'

They asked no further questions. Matthew and Robert removed his boots, undressed him and rubbed his body dry to restore the circulation. Once he was wrapped in warm blankets Mam doled out a hot dumpling stew and Lucy bathed his eye.

'Ee better get off to bed now, son,' said Peggy. 'Tell us all aboot it in the morning. We canna do anything more tonight.'

While her two younger sisters slept soundly Lucy tossed and turned. Heavy snow always fed her insecurities. She had seen how weary her father looked when they returned with the rescued sheep, and noticed how he now used a stick as a constant support. Last year there had been nine weeks when the mountain tracks had been impassable and contact had been impossible with Jonathon, or even her eldest brother James at nearby Orton. The state in which Tom had just returned frightened her, and made her realise how dependent the family were on each other. Her plans for flight were now plagued with concern for those she would leave behind.

Later, trapped in the void between sleep and wakefulness, she suffered again the assaults she had been subjected to by Tom and Jos. Aware of her naivety, the narrow divide between love and lust, passion and violence still bemused her. For the umpteenth time she questioned her own behaviour: continuing to swim naked as she had as a child; not fighting back when Tom, drunk and incapable, assaulted her; submitting to a lone visit to Hugh's Cave. Maybe it was all her fault. And most troubling of all was her reaction to Tom's misplaced desire. Since that traumatic night, he had invaded her dreams in an unsettling way.

She crawled on her knees to peer through the window at the re-sculptured landscape. It had stopped snowing. She tiptoed downstairs. The hands on the long case clock, her da's most precious possession, stood at five o'clock. She busied herself attending to the fire and then lifted the latch on the heavily studded porch door to venture out for water. With her shoulder thrust against the wood, it took all her strength to shift the compacted snow sufficient to squeeze through. Once outside the scentless air was deliciously fresh and cleared her head. Movement above suggested Matthew and Robert would soon be down to take hay to the sheep.

Over creamy oatmeal porridge, Tom recounted the events of the night before.

'Did ee cut your eye in a fall?' asked Mam.

Tom shook his head in a manner that precluded any further interrogation.

'You and I will visit the Teasdales this morning,' said James decisively. 'T'offer our sympathy and some recompense. We can spare a few ewes now and maybe some lambs in the spring. I know it wasn't all Tom's fault,

107

Jos should never have been in that position on his own, but it was our Rock who precipitated the disaster.'

'Can I come along too?' asked Lucy.

'Aye.' Mam tapped her daughter's hand. 'I think that might help to calm the situation. And tek some tea and sugar with yer.'

Lucy picked up the prized caddy and infuser and put them in a leather bag. Dressed for the bitter weather, they each threw a sack round their shoulders for extra warmth and protection.

T om's head thumped, and every muscle in his body seemed to ache when he bent down to tie his laces. He knew his father was right, but he was apprehensive about the impending confrontation with the Teasdales.

The snow squeaked beneath their boots as they followed in the footsteps and sled tracks of their neighbours. Lucy took her father's arm and gave Tom an encouraging smile as they approached the Teasdales' dilapidated farmhouse. The rank smell he remembered from childhood assaulted his nose as soon as Edmond opened the door.

'We were expecting yer,' he said. ''Twas a bad do last night, come on in.'

Sitting crouched by the smoky fire, her head in her hands and coughing distressingly, sat his wife. Edmond motioned them to take the other stools and then went outside to call Jos.

'We're really sorry about what happened up at the tarn,' said James. 'Tom only went t'look for Jos, to help. Ee didn't expect Rock to react as he did… ee's a young dog. But Tom should've known better.'

Edmond nodded slowly but made no response.

Da turned to Lucy. 'Mek us a cup of tea, lass. We've

brought some with us,' he said in an aside to Martha. Lucy picked up the blackened iron kettle and was putting it on the ashes when Jos walked through the door. A look of surprise, and flash of colour, rose to his cheeks on seeing the visitors.

''Ello lad,' said James. 'Tom has told us all about the tragedy out on the tarn last night. It must've been a horrifying experience for 'ee.' Full of sympathy, James's eyes never left Jos's face. 'We've come today t'try and make amends for some of yer losses. We thought ten ewes now and the same number of lambs in the spring. D'you agree?'

Jos nodded gloomily, but made no comment. Nell stood up and turned in a circle, before slumping down on the same patch of damp earth. Edmond stared into the embers and Martha clasped her cup as if to warm her skin. The fight seemed to have gone out of the whole family, and Tom wondered if they ever conversed with each other.

James turned to Edmond while they waited for the water to boil. 'You've been badly missed at church, Ed, and at the meets. No one hereaboots can handle a fiddle quite like you, but you've taught yer sons well. Jos and Simeon were the toast of the district on Saturday night.'

Lucy handed round a selection of chipped earthenware mugs, and Edmond supped his tea noisily. Once it warmed his stomach, he began to talk.

'I dunno what's t'become of us, Jas. Since the common land was taken we have to graze our sheep further and further away. That's why Jos was so far from home last night.'

'Aye, I know it's hard,' said James.

'Ee seem to be managing alreet,' said Edmond grudgingly. We started on the downward spiral years ago and Martha gets so depressed. It's the lads I worry aboot. There was a time when we could hold our heads up high… but I know what they say aboot us now, and the way we live. We're not totally deaf t'the wagging tongues. We lost our self-respect some years ago.'

'Your Simeon seems to be doing well. I hear ee goes up to London with Sir William now.'

'Aye, but he's different from us… ee's not really a Teasdale, summat wrong there. Ee's no longer welcome in this house.' Edmond looked meaningfully at his wife.

James pulled out a pouch of tobacco from his pocket and handed it to Edmond. Both men filled their clay pipes, and started to draw the smoke.

'Ee have to respect him for adapting to changing circumstances, Ed. It's something we'll all have to respond to sooner or later. That's why Tom here has started a proper education. I just hope I'll be able t'do the same for young Robert.'

Tom began to relax, relieved that the Teasdales were taking the tragedy so stoically. Jos never looked in his direction, but his gaze kept straying towards Lucy.

'I'm more concerned aboot my lasses,' James continued. They'll need t'find husbands who are prepared to move out of the dale. But I shudder to think of them having to work from dawn till dusk in the heat and noise of a factory.' The two men supped their tea in empathetic contemplation.

'Couldn't Simeon help Jos find work on the Lowther Estate?' James asked.

'Aye, but Jos doesna like teking orders, and the land's in his blood. Ee's a proper Teasdale.' Edmond sucked deeply on his pipe, filling the air with the sweet scent of tobacco.

As they prepared to leave Jos stepped forward and placed the sack over Lucy's shoulders. 'Thank you,' she said, but her smile was formal, distant. Tom suspected they had had some form of liaison, or possibly a conflict, he couldn't be sure.

Once out in the crisp air a pale sun suffused the sky, painting pink tinges on the sparkling white world. A soft white blanket had swallowed up familiar landmarks, and the sheep moved soundlessly in their search for exposed grass under the protection of the trees.

'Look, Lucy,' said Tom. 'The gateposts are wearing woolly hats.' She giggled. 'That went well,' he continued.

'Aye, that was the old Edmond I knew as a youngster – just for a brief moment we saw him as he used to be.' Said his father.

Tom deliberated on the Teasdales' situation, conscious he had been unfair in treating Jos so coldly. Now he wanted to make his peace, but Jos seemed disinclined for reconciliation. The undercurrent he sensed between his old friend and his sister was also intriguing.

'I heard you had a day out with Jos recently,' he said to Lucy. 'I know I've been aloof towards him in recent weeks. Did he mention it?'

'Nah,' Lucy replied guardedly. 'He just wanted to show me where the eagles nest each year... it was an unforgettable experience.'

Chapter 13

There were many stories to exchange following the shepherds' meet. However, it was Tom's tale of the drama at the tarn that took centre stage. The younger boys clustered round to hear the details and he found himself enjoying the attention, and the way he was able to hold an audience.

Shortly before the Christmas break George's family invited Tom to stay for the weekend. Steele Hall was a revelation. A wood fire roared in the hallway and a Persian carpet graced the floor. In the dining room family portraits of elegantly attired men and women, in rural settings, stared down, and silver candelabra and tureens were displayed on walnut side tables. Having always had to share a bed, not to mention a bedroom, Tom was overawed to be shown to a spacious bedchamber with dressing room, for his exclusive use.

It was at dinner that Tom was introduced to the family. 'Good evening, Thomas,' said George Bland Senior, extending his hand. 'We are pleased to have a colleague of George joining us.'

'Good evening, sir.' Tom tried not to make his voice sound too reverential.

'Now come and meet the rest of my family.' Mr Bland

led the way into the dining room. Here his wife and daughter Catherine were sitting each side of the fire while George, and his brother Christopher, hovered in conversation by the bay window. Outside stretched a well-tended lawn sweeping towards acres of prime agricultural land. Beyond, the purple mountains provided the perfect backdrop. George smiled an encouraging greeting, for which Tom was grateful. Although he had put on a clean shirt he was uncomfortably aware of the patched elbows on his jacket, and the shabbiness and rustic nature of his clothing.

The range and depth of topics discussed over dinner engrossed Tom. Mr Bland made regular trips to London on business, was an avid reader of *The Times*, and took a great interest in affairs of state. Tom listened attentively, finding his assessments enlightening.

It soon became apparent that all those sitting round the table were expected to contribute to the conversation. Tom could switch easily between the vernacular and perfect English, but his knowledge of the politics of the day was limited to the small geographical area in which he circulated. However, when the discussion turned to the relative merits of the English poets he was on more familiar ground, and contributed an opinion on the new rising star, William Wordsworth. Mr Bland responded animatedly.

'Did you realise he was a well-known political agitator in his youth, and even supported the demise of our royalty? I've had dealings with the family over many years, always complaining about the debts they were owed by the Lowthers. Sir William has been good to the family; Wordsworth needs to appreciate that. He even gave him his current post.' He wiped his mouth on his napkin in obvious irritation.

'And what d'you think of his poetry, sir?' Tom asked.

'He's had some dreadful reviews; particularly by Lord Byron and that fellow Jeffrey of the *Edinburgh Review*.' His host broke off a piece of bread to mop up his gravy. 'I've been told the preamble he includes with each of his little offerings is particularly pompous. Typical arrogance of a Cambridge man I fear, and to be expected from one who supports the ideals of Tom Paine and his ilk.'

'I cannot agree with you, sir,' Tom challenged. 'I think his work is outstanding.' George and Christopher looked up abruptly from their plates. Tom pressed on. 'He champions the shepherd and farmer, and writes with simplicity using the language of the common people. When I read a selection of his poems to my sister and a friend they just couldn't believe poetry could be so meaningful.'

An amused look flashed across Mr Bland's face. 'How were you able to get hold of his work, Thomas?'

'I've a brother who teaches in Ambleside. Mr Wordsworth mentors the school and gave Jonathon a signed copy of *Lyrical Ballads*. He loaned it to me.'

'I have read some of his poems,' Mrs Bland joined in. 'They lack the traditional format and classical connections for my taste; and I find some of the topics he addresses are really quite trivial.'

Tom's lips tightened. 'They may seem trivial to you, Mrs Bland, but they can inspire those of us who identify with the language and subjects.' Out of the corner of his eye he saw Christopher give a nod of approval. 'For us it's about real people. My sister wept when she heard his poem *Michael*. Surely verses that strike so hard at the emotions must have some merit?'

'I have heard his work is much admired,' his hostess responded quickly with a patronising smile. 'Particularly by the young.'

Tom was aware Catherine's eyes had never left his face, and he felt the colour rising in his cheeks as he ploughed on. 'It was being introduced to William Wordsworth's poetry that motivated our Lucy to teach herself to read and write. Like all the girls in our dale she has been denied a basic education. Surely that has to be celebrated.'

'Of course, of course,' said Mrs Bland hurriedly, getting up from the table. 'Now let's all sit by the fire and Catherine can entertain us on the piano.'

Tom had held his own, and he noticed Catherine giving him shy, approving glances.

Tom was woken the following morning with a crisp tap on the door. He pulled himself up on his pillows.

'Good morning, sir. I trust you slept well.' Tom watched bemused as an elderly butler set down a pitcher of hot water for him to wash, and then knelt down on arthritic knees to attend to the fire.

The rest of the weekend went well. The Blands had permission to hunt locally, and with a borrowed gun Tom and George spent the next day stalking red deer in the nearby forest. George narrowly missed a solitary hind, well obscured in its greyish-brown coat amongst the decaying vegetation. George cursed as it bounded away, but Tom was not unhappy; it was a beautiful, harmless animal. That night at dinner they were served venison.

'I expect this will be a treat, Thomas,' said Mr Bland. 'I doubt you've tasted venison before.'

Tom hid as smile as he remembered the escapees from the Lowther herd that had arrived in Ravendale over the years – never to return!

L ucy had a dream. With the pocket money her father gave her to spend at Shap Fair she purchased paper and

115

sealing wax, and in her head she composed the letter she would send to her aunt. She desperately wanted to discuss it with Tom, but the emotional distance between them seemed unbridgeable, and she knew Jonathon did not approve of her plan. Regretfully she decided it would be better to maintain secrecy, and wait for a positive response from Aunt Mary before broaching the subject with the family.

The immediate objective was to find her aunt's address. She knew there was a bundle of documents, wrapped in linen and tied with tape, in the settle. She had never been curious about these before, but now hoped they might include some correspondence from her relations. An opportunity to investigate came one morning when her father was out repairing a collapsed wall, and Mam had gone to visit an elderly neighbour at Bombay. Her stomach muscles tightened as she furtively untied the bundle and scanned through the papers.

Amongst the wills, mortgages, conveyances, receipts and miscellaneous correspondence she found two short, formal letters from a Mary Ernest in South Kensington. These related to some money matter she couldn't understand, but in the absence of anything more definite she had to assume these were from her aunt. She smoothed the paper, noted down the address and replaced the package.

Sitting by the waterfall, with the sun over her shoulder, she meticulously penned her letter in what she hoped was appropriate language and tone.

Dear Aunt Mary,

I hope I find you and Mr Ernest in good health. You may not remember me. I am your sister Margaret's daughter and I will soon be eighteen years of age. The main purpose of this letter is to ask a great favour. Do you know of any situation I could apply for in London? As you will no doubt recall there are few opportunities for young women here in Westmorland.

You will note from this letter that I am literate, but self-taught. I am also fully conversant with the running of a house and dairy, but only in the ways of the area in which I live. I like to think I am adaptable and can learn quickly.

I sincerely hope you will be able to comply with my request and anxiously await your response.

Your affectionate niece,
Lucy Shaw

Lucy folded the paper neatly, wrote the address and sealed the join with wax. She now had to wait for an opportunity to visit Shap – alone.

Chapter 14

The festive season was soon upon them, and as was the local custom each family took turns to entertain their friends and neighbours with the best they had to offer. On Christmas night the whole valley would gather at Ravendale Head, and in preparation holly and ivy were collected from the woods, a lamb roasted on the spit, and a hock of salt bacon boiled. Elizabeth and her children would be missing this year; their loyalty now lay with her husband's family.

'I'll walk over to Knipe on Boxing Day with the gifts Da has made for the youngsters,' Lucy offered.

'A good idea,' said Mam. 'Ask Matthew or Robert to go with you.'

'Nah, I'm sure they'd rather stay here with their friends. I'll leave early and be back in the late afternoon. I'll just tek one of the dogs for company.' She flashed her mother a confident smile.

Tom returned from tending the animals to find several ponies tethered in the yard, and the flickering lights of a roaring fire glimmered behind the windows. His da, who was clearing the snow from the path leading to the privy, gave him a wave. On reaching the farmhouse, the merry music of a violin wafted on the air. *Good*, Tom thought, *Jos is there and maybe Edmond too*. He paused outside the porch to knock the compacted snow from his working boots, and combed his fingers through his hair. Gently he lifted the latch and edged his way inside.

All eyes were concentrated on Lucy, who was standing on a low table. Her Sunday dress, of fine grey wool with a white crocheted collar, skimmed her slight body, and her hair floated loose on her shoulders. Her voice had a husky edge, and there was a natural rhythm to her movements as she swayed to the music of Robbie Burns, *Ye Banks and Braes o' Bonnie Doon*. He switched his attention to Jos, who was standing behind wielding his bow, tapping time with his foot. There was a tender expression on his face, a look Tom had never noticed before. The ballad came to an end to wild clapping, and the stamping of boots on the flag floor. Acknowledging the applause Jos hung his fiddle on a hook on the wall, before retrieving the ball of mistletoe suspended in the inglenook. Coming from behind he threw an arm round Lucy's waist, lifted her down and planted a kiss on the side of her neck.

Tom was overwhelmed by the pang of jealousy which swept over him as he watched Jos embrace Lucy before all their family and friends. He stepped brusquely between them and took her arm, whispering, 'Da's outside clearing a path through the snow. He needs our help.' He propelled her towards the door. Relaxing his grip, he realised he needed to respond to her obvious euphoria. 'That was an exhilarating performance, Lucy,' he said more gently.

She cleared her throat. 'Thank 'ee, Tom. They're such an appreciative audience, I could sing all night.'

The liquor flowed freely and the communal singing and dancing began. Edmond joined his son in providing the music, young Robert led the dancing and the older generation clapped in time to the familiar tunes, the whole room bound together by the rhythm of the music. The menfolk took it in turns to introduce the songs and ballads, which became bawdier as the evening wore on. Alice and her brothers contributed a Welsh carol, which was greeted with a good-natured mixture of derision and enthusiasm. When midnight drew near Lucy, by popular demand, led the singing of the dale's favourite carol, *While Shepherds Watched Their Flocks by Night*. Tom noticed a high colour had crept up on her cheeks.

The guests began to drift away, their lively voices and laughter floating back in the clear air. Alice snuggled up to Jos.

'Are you going to walk me home?' she asked with a teasing smile.

'Yer'll be alreet. You have yer brothers as chaperones. Da and I will be going in the opposite direction, escorting Hannah and her family.' Father and son stored away their instruments in the cases and prepared to leave.

'Thank ee for cumin.' James shook Edmond warmly by the hand. 'We couldn't have celebrated in such style without you.' Edmond and Jos slapped each other on the back, a joyful moment for them both.

'Where's Lucy?' Jos asked, looking round. 'I'd like t'thank her for a great neet.'

'She's already gone up to bed,' said Tom. 'She was tired and has to be up early tomorrow to visit the family at Knipe.'

Boxing Day dawned bright, but with a heavy frost glazing the snow. Lucy's head thumped as she struggled to rise from the hair mattress. Her skin felt hot and dry to the touch, and she had a tight sensation in her chest. Today, of all days, she could not afford to be ill. A long, circuitous journey lay ahead; first to Shap to deliver her letter, and then on to Knipe to cover her tracks. A round trip of many miles.

'Pass on our love and blessing,' called out Mam. 'We hope they like their gifts.' In Lucy's basket were stowed the wooden toys their grandfather had made, whittled away by the fire during the autumn evenings. 'And let 'em know what a good evening they missed,' she added.

Lucy gave her mother what she hoped passed for a cheerful wave, and tapped the letter secreted in her pocket.

A rasping dryness in her throat, and stabbing pain behind her eyes troubled her as she crunched her way up the track. The brief elation of the Christmas festivities was now drowned out by a problem she had tried to ignore for too long. She was carrying Jos's child.

Lucy was confident Jos would offer to marry her, and her parents would encourage their union... but she had more ambitious plans. Alternative courses of action spun in her head. Maybe, if she received an offer of employment within a couple of weeks, she could hide her condition, go to London and await the consequences. Maybe, if there was the prospect of a position in the future, she could keep the name of the father secret, and leave the baby in her sister's care. She knew any money she sent back to support the child would be welcome in Elizabeth's household. Until these options had been ruled out she resolved not to tell Jos.

Preoccupied with these thoughts her footsteps propelled her forward until she heard the faint rumble of wheels and the clatter of horses' hooves. She had nearly reached her destination. The main street was empty of pedestrians and she had passed no one on her journey. She now adjusted her shawl to obscure her face as she handed over and paid for her letter at the King's Head. The elderly licensee at the inn assured her it would leave on the evening coach to London.

A heady mixture of fear and excitement had carried

her to Shap. Now, with her mission accomplished, she felt unutterably weary. She yearned to lie down, to rest her burning cheeks in the soft snow and sleep.

Lucy was lost in an unfamiliar world. Kneeling in a walled garden, she planted spring bulbs between scented rosemary. On the westerly wind a plume of black smoke drifted across from a nearby factory, and a baby cried constantly from the far side of the stone wall. At the top of the hill she could see a church. Her knees ached as she struggled to her feet and set about the climb. She was on her knees again, but this time in prayer. The morning sun streamed, mauve and azure, through the stained glass windows, and threw shadows across the stone floor. Fashionably attired men and women rustled in their seats, and all eyes were riveted on the pulpit. Lucy followed their gaze to see a fine-looking, dark-haired man in a white vestment – with tears rolling down his cheeks. She kept reaching out, stretching, hoping just to touch his hand, his surplice; but he was always, always just beyond her reach.

'Turn 'er over. Is she alive?' A rough voice from far, far away interrupted her semiconscious state, and a hand pushed her gently on the shoulder.

'She's just a young lass, poor mite... but she's dressed well fer the cold. She's not a vagrant... and t'dog looks healthy enough.'

'D'yer recognise her?' said his companion. 'Look in her basket, see if there are any clues.' Lucy felt someone tapping her cheeks.

'Can ee tell us yer name, lass?'

Lucy could hear Remy whining softly, but could not marshal her thoughts or summon the energy to speak.

'She canna hear yer, she's not conscious.'

Chapter 15

Having returned jubilant from the evening's festivities, Jos spent a sleep-deprived night thinking about Lucy. Up early, he completed his morning tasks at record-breaking speed, hoping to contrive an accidental meeting with the woman he idolised. His excuse to his mam, as he set off, was that he needed to clear his head.

A light fall of snow in the early hours had obliterated the footprints of the previous night, so Lucy's tracks were easy to follow. When the path divided, at the point where she should have diverted for Knipe, the steps and paw marks carried on towards Shap. He was confused but carried on doggedly until he reached the high road, but found no sign. Acutely aware he was stalking her, he retraced his steps to follow the direct route to Knipe.

Jos hadn't travelled more than a mile when Nell's ears pricked up, and in a flurry of soft snow she bolted across the open moorland. He whistled and called, but uncharacteristically she was slow to respond to his command. When she did finally return she jumped all over him in excitement.

'What is it, ol' girl? Have ee found something? He turned up his collar and quickened his pace. A copse came into view, and a collie bounded towards him out of the trees. He instantly recognised Remy, and deeper in the wood he could make out a couple of figures, crouched over a heap of clothes. He broke into a run.

'Is she hurt?' he called out to the two farmhands who were leaning over a young woman.

'Not that we can tell. She seems t'be drifting in and out of consciousness, so may have hit her head. Do ee know who she is?'

'Aye, I do.' He knelt down, cradled Lucy's head and caressed her cheek with a rough hand. He whispered in her ear, but she didn't respond.

'I need t'get her home.' He scanned the sky.

'How far do ee have to go?' asked the younger of the men.

'A few miles east of here, beyond Hallswater.'

'You canna be carrying a lass that distance. I live just over the rise, you can borrow my pony,' he offered. 'That's if ee can handle him, ee's a bit frisky.'

'Will it carry us both?'

'Nah, he's only a babe, but you can walk alongside.'

'Thank ee,' Jos said. 'That'll be grand, and if ee've got an old rug to keep her warm, I promise to bring them straight back.'

Jos wrapped Lucy tightly in the rug and lifted her onto the animal's back. The pony seemed to understand what was needed, allowing him to hold the leading rein loosely while he supported her limp body. The snow held off, but it was an agonisingly slow journey. On the final decline Jos saw Tom in the yard, breaking up the ice on the duck pond.

'Tom, come here, quick as ee can,' he shouted. 'Summat's happened to Lucy.'

Tom threw aside his pick and ran to meet them.

'A couple of farmers found her out on the fell; they've lent me their pony to bring her home.' Together they lifted her off her mount and carried her indoors, her hands and cheeks papery white and frozen.

'Whatever happened?' asked Peggy, her hands shaking as she undid her daughter's cloak.

'Nell found her, or rather Nell nosed out Remy in the copse near Dingle Bottom.'

Peggy looked puzzled. 'But she was on her way t'see Elizabeth. Why was she so far off the track?' She rubbed Lucy's hands with her own to restore the flow of blood. 'D'yer think she'd been lying there for long?'

'I dunno,' Jos replied shakily.

Peggy touched him gently on the arm. 'Thanks for bringing her home, Jos. Now could yer fetch James for me? Ee's with Matt and Robert, down in the threshing barn.'

Within a few minutes all the family had gathered round. No longer needed, Jos stepped out into the fading light to start the long trek back with the pony.

The next few days dragged by, the family powerless to help Lucy, who had a high fever and debilitating dry cough.

Tom climbed the stairs, mildly nauseated by the mingling smells of baking bread and dried lavender that hung in the air. Lucy's eyes were shut tight, but he was relieved to see her breath no longer rattled deep in her chest. He dropped down on his knees beside her bed. He could not forget the desire he had felt for her, and questioned now whether this was his punishment. Not sure whether she was asleep or awake, he took her hand.

'Lucy, I need to tell you something…' His mouth was as dry as sun parched grass. He moistened his lips and began to recount his version of the assault after the game of hide

125

and seek. 'Please forgive me, I didna know it was you or even what I was doing.' Lucy's thumb twitched, and then stroked the dark hairs on the back of his hand in a gentle rhythm. He sat, unsure what to do or say next. 'Would you like me t'read t'you?'

'I'd like that,' she said in a hoarse whisper. 'Read me *The Brothers*.'

He fetched the leather folder, and a few loose papers fluttered to the floor. Tom gathered them up. 'I thought you'd copied out more than this,' he said.

'Aye... a book,' she said wearily, and mumbled something he was unable to decipher. He picked up her hand for the second time and started to read. Her lips moved with the vestige of a smile, and her chest now rose and fell with a regular beat. Partway through he felt the pressure from her hand slacken as her fingers spread and went limp. He studied her face for a full minute as it lay on the rough pillow, her complexion as smooth as the effigies in Carlisle Cathedral. The harsh winter winds and days spent toiling in the sun had not had time to leave their mark on her young skin, and perhaps they never would. A childish image of Snow White flashed across his mind. He moved quietly from the room to join his mother, who was sitting by the fire peeling vegetables.

'She's sleeping, Mam, and breathing quietly.'

A bright smile lit up her weathered face. 'So the crisis has passed. Thanks be to God.' She ladled the potatoes and carrots into the stockpot and crept upstairs to check on her daughter. 'She'll sleep for hours now. We won't disturb her,' she said to Tom as she went out into the dairy.

Lucy opened her eyes. Sunlight was streaming through the low window. Why had they let her sleep so late?

She raised herself up on the pillow and looked round the room. There was a jug of water and a towel on the box by her bed, and a thick blanket had slipped onto the floor. Something was amiss. She felt normal, well even, but disconnected from her situation. She banged her head with her fists as she struggled to recall what had happened the day before. The rope tail of a wooden horse poking out of a basket caught her eye, and slowly it came to her: the party on Christmas night; being the toast of the evening. Today she had promised to take the presents to her niece and nephew and she was already late.

She held her breath, her ears strained to listen to the movements in the house: a bird scratching on the roof; a creaking timber; the dripping of water. She seemed to be alone. She clambered out of bed, momentarily steadying herself against the wall as her head spun. A single thought hammered in her brain: she must get to Elizabeth's farm and back before the family returned for their evening meal. She pulled on her clothes and took a clean pair of stockings from the box by her bed. On impulse she picked up the linen bag in which she kept her money, pen and a few trinkets. She tied it round her waist and pushed it under her skirt.

Why did she feel so weak? Passing through the pantry she helped herself to a flat loaf and hunk of cheese which she ate hungrily. The food gave her energy. She rubbed some goose fat into her chilblained hands, laced her boots, picked up the basket and quietly closed the door behind her. Her brothers must have taken the dogs; she would have to travel alone.

The incline on the road leading from the farm was not steep but her breath did not come easily and her joints ached. The weak warmth of the sun maintained her spirits, and with each laboured step her memory cleared as if she was climbing out of a black pit: the excitement of the festivities, Jos's attentions, the tortuous journey to Shap and the posting of the letter.

The irregular drum of iron shoes hitting the hard stones on the lane broke into her thoughts. She turned and stepped back to let the rider pass. The horse whinnied as it drew to a halt and the rider, a middle-aged man, leant forward to pat its neck. He smiled down at her. 'A lovely morning for a ride,' he said. Swaddled in a thick scarf Lucy did not recognise the face, but there was an openness about him which she found comforting. 'I've been spending a few days in Askham,' the stranger continued. 'Some old family business. I wanted to take in the beautiful scenery around here before I returned to the city, so borrowed my host's mare.'

Lucy smiled and nodded.

'And where are you heading, young lady?' he asked in a kindly tone. 'You look weary, as if you might appreciate a lift.'

Peggy had scarcely left Lucy's side for a week. Now, at last, she was free for a quick visit to see her neighbour Jane Yarker. It was a sparkling day, and her mood was carefree as she wandered up the lane, keen to catch up on the local gossip and attempt to unravel the mystery surrounding Lucy's escapade.

Bustling home an hour later to prepare the midday meal she was hailed by Tom, who had returned ahead of her. 'Mam, where's Lucy? The house is empty.' His voice shook with concern.

'She canna be far away, son, she's too weak. Have ee checked the privy and all t'barns?'

'Aye, I've looked and called out everywhere. D'you think she's passed out somewhere?'

Peggy hastened up the stairs. The room was immaculate, the blankets neatly folded on the bed. But Lucy's clothes, which had been hanging on a chair by the window, had gone, together with the basket containing the bairns' toys. Peggy lifted the lid of the box by Lucy's bed; her grey Sunday stockings were missing, and the bag with the money she had saved from the butter they sold at Shap.

'The basket and toys aren't here. She must have gone to see Elizabeth,' she called down. 'What was she thinking of?'

'The others should be home any minute. We'll tek the dogs to look for her,' Tom shouted back.

James and his sons split up, each following different routes to Knipe. Robert was the first to arrive at the farm. By the entrance gate, sheltered under the hedge, he found the basket of toys.

The family and neighbours scoured every local track until finally James was forced to seek out the parish constable at Askham to recruit volunteers for a wider search. For the next few days everyone in the district combed the area looking for Lucy, but no one had seen her, and no further clues were found.

Peggy was hanging out the blankets from Lucy's bed when the local constable marched purposefully down their lane. She called to her husband, and together they walked hand-in-hand to the farm gate to meet him.

'I've grave news, Mr Shaw.' The constable removed his hat. 'They've found the body of a young girl, answering to the description of your daughter, in woods just south of Penrith. They think she may've been robbed and then murdered.'

'But she wouldn't have had anything with her worth teking,' said James.

Peggy grabbed his arm, her eyes large and unseeing, as though caught in the bright light of the evening sun. 'I think she may have, Jas. I don't understand why, but it seems likely she had the money she's been saving with her. I thought it was to buy writing materials, but mebbe she wanted to give some to her niece and nephew. It's certainly gone from the box by her bed.'

For a brief moment the impenetrable mask that always settled on her husband's face in times of crisis slipped. She squeezed his hand.

'Ah, so robbery could have been the motive,' said the constable with a satisfied air of finality. 'I'll need someone to come and identify the body.'

'I'll saddle up my horse,' said James.

'I must warn 'ee, sir, they say she's been badly mauled. The winter scavengers have already done their work.'

'Wait till Tom comes back. Tek him with you,' Peggy pleaded.

'Nah, lass. This is something I can protect my family from having to witness. It's something I must do for you all.'

Peggy slumped uncomprehendingly into her rocking chair. She swung endlessly back and forth, trying to make some sense of it all. How could her daughter have travelled so far – and why?

Later that day, as the shadows lengthened and the cold began to bite, she stood alone at the gate waiting for her husband to return. At last the outline of a man leading a horse appeared on the horizon. Immune to the pain in her aging knees she picked up her skirts and ran and ran. James had returned with Lucy's body, wrapped in several blankets bound with twine and strapped to the back of his pony. He threw an arm round his wife's shoulders as together they brought their daughter home.

'Jane Yarker will be cumin along later to help yer lay her out,' James said. 'But please, lass, don't under any circumstances unwrap the bindings.'

Peggy nodded assent. 'Cud they tell how long she'd been dead?'

'Nah, the doctor cud tell me verra little. Neither how she died, nor when. She may have collapsed again, or she may have been attacked. He could not tell from her injuries.'

Curious, Peggy asked, 'But what about her clothes? Did ee notice what she was wearing?'

''Twas difficult to tell, lass, they were all torn and covered with mud. I think it was her usual tweed skirt and brown stockings.'

Peggy bit her lip, but remained silent. She helped James lift the light body from the back of the pony and carry their daughter into the silent house. Afterwards she walked purposefully to the end of the garden where the bee skeps nestled in the wall behind the orchard.

Peggy and Jane laid Lucy's swaddled body in a simple wooden casket, padded with sheep's wool and lined with white linen. James nailed the lid firmly in place and James and Matthew balanced the casket on two upright chairs, well away from the fire. The family took turns to sit with her, day and night.

Tom approached the coffin warily, laying his hand tentatively on the polished wood.

Mam caught his eye as she raked the wood-ash in the hearth. She smiled encouragingly. 'She's at peace now, son. We were reet lucky to have had her for those few years.' She wiped her smudged cheeks with the corner of her apron.

A knock at the door signalled the arrival of the first of a string of neighbours, each bringing small gifts for the family. Mam went to greet them and Tom took over the vigil.

Meanwhile James was kept busy informing the extended family and making arrangements for the funeral. By the light of a blazing fire he wrote letters late into the night, and the following morning set off at dawn to catch the mail coach at Shap.

The heavy oak door squeaked as Jos lifted the latch. The house seemed too quiet. He felt like an intruder. From under his jacket he produced a pair of ducks, ready plucked by Martha. Peggy didn't question their provenance, but thanked him warmly and took them to the dairy to salt, leaving him alone with Lucy. Jos hadn't seen her since the afternoon he brought her safely home. Day after day he had found an excuse to pass the farmhouse. He had lingered at the threshold but each time his nerve failed and he had walked on by. Now, alone with her coffin, he stood paralysed in the doorway.

His eyes travelled round the familiar room. In every corner he felt her presence. The panelled cupboard, where he had hit his head as a child and she had kissed it better; the window ledge where her mam had displayed the daffodils; the spice cupboard, where he and Tom had been caught stealing pinches of sugar; the hook on the wall, where he had hung his fiddle on Christmas night.

Mustering all his emotional strength he walked to where her casket lay. He leant across and laid his cheek against the polished wood and his mind returned to the last time he had been in this room. It was on Christmas night, when he had placed his hand round her waist and felt the swelling in her belly.

Chapter 16

The single bell tolled, calling friends and neighbours. Tom stood, his arm round Robert's shoulder, and watched the slow-moving silhouettes appear on the horizon. From north, south, east and west, across the common and adjoining dales the mourners came. Most travelled on foot, but some on ponies, which they tethered in the field next to the farmhouse. Dressed in their carefully brushed Sunday best, everyone gathered in the chapel yard for the simple service. Elizabeth cradled her baby and Mam gripped the hands of her grandchildren. Hannah stood, head bent, at the back with her father and brothers.

Accompanied by Edmond Teasdale, the dalesmen raised their voices to the hymn Lucy had sung so memorably at the Easter service, *When I Survey the Wondrous Cross*. The melancholy strains, lifted by the light wind, echoed evocatively around the snow-capped crags.

Tom drew a piece of paper from his pocket and carefully unfolded it. He straightened his back, lifted his head and read the last stanza of the poem he had shared with Lucy and Jos, on that life-affirming day last summer.

> '*She dwelt among the untrodden ways*
> *Beside the springs of Dove*
> *A Maid whom there were none to praise*

And very few to love;
A violet by a mossy stone
Half hidden from the eye!
Fair as a star, when only one
Is shining in the sky.
She lived unknown, and few could know
When Lucy ceased to be;
But she is in her grave, and oh,
The difference to me!'[8]

His voice faltered when he came to the last line, and he cast a sidelong glance to where Jos stood alone under the shadow of the sycamore trees. His head was bowed, his shoulders shaking. The three of them had spent so much time together when growing up, now Tom pondered just how close Jos had been to Lucy in recent weeks. A blackbird sang lustily from a high branch, and he saw Alice step up from beyond the clump of trees and grasp his arm.

The Reverend Stephen Wilder delivered the final prayer, and the coffin was strapped to the back of a piebald pony, supported on each side by his two older brothers. Mam said her last goodbye before joining the women and children as they turned towards the mountains and home. Led by Stephen, the men shuffled into a rough line, and the sad procession moved off along the Corpse Road towards Shap.

Jos muttered a few ill-chosen words to Tom as he pushed past to take his place near the back, adding, 'I nivver even had the chance to say goodbye.'

Tom shook his head. He could think of no reply. Remy rubbed against his leg, almost causing him to lose his footing. 'Go home girl, on yer way,' he growled at the dog in irritation.

The path took them over the fells, where the boggy land had frozen hard. Alongside the crumbling ruins of the abbey, it narrowed between dry stone walls covered in bright green moss. Tom dropped back to join Jos.

'Here, have this,' he said, offering him the poem. 'I know you loved her too.' Jos ignored his gesture and they walked on in silence. 'Lucy would have wanted you t'have it,' Tom repeated encouragingly.

'What's the use?' said Jos disconsolately – but still he took it and stuffed it in his pocket.

A rattling of loose stones made them both look back. Skulking along, about fifty yards behind, as though herding a flock of sheep, was Remy. Tom was about to shout a rebuke when Jos intercepted.

'Leave her be. She's doing no harm and we've no way of knowing what she knows or feels.'

The cortege was met at the lychgate by the vicar of Shap, and escorted to the open grave. Here Tom's attention was drawn to a striking woman in a gown of fine wool, topped with a Black Watch tartan cape. Too smart for a local, she looked out of place. He wondered why she was there. Just a tourist, maybe, who happened to be visiting; or perhaps she had relatives buried in the churchyard. She stood with her back to the church wall and the hood, which partly covered her face, was blown back by a sudden breeze. Her expression was sad, but had about it the composure that was typical of the local community. To Tom's great surprise his father walked over to speak to the stranger, took her arm, and drew her in to join the mourners round the graveside.

'That must be Aunt Mary,' Jonathon whispered. 'The one who escaped to London; twenty years ago.'

Tom studied her discreetly. She had the dark eyes of the Whitesmiths, but it was hard to believe this tall, elegant woman had once been a country girl like his mother. Living in London had certainly removed all trace of her rustic inheritance. And what had brought her to Shap at this time? Young deaths were not uncommon, so it seemed unlikely she would have received word from the family, or considered it her duty to be there.

Numbed with cold and grief, the entourage stood in silence as the coffin was lowered into the earth. Tom scanned the respectful faces of the mourners before self-pity took control of his thoughts. He closed his eyes and dug his nails deep into the palms of his hands as the last ceremonial handful of earth was scattered on the lid of the casket… Ashes to ashes, dust to dust.

'What brings you here, Aunt Mary?' Tom heard his brother address the outsider.

'Ah, you recognise me, Jonathon,' she replied with obvious pleasure. 'I was on my way to Scotland to visit my husband's relations when I heard of this sad event from the proprietor at the inn where I slept last night. The circumstances of your sister's death sounded so dreadful I delayed my departure, thinking it would give me an opportunity to pay my respects to my own family. I'm sincerely sorry. I've heard tell she was a talented girl.'

'Aye, she could sing like a nightingale and, like you, had the drive to improve her status in life. She could have gone far,' Jonathon replied.

Aunt Mary seemed to falter for a moment before responding. 'I understand from your father that you now hold a position of responsibility in Ambleside. Congratulations. How do you like living there?'

'I like it well enough, and we are delightfully entertained by the visitors who come each summer with their London ways and extravagances.'

She acknowledged his telling comment with a smile, before asking, 'Have you ever come across Mr and Mrs Wordsworth, or his sister Dorothy?'

'I know William quite well. He's a good friend of the school and often calls in for a chat. Why do you ask? D'you perhaps know him?'

'I know his work of course, which I much admire, and I did meet him many years ago when he was in London. It was during his youthful militant years. He was an old Oxford friend of my employer at the time.'

James strolled across to join his sons. 'It's time to be on our way. Will ee be coming back with us, Mary?' He clasped his arm round his sister-in-law's shoulders. 'Peggy would so appreciate it if ee did.'

'I only wish I could, but my coach is booked and I am expected at Carlisle. Please give Margaret my condolences and tell her I will be writing.' She pulled up her hood and turned towards the highway, while the funeral party regrouped to return to the dale for tea. Jos did not join in the wake. Tom watched him divert towards the slate quarry, and no doubt the comfort Alice could offer.

Once the mourners had departed Tom took the path leading to Ravendale Force. Following the contours of the beck he picked up a stick to throw in the water for Remy to fetch. The anticipation and eagerness to please that pulsated through his dog's body finally melted his heart. After the rigid self-control of the day he threw himself down on the heather, and slapping his hands on the turf he cried out like a stricken animal.

Jos whistled for Nell. Together they walked resolutely along the path leading to Ravendale; an evening stroll he had often taken with his father in happier days. A rabbit scuttled across the path, reminding him of the many times he and Tom had gone ferreting as boys. The cold northerly wind whipped his face and his eyes started to water. Jos had felt like an outsider at the funeral and now he was determined to get his own back, to have something tangible to remember Lucy by.

On reaching the Shaws' home all seemed quiet. The farm dogs barked, but in a half-hearted way as though they recognised his step and the smell of his dog. He slipped past the farmhouse and stood quietly outside the door of the stone barn, checking no one was coming. When satisfied he lifted the latch and sneaked inside. It was coal-black – maybe he should have chosen a night with a brighter moon. Standing on tiptoe he started feeling along the top of the wall, just below the roof as Lucy had specified. He stiffened when he heard a door bang shut, but it was only one of the womenfolk going to the closet. There was a clatter of clogs on the flagstones – then silence. He hardly dared to breathe as he searched systematically behind the piles of hay, stored wood and farm equipment. Finally, in the corner furthest from the door, his hand touched the glassy smoothness of a polished slate. On closer inspection he found they were the two slates Lucy had described, and concealed between them a thin package enclosing her commonplace book. He replaced the slates and hid the packet deep in his overcoat pocket.

To avoid passing the farm for a second time he waded through the beck and squelched back home to Highburn. The following day he carefully stitched an inner lining into his violin case. 'To protect my fiddle', he told his parents. Behind it he secreted the package.

Chapter 17

Heartbroken, the Shaw family coped with their loss in the only way they knew how. For James and Peggy, who had lost two children in infancy, it was the Lord's wish, and their duty to endure it stoically. They put their energies into the daily round of activities and encouraged their children to do the same. Peggy struggled with the extra work, particularly in the dairy where Lucy had had a strong wrist for turning the butter. James and Robert rose early and returned late, having spent the daylight hours out on the fells. Tom, meanwhile, knuckled down to his studies but ached for someone to talk to, to share his pain. Jos, who he felt sure was equally grief-stricken, had withdrawn all contact with Ravendale.

With the mental isolation from his kinfolk Tom's friendship with George Bland blossomed, and he became a frequent visitor at Steele Hall.

'I heard some interesting news today,' said Mr Bland as Tom joined the family for dinner. 'There's going to be a challenge to the Lowther brothers in the forthcoming election.'

'Surely not,' said his wife. 'Their family has represented Westmorland unopposed for decades. Who's daring to put up against them?'

Her husband picked up his napkin and tucked it into his shirt. 'Henry Brougham, a Penrith man.'

Meaningful glances were exchanged between the young people at the table.

'He could be a strong opponent, Father,' Christopher ventured. 'He already has a national reputation as a supporter of the campaign against slavery. If elected it could reflect well on this area.'

'Mr Baxter directed us to an article in the *Kendal Advertiser*,' George added. 'It was an account of his brother's visit to Kendal to set up an election committee. He had some harsh words to say about the Lowthers, and even referred to Westmorland as a "rotten borough".'

Tom took a long drink from his glass, and cleared his throat. 'My father tells me the talk at Shap Market is about how well Brougham can rally the support of the crowds. He's gaining a reputation locally as a good orator.'

'You mean he curries favour with the mob to whip up discontent?' countered his host.

'You could say that, sir, but he undoubtedly appeals to the nonconformists who are thriving in towns like Kendal. He might not make much impact this time round, but it could be the first step towards major reform.'

Mrs Bland handed round tureens of vegetables, fresh from the garden, and Catherine turned to Tom. 'Does your father have the vote?' she asked shyly.

'He does. But several of our neighbours, who are working similar amounts of land, aren't so fortunate; and neither are my brothers who are educating the next generation. That hardly seems fair… or indeed a sensible way to run the country.'

'The present arrangement works best for all levels of

society; leave well alone is my advice,' said Mr Bland. 'The Lowthers have always looked after our interests.'

Tom noticed two bright spots of colour on Christopher's cheeks when he spoke up. 'But Father, we live in the middle of nowhere and are protected from the realities of political life. They'll have to extend the franchise someday. As Tom has pointed out there are a lot of educated, articulate men around, particularly where industry is flourishing. Why should these men, who contribute significantly to our economy, be denied the right to vote just because they don't own land? Surely they are entitled to a say in the way the country is run.'

Mr Bland gave his younger son a dismissive look. 'I can't think of any examples round here.' He grunted.

A sudden draught of wind came down the chimney, filling the room with smoke. Mrs Bland gave a delicate cough. 'Whatever the outcome, the canvassing and propaganda will soon be starting in earnest. We'll all have to watch what we say.'

'And don't believe everything you read in the newspapers,' her husband added. 'Particularly from anonymous contributors.' He pushed back his chair and rose to his feet, precluding any further discussion. 'Now what are you young people planning to do this weekend?'

The hunt was scheduled to meet near Ravendale, and Tom had invited George to join his family and friends.

'It's about time you saw how the other half live,' he said with a grin. 'Christopher will be welcome too.'

It was a crisp February morning when Tom and Luke Yarker met the Bland brothers at the crossroads and escorted them to Ravendale Head. Here Tom introduced them to James, Peggy and the family.

'It's a good scenting day and likely t'stay calm,' said James as he shook their hands warmly. 'Yer in for a good day's sport. I just wish my old legs would let me join 'ee.'

They climbed steadily until they gained two thousand feet. Here the snow lay in patches, giving them a panoramic view of several dales. George and Christopher joined wholeheartedly in the holloaing, and they all stood spellbound as a crafty fox ran for several hundred yards along the top of a wall to confuse the hounds. To Tom's relief Jos and his gang were nowhere to be seen. He assumed they were working at the quarry, and this was confirmed when a loud report shook the fells.

The sky had a pink glow by the time they returned to the inn for a meal. Two carcasses hung prominently from ceiling hooks; the prize for today's effort, and a glowing fire and the aroma of roasting meat completed the welcome.

James was sitting at a table with a group of elderly farmers, and congregated in the nook sat Jos, Alice, her brothers Dai and Bryn and a few other men from the quarry; all buried deep in conversation. Alice, with her usual enthusiasm, bounded over to meet the new arrivals and Tom introduced her to his guests.

'Alice has a very outgoing personality,' he said, patting her bottom before adding, 'she comes from Wales!'

'What are yer companions up to?' Luke asked Alice. 'They look as if they're plotting some mischief.'

'We're all off to Kendal tomorrow,' she said excitedly. 'The Lowthers are starting the canvas for votes and we're joining the demonstration in protest.'

'You're going along too, Alice? Is that wise?' Tom asked.

'We'll have a lively time, and the boys'll look after me.'

George frowned. 'Are you telling us you support the Whigs?'

'Indeed I am. My family are Congregationalists, and most of the lads sitting over there were Cornish tinners, and Methodists... though I doubt any of them have seen the inside of a chapel for many a year.'

She was still laughing when Christopher asked, 'Didn't Brougham use to represent Camelford?'

'So the lads tell me; that's another reason they back him.' She waved her hands dismissively. 'Anyway we hear they'll be laying on free ale. It's an excuse for a bit of fun.'

James, who had been listening attentively, puffed on his pipe. 'Yer reet, Alice, 'tis the dissenters Brougham's appealing to, though his own background isn't too different from the Lowthers, and I reckon he's equally self-serving in his outlook.' He tapped the tobacco from his pipe and turned to George. 'What does your father think aboot it?' he asked in a kindly tone.

'He thinks we should maintain the social order as it stands. It's a tried and tested system.'

James nodded. 'I understand, lad. Like me your father has a loyalty t'the Lowthers which is hard to ignore.'

Jos wandered over.

'We've been discussing the demonstration you're planning to join tomorrow,' said James, addressing Jos. 'Just remember, lad, you've more t'lose than yer companions. The earl owns the land your da farms, and ee pays your brother's wages.'

'Mebbe, but ee doesn't own me,' Jos replied defiantly.

The chat and warm ale flowed, and when a young farmer struck up a tune on the harmonica the customary singing began. Jos was in good humour and Tom was able to engage him in a conversation relating to the hunt. Meanwhile Alice sat talking to Christopher, and when she slipped outside Jos rose with undue haste to follow her. George flashed Tom a concerned look.

'He'll be all right,' said Tom with a wink. 'Alice can be a bit wild, but she's plenty of common sense. She'll look after him!'

It was after midnight when they walked in a silent procession back to Ravendale, their way lit by the lantern of the moon meandering in and out of the clouds. As they threw themselves down on the straw mattresses in the upper room Tom felt confident that George and Christopher had enjoyed the day, and were too exhausted to notice the paucity of their surroundings.

Candlemas had been celebrated, and the first snowdrops were pushing through between the gravestones when Mr Bland rode into Bampton. Spying his sons with Tom and a group of youngsters behind the lychgate, he reined in his horse to speak to them.

'Have you heard of the goings-on in Kendal?' His voice was brusque.

'I did hear that there had been a bit of a riot,' said Tom. 'No doubt we'll read the full story in the *Advertiser*.'

'Some of the troublemakers came from your dale,' said Mr Bland accusingly, 'and there was a woman involved. I hope they aren't friends of yours, Tom.'

'Were any names mentioned, sir?'

'Two brothers by the name of Watkins, and a lad called Teasdale. Do you know them?'

Christopher lowered his eyes.

'I do,' said Tom, 'but I doubt they meant any real harm. The rumour I heard is that they were plied with free ale by those representing the Lowthers, and that's why matters got out of hand. Did you hear what actually happened, sir?'

Mr Bland sat up straight in his saddle. 'I've been told by one of the escorts that Lord Lowther's carriage was travelling down the main street in a triumphal procession when it was attacked from all sides with mud and stones. The horses had to break into a gallop to get to safety. It was all most undignified, dangerous too... an absolute disgrace.'

Tom swallowed hard. 'It happens all the time at the markets and fairs, sir. Anywhere there's a free drink.'

Mr Bland looked sharply at his two sons. 'Tom is always welcome at Steele Hall, but I cannot condone you mixing with such riffraff. You boys are not to visit Ravendale again.'

Chapter 18

Their last school term had ended. George had been accepted at Oxford, to start in the autumn trimester. Tom was to spend a year at the newly opened theological college at St Bees, and Luke was to assist at the grammar school until a more permanent post could be found.

Before moving away to finish his education Tom was looking forward to a summer back at Ravendale, and the opportunity it afforded to rekindle his old friendships. He began by helping out the Jackson family.

'D'you still miss Lucy?' Hannah asked as she led the pony and sled up the pre-cut track through the bracken.

'All the time. Whenever I'm at home I imagine how she used to be. When I hear a light footstep on the stairs, or brush past the lavender bushes in the garden. Sometimes, when I see the silhouette of one of my sisters spinning by the window, just for a brief moment... '

Hannah halted the pony, enabling her brothers to pile the bracken neatly round the edges of the sled. 'Aye, that's just how I see our mam.' She wiped her hands slowly up and down the front of her leather apron as if in deep thought. 'Tom, d'you believe there's another life beyond this world?' Her question took him by surprise.

'If I'm to follow a career in the church I'll be obliged to,' he responded in a matter-of-fact voice.

'Ee don't sound verra convinced.'

'You're reet. My memories are the only life-after-death experience I can make sense of. I don't have your unconditional faith, Hannah – but I'll be working at it.' He attempted a laugh.

''Twas a lovely poem ee read at Lucy's funeral.' Her voice sounded wistful. 'It cud've been written for her. I wish I cud read like that.'

'I helped Lucy,' said Tom. 'I could help you while I'm still around.'

Hannah dismissed his offer with a shake of the head. 'I'd be no gud at schoolwork, and when would I have the time? My da and brothers always seem t'need me.'

Tom stood back to watch her brothers, their shoulders already muscular, their bare backs gleaming in the sun. 'It won't be so long before they find wives of their own and move away,' he said. 'Then you'll be left with just your father. You have a future to plan for too, Hannah.'

She looked unconvinced, and turned the conversation by asking, 'Now tell me, Tom, aboot yer plans?'

'First to be ordained, and then to move t'somewhere where they need priests; which is likely to be a long way from here.' He kicked at a loose stone with his boot as he weighed up his prospects. Ideas had been slowly gestating in his head. William Wordsworth's talk of the French Revolution; the reasons behind the recent riots in Kendal; the challenging discussions at the dinner table at Steele Hall – all had sparked an interest in the politics of the poor and oppressed.

'Y' mean t'some city slum? Is that better than what ee have here?'

'Perhaps not, but I won't know till I've tried. It's what Lucy used to dream of. She had aspirations,' he added with some irritation. He unhitched the pony and retied it to the front of the sled for Hannah to steer back to the farm. 'You seem to be seeing a lot of Jos these days,' he said, handing her the reins. 'I'm not sure what path he's following, but he seems to be drifting away from his roots.'

'Yer reet. Ee has some strange opinions and tells me he hates the lords and ladies for their power and influence. I just don't know where his ideas come from.'

'It's his companions up at the quarry,' said Tom. 'Most of them have travelled the country. They're aware of the agitation which is brooding and the excitement that can bring.'

Hannah sighed as she pushed back a stray wisp of hair. 'And now it looks like yer'll be joining them.' Tom thought he noticed her chin tremble as, averting her head, she tugged at the halter of the pony and stalked off down the slope. He concentrated on cutting more bracken to fill the second sled, and by the time she came back her smile had returned. On impulse he leant across her soft body and planted a kiss on her cheek.

'I luv yer, Tom Shaw,' she murmured.

'I hear the Lowthers had an easy ride at the election,' said young George as the family gathered round the fire.

'It seems so,' said Christopher, 'though there was trouble afterwards and the military had to be summoned – yet again.'

Their father took a glass from a silver tray and handed it to his wife. 'I hope that silences the opposition for a while. Better the devil you know – every time.'

'I don't agree with you, Father,' said Christopher. 'I hope this is just the beginning, not the end of resistance.'

'And I'll be damned if I'll be given a lecture on how this country should be run by my own son.' George Bland flashed an angry look at Christopher. 'We don't want to repeat the experience of France on English soil.' He downed a large gulp of whisky before continuing in a more measured tone. 'Now let's concentrate on more important matters. Has your father decided on your future, Tom?'

'Yes, sir. I'm going to St Bees Theological College for a year, and will complete my training as a curate at Newton Rigg. It's not a big living, a population of five hundred or so, but there's free accommodation in a one-roomed cottage owned by an elderly widow a couple of miles from the village. Being independent will suit me well.'

'That's a good start, Tom. It's a fair-sized parish in which to get the necessary experience under your belt. Once you're ordained I may be of some help to you.'

The following morning, as Tom was leaving Steele Hall, he noticed Christopher in the yard grooming his horse. Curious, he diverted to speak to him.

'Have you been seeing Alice?'

Christopher nodded and tapped his nose. Tom touched him lightly on the shoulder. 'Be careful my friend, she may not lead you the way your parents expect you to go.'

Tom walked on briskly, making for home. His mind returned to Hannah's unexpected response at his impending departure. It seemed she was not as committed to Jos as he had thought. There were few eligible women in the dale and he was aware his choices were limited. Hannah was warm and caring – and physically strong and capable. Perhaps she would make a good wife. When their paths crossed at the Sunday morning service he approached her.

'Hannah, once I've graduated from college would you consider joining me at Newton Rigg?'

A look of surprise and pleasure crossed her face, but her brow soon furrowed and she was slow to respond. 'Nah, I canna do that, Tom, but I'll wait for 'ee… wait till ee come back to Ravendale.'

'I have to sever my ties here,' he said bluntly. 'I doubt I'll ever return. But for the next few years it's likely I'll still be in Westmorland. You could join me as my housekeeper. We might even consider marriage if that's what you wanted.'

'I wouldn't want t'be away from all I know here. I'm happy living in Ravendale.'

'It's not Botany Bay you'd be heading for,' said Tom, unable to disguise his growing impatience. 'It's just the other side of the fells. You could be home within a few hours.'

'I'm sorry,' said Hannah, 'but I canna do it. I have t'think of my family.'

Tom appreciated this was where her loyalties should lie, but her passivity irritated him. 'It's your choice,' he said over his shoulder as he quickened his pace to rejoin his family.

For the rest of the summer Tom passed most of his leisure hours with Hannah, and the older generation smiled knowingly. But the following year, when he had settled permanently at Newton Rigg, word got back that Hannah was once again spending time with Jos.

Tom served Newton Rigg well. He inspired the children at the village school; read and wrote letters on behalf of parishioners to families now dispersed across the country and the New World. He delivered familiar sermons, directly related to the biblical text, and watched the old men nod their heads in agreement, before drifting off! He held squealing babies at baptisms and gnarled, veined hands at burials. He walked miles to outlying farms to support the sick, and on the same visit chopped wood, collected peat, delivered lambs and rekindled fires. He caught, and resisted, the eye of some of the young and not-so-young women of the parish. His manners were courteous and his behaviour beyond reproach. He was ordained as a deacon at the parish church in Windermere in 1820 and was now, a year later, ready for ordination into the priesthood.

The day before the ceremony Tom returned home for a celebration picnic which Luke, who was now the Ravendale schoolmaster, had organised at the head of the lake. Only Jos was missing as the old gang relaxed and chatted, reliving their childhood memories. As the day wore on the heat became oppressive.

'Luk at that sky.' Richard pointed upwards. 'We're in for a deluge. It's time we made for shelter.' Thunder rumbled overhead, petering out in the hills to the north, and the first big drops of rain pockmarked the dusty earth.

Luke gathered together the remains of their picnic and pulled Agnes to her feet. 'Let's make for the shepherd's hut over yonder. It's just a summer storm; I doubt it'll last long.'

'There won't be room for us all up there,' said Tom. He held out his hand. 'Come with me, Hannah.' Running and laughing, they made their way to a sheep shelter on the other side of the beck. 'A bit cramped, but it's clean and dry,' Tom shouted above the downpour which pulsated on the galvanised roof of their refuge. Hannah shook the rain from her shawl, and Tom crossed his arms and wriggled his shirt free from his trousers. He laughed as he wrung out a stream of water before putting it back on.

An hour passed and the deluge continued, with the beck rapidly gathering water from the fellside crevice.

Flashes of lightning streaked across the sky and claps of thunder reverberated menacingly around the mountains.

Hannah shivered. ''Tis God talking, ee can feel the power.'

Tom bit his lip. 'I had hoped to see Jos today,' he said, changing the subject. 'Is everything going well with you two?'

'Aye, we understand each other. But I worry aboot the company he keeps.'

'Is that where he is today?'

'I canna say. Ee says the less I know the better. They seem to do a lot of drinking and plotting. Ee thinks all working men should have the right to vote. What aboot t'women I say? Ee doesn't agree with that.' She laughed and moved closer.

'I can appreciate his frustration with what life has thrown at him,' said Tom. 'I just hope he doesn't get himself into serious trouble.'

With the coming of the rain the temperature had dropped. Hannah slipped off her shawl. 'Tek off that wet shirt and put this round yer shoulders,' she said. Tom shivered from the coolness of the air as she tugged at the second sleeve. Perhaps misinterpreting his response her hand wandered to his groin, and she began to unbutton his flies.

'I won't ask anything of yer, Tom, I won't cause trouble... we can just enjoy ourselves.'

Tentatively Hannah wriggled herself to lie on top of Tom. 'Do you...' she began, but overtaken with embarrassment didn't finish her sentence. She kept her eyes on his face, willing him to let her in mentally; to stroke her hair, caress her skin, whisper in her ear. But Tom's eyes remained shut; his hands still; his countenance an unreadable mask. She knew he held her in no high regard. He did not want her in the way she wanted him. His mind was probably elsewhere. She had to accept that.

For years Tom had been her secret passion, something over which she had no control. To be near him as she was now, to absorb the rain-washed smell of his skin, to touch him in an intimate way; her heart danced with the indescribable pleasure. Her soft flesh rose and fell with every breath he drew as she transferred the warmth of her body to his.

Tom felt no great desire for Hannah, but with her mothering ways she was a gentle reassuring presence. He slid slowly into her and she responded with shivering delight. Afterwards she gave him a furtive sideways look, a glance which seemed to reflect the same fears and uncertainties he was experiencing. He knew this wasn't love, but comforting it certainly was. He wondered how many relationships were built on similar foundations.

'Mebbe I can now keep some of you in the dale,' she whispered as they lay under her shawl, listening to the steady metronomic beat of the rain.

Hannah's comment unnerved him, and as voices from the past resonated in his brain he thought of Jos, and began to question her motives.

Sunday 12th August 1821 was a momentous day, with an early start for Tom and his father.

'I'm reet proud of you, son,' Mam said. 'Put this on yer finger – once the bishop has blessed you.' She dropped a plain gold ring into his hand. In mint condition, he examined it with interest.

'Where's this come from?' He rotated it, round and

round with his index finger. 'There's an M inscribed on the inside, is that for Margaret?'

'It's been in the family a long time and was intended for Lucy when she reached twenty-one. I know she'd have liked you t'have it now you are starting out on a new life. I had the blacksmith enlarge it for you,' was her noncommittal reply.

A heady scent of honeysuckle, damp from the morning dew, permeated the air when Tom and his father reached the Kings Arms. Today he found it nauseating. The stagecoach pulled up promptly at nine o'clock with Geoffrey Parsons, his sponsor, already on board. An hour travelling along the Carlisle to Lancaster road brought them to Kendal and the parish church by the River Kent. Dating from the early thirteenth century, it had recently been enlarged and renovated. When full it could accommodate over a thousand worshippers, and glancing round Tom could see few spare places in the pews. Polished boots clicked on the stone floor and the organ played quietly in the background as the choir filed in. Tom sat nervously with the other ordinands to await the arrival of the Bishop of Chester.

'Here he comes,' murmured Geoffrey. The building throbbed as the organist thumped the bass notes before the music swelled to a crescendo. A tall, overpowering figure in full regalia floated down the nave. He paused at the crossing in front of the carved rood screen, turned to face the congregation and cleared his throat.

'Priests are ordained to lead God's people in the offering of praise and the proclamation of the gospel. They are to set the example of the Good Shepherd before them as the pattern of their calling.'

Tom smiled to himself; this was an analogy he appreciated.

The bishop's sonorous voice droned on as he worked down the line. 'Send down the Holy Spirit on your servant Thomas Shaw for the office and work of a priest in your church.'

He laid his hands on Tom's head and a shudder passed through his body, like the shaking of the ground when the rocks collapsed in the borran. Tom knew he was now committed; but he also knew it wasn't a free choice or a calling. For him it would be a job. He fingered the plain gold band his mother had given him that very morning; a symbol of the priesthood he had joined.

It came as no surprise to Tom when he heard that both Edmond and Martha Teasdale had died, within ten days of each other, from the pneumonia that had afflicted Lucy. The harsh winter weather meant the funerals had taken place a month before the news finally filtered through. He waited for the snows to clear, and then took a few days' break to pay his respects to Jos and visit his own family.

Approaching Highburn the dogs charged out to greet him but, unusually, there was no one about. He tapped lightly on the open kitchen door and called out. In response came a shout of distress. Alarmed, he pushed through into the dark interior to find Hannah lying prostrate on a horsehair mattress, beneath a jumble of old blankets.

'What are you doing lying there?' he asked in shocked surprise. 'Are you ill?

'Tom! Thank God someone's come.' Her face glowed white, beaded with cold perspiration. 'I knew my prayers wud be answered. They don't call this labour for nothing.'

'Where's Jos? Is he somewhere around? Can I fetch him?'

'Nah!' She arched her back and groaned.

Tom instinctively knew it was too late to summon help. He would have to rely on his experience of bringing lambs and calves into the world. Fortunately Hannah was young and healthy, and responded well to his instructions. He spoke gently as she struggled with the spasms of pain; squeezed her hand hard as she summoned the strength for the next push; encouraged her when she seemed distraught.

'I can see a dark head,' he said. 'A final push should do it.' As he spoke a baby boy slipped easily into his hands and started to wail. Lost in wonder at the miracle of human birth he wrapped the newborn in a folded sheet, and laid him on his mother's belly, as though he was a lamb to be licked clean.

Hannah smiled up at him. 'Thank 'ee, Tom. I'm that grateful you dropped by when you did. You may not have heard – Jos and I got married on Boxing Day. Ee'll be so pleased ee has a son.'

Tom nodded, his mind in turmoil. 'So where is Jos?' he asked once he felt calmer.

'Ee went into Kendal – some unfinished business, ee said. We weren't expecting the birth yet. Baby wasn't due for at least three weeks.'

Tom stroked the downy head. 'He looks a big, healthy lad to me. Well done both of you.' He was bending down to put the kettle on the fire when the dogs started barking.

'I think yer da's back,' Hannah panted excitedly, clutching the baby to her breast.'

'I'll be on my way,' said Tom, pulling on his boots and grabbing his stick.

'Won't ee stay and wet the bairn's head with us?'

'Nah, lass. This is the time for you to be alone with your new family.'

'I can nivver thank ee enough, Tom.' She smiled and held out her hand. Tom gave it a squeeze and took his leave.

Outside he met Jos in the yard splashing water on his face from the rain barrel.

'Congratulations, Jos,' he said, patting him warmly on the back. 'You've a beautiful baby boy in there.'

Chapter 19

'For God's sake keep your voices down… and tread on the bleedin' grass,' muttered Davy Pascoe.

Jos, Dai and Bryn followed in single file, led by the weak light of a crescent moon. They had unknotted the handkerchiefs round their necks and retied them over their mouths. Each man carried a stave; one end wrapped round with old cloth and soaked in tallow. Stuffed deep in Davy's pocket was a tinderbox. A light west wind cooled their sweating brows as ahead loomed the turrets of the castle; stencilled outlines against a pewter sky, like an etching from a medieval fairytale.

Jos was ill at ease with the whole clandestine expedition. His enthusiasm for reform and energy for political agitation no longer matched that of his companions; particularly that of Davy. Davy had had a brother killed in the Peterloo massacre, and since turning up at the slate quarry had used his powerful personality to coerce the other miners into rebellion against authority. A heavily built man, he carried a grudge against the world and the aristocracy in particular. Tonight's escapade was part of his plan to take vengeance.

Jos had to confront his own demons where fire was concerned, but he was also aware that arson could lead to hanging, or the very least transportation. He now had a wife and son to consider. There had been a long spell of dry weather so the hay lay tinder-dry, and he had argued in advance of the escapade that now wasn't the right time to be carrying out such an attack.

'The wind's not reet,' he kept telling them. 'I know it's only a light breeze but it keeps changing direction, it could drive the flames and sparks eastwards.' He shook his head anxiously. 'That would take it towards the barns and stables.'

'All the better,' scoffed Davy. 'We'll give them a good roasting.'

Bryn tried to reassure Jos. 'The walls are solid stone and the roof's slate. We can't do any harm to the buildings, even if the sparks fly.'

The night was unusually silent. The thumping of Jos's heart resounded like the tick-tick of a grandfather clock, and he jumped when a small creature scuttled across their path, rustling the dry, dead leaves.

'This is it, lads, the ricks are just beyond that wall,' muttered Davy. He unhitched the gate soundlessly and they crept towards a row of black shapes in the corner of the field. A dog barked from somewhere near the home farm. They froze until it tailed off into a few desultory yaps. The three men huddled in a circle round Davy as he blew the tinder alight, and transferred it to the first rick. For a brief while, it smouldered. Then a wisp of smoke floated upwards, followed by a crackle and the first flame burst forth. Within thirty seconds, a fire blazed.

'Come on, light the rest of 'em – let's get out of here,' Davy commanded. The Watkins brothers plunged their staves into the flames, and ignited two of the remaining ricks. Fanned by the breeze they were soon infernos, roaring through the hay. The heat scorched their faces, and sparks exploded in all directions, singeing their hair. Jos beat out an ember with his hand when it landed on Dai's shirt.

'Get on with it, Jos, the last one's yours,' said Davy impatiently.

Jos regarded the fires in a panic of indecision. 'I canna do it, it's madness.' He threw down his stave as ferocious barking started up at the castle, and shouting from the nearby village.

'Run for it!' hissed Davy. They needed no second bidding. Jos, being the only one with an intimate knowledge of the locality, vaulted over the nearest drystone wall, and using it as cover ran on its lee side, like a fox escaping its pursuer. From there he waded through the river and made for the common. He didn't look back until he was within sight of home. Finally, gasping and gagging, he sunk down on his haunches and turned to see the eastern sky ablaze. What had they done?

'Luke, Luke, wake up!' Richard shook his friend repeatedly by the shoulders. 'There's a fire over towards Askham.'

Luke threw off his cover and crawled on his knees to look out of the attic window where a pink glow lit up the horizon. 'It's coming from the direction of the castle. Surely the earl's home hasn't gone up, not again.' Luke started to pull on his trousers. 'We'd best get over there right away. You bridle the ponies and I'll pick up some buckets. We'll call for Jos on the way.'

Richard looked doubtful. 'We can't afford the time. Anyway, ee'll likely 'ave seen it and be over there ahead of us.'

With their eyes fixed on the crackling display ahead they gripped the ponies with their knees and urged them into a canter. When they reached the castle grounds a pall of smoke hung over the ornamental lake from where a chain of men were drawing buckets of water. Tethering their ponies by a stream they ran towards the outbuildings. Here Luke had to raise his voice to be heard above the pandemonium.

'Which way, which way?'

'Through the walled garden t'the stables,' said a bystander. 'They've lost the hayricks, and a spark has ignited the hay inside the barn adjoining the stables. "Tis the horses they're trying to save now.' They handed over their pails and made for the stables, where tongues of flame and smoke were drifting towards the looseboxes. Standing well back, conducting the rescue attempt, was the earl's son, Sir William.

'Have they got the horses out, sir?' asked Luke. 'I don't mind going in.'

'Simeon is with them. He said he could manage better on his own. They know and trust him.'

A shout from behind made them turn to see Jos arriving wet and dishevelled. 'What the 'ells goin' on?' he spluttered.

'The earl's hayricks were set alight, and the wind has carried sparks and embers in this direction. The whole building is full of smoke.'

Jos paused to assess the situation. Horror-struck, he could hear the horses coughing, their hooves sliding and clattering on the worn cobbles and bashing against the wooden stalls.

'Simeon's in there, trying to encourage them out,' Richard shouted above the hubbub. 'How did yer get so wet?'

161

Jos ignored his question, and pulling the ragged handkerchief from round his neck dipped it in a bucket of water. 'They're in a panic. I've gotta help Sim.' He started to run towards the stable door.

'Hold on,' said Luke, 'here he comes.' The door flew open, and with his head buried in his charge's neck Simeon led a black stallion, smeared with lather, out into the fresh air and handed the distressed animal over to Sir William's care.

'Sim!' Jos yelled out. 'What can I do?'

Simeon turned abruptly, a wave of relief passing over his dirt-streaked face at seeing his brother. 'There're three more horses in there. You tek the horse in the first bay on the left. Ee's a steady animal.' He threw Jos a wet towel. 'Blindfold him, and try to keep him calm. I'll follow close behind with the filly. She's much livelier and he'll be a comfort to her. It's impossible t'see with all the smoke and they keep prancing about.'

Jos knew he didn't have his brother's experience of handling thoroughbreds, but he was confident his empathy with animals would see them through. 'What's his name?'

'Benbow.'

Inside the smoke was choking, the horses whinnying and kicking out. Jos laid his hand on Benbow's collar, slipped on the head cover and whispered in his ear. Together the brothers led both animals to safety.

Simeon mopped the perspiration from his forehead with his sleeve. 'There's still the master's old mare Patience to be got out,' he said, turning back towards the stable door. 'I'm going back for one last try.'

'I'm cumin' with yer,' said Jos.

'Nah, leave this one to me,' said Simeon. 'She's an old horse and we might be too late.'

The door slammed closed behind him, followed by a gut-wrenching thud of crashing timber. Jos charged forward and manically pulled at the handle. From behind a strong hand circled his neck in a crushing grip. It was Sir William.

'Leave it, man, you'll do more harm than good. Any further rush of air will fan the flames.'

Jos stood impotently beside Sir William, their eyes riveted on the only exit.

Miraculously the door crashed open once again. Patience galloped off into the night, and Simeon collapsed, spluttering in the doorway to be pulled clear by Sir William, who cradled him in his arms. Dazed, Jos stood by watching the pair.

'I'll make sure whoever did this pays,' growled Sir William, clenching his fist in an angry gesture. 'If it's those belligerent workers up at the quarry I'll have them all arrested.'

'What meks ee think it was arson, sir?' Jos asked.

'It has to be: three ricks going up at the same time!'

Throughout the night the village constables, and ground staff from the castle, made extensive enquiries around the hamlets, villages and outlying farms. Rumour was rife. Some said two strangers had left the scene in a hurry and disappeared into the woods making for Martindale. Others reported a lone masked man taking cover on the road towards Penrith.

The following morning all the workers at the quarry had reported for work except a Cornishman, David Pascoe, who had been taken on just a few weeks previously. Everyone was interviewed by representatives from the Lowther estate. Jos and the Watkins brothers were able to supply alibis, and later that day Jos questioned Bryn.

'Yer got home alreet then?'

'Yes, only Alice noticed the burns on my shirt, and she knew better than to ask any questions. What happened to you?'

'I went back and joined in the rescue... I had to. I thought we'd lost Simeon at one stage. Ee went back into the stable for the last horse when part of the roof collapsed... I've nivver been so scared.'

Shortly after midday two constables stopped by at Highburn. Hannah was able to confirm Jos had been out tending the sheep, and had joined in the rescue attempt as soon as he had seen the flames.

In the evening, when Jos set about chopping some kindling, Hannah noticed him wince as he gripped the axe. 'What's the matter with yer hand?' she asked. 'Let me see.'

'It's nowt,' he said, pulling his hand away. 'It's just a blister, from hauling the sled yesterday.'

Chapter 20

Tom served as a country curate for thirteen years. An able, conscientious assistant, he was encouraged by the aging incumbent, Geoffrey Parsons, to remain in post until his retirement, when he confidently told Tom he would be offered the living. When he finally stepped down, his son, who had been serving a parish in Manchester, applied to come home. The local landlord and patron offered the post to Gabriel Parsons.

During his years at Newton Rigg, Tom made regular forays back home to Ravendale. Having delivered Edward into the world, he felt a special bond with the boy. In the early days, Edward would toddle towards him on sturdy legs, chuckling as Uncle Tom swung him onto his shoulders. As the years went by, he sprinted up the lane like a young deer on hearing his whistle. Taking Tom by the hand, the pair would wander back, lost in conversation in their private world. Sometimes, Tom admitted to himself, it was this frequent contact with Edward that deterred him from moving on.

Jos was rarely about when Tom called by and he gathered, from Hannah's comments, that he had also withdrawn quite suddenly from socialising with his comrades at the quarry.

'Ee really enjoys Edward's company though,' she

said. 'Ee teks him off into the fells whenever there's an opportunity.'

'That's splendid,' said Tom. 'He'll teach him his shepherding skills, and an appreciation of the natural world. He's a good da.'

'That ee is,' Hannah agreed happily, 'and ee makes sure Edward goes to school regularly. Luke Yarker says he's doin' really well.'

On what was to be his final visit to Highburn for some while Tom found Hannah sitting with Jos on a bench, overlooking her well-stocked vegetable patch. He squatted down beside them on an upturned log.

'So when are yer moving on?' Jos asked. 'You used t'have great plans.'

Tom acknowledged the comment with a wry smile. 'That's why I've dropped by; it looks like any time now. I've stalled for too long, but I've finally had some good news. D'you remember my old school friend George Bland? He now serves alongside his uncle who is the rector of a large diocese in Lancashire. I've had a long letter telling me the population is growing at such a rate they are overrun with work and he is recommending me for a curacy.'

'Manchester?'

'Closer to the Yorkshire border, a market town called Halesden. George lives in a cottage in the grounds of the vicarage with Catherine, his sister, who acts as his housekeeper.' Tom threw Jos a meaningful look, but there was no reaction. 'He informs me it will be quite a change from what I've experienced here; full of smoking chimneys and clattering machines.'

Hannah stared uncomprehendingly into the distance. 'Will yer be George's assistant?' she asked.

'No. There are half a dozen parishes under the rector's control, and I'll be employed in the main town, directly under the Reverend Anderson.

Hannah turned to face him, a bleak expression on her usually cheerful countenance. 'So yer'll be moving away for good then? Edward will miss yer.'

'Aye, but I'll write. And from what you've told me he'll be able to read you my letters and even reply.'

Jos stood up abruptly, threw the dregs of ale on the garden, and marched indoors. A long silence followed his departure as Tom and Hannah sat with their own thoughts, watching the bees humming busily around the broad bean flowers. Finally, Tom rose to take his leave.

'I must be off to give my parents the news,' he said. 'Take care of yourself, Hannah, and look after Jos and your boy.'

Her eyes remained downcast. 'Aye, I will,' she promised.

George and Tom had corresponded while he was at Oxford, but as the years sped by their communication had all but ceased. When news reached Tom that Christopher Bland had eloped to Canada with Alice, he thought he was probably persona non grata where the Bland family were concerned, and would never hear from them again.

The unexpected arrival of George's invitation had been timely, and Tom accepted with alacrity. He wondered whether George Bland Senior had had any influence, perhaps having heard of his situation through local gossip. Whatever motivated George's offer he looked forward to renewing their friendship, accepting the challenge, and reawakening his interest in tackling the inequalities in society.

Jonathon came to visit the day before Tom was due to

leave, which gave the brothers an opportunity to discuss the future. It was a balmy evening as they strode across the common, and sat on a convenient rock looking down on the still, brown waters of the lake.

'I'm going to miss all this,' said Tom.

'For certain you will.' Jonathon pulled out a pipe and tapped it on the rock. 'You'll find the way of life very different in Lancashire. Since the war ended there's been this smouldering anger with the way the country is run… we saw it with the Luddites and we saw it at Peterloo. We might think times are hard here but there's always fuel for the fire, food to eat, and most important of all the support of our neighbours when things go wrong.'

Tom swatted at a horsefly that buzzed round his head. 'I'm wondering what I should address in my sermons.'

Jonathon packed his pipe systematically with tobacco before answering. 'Remember, Tom, many of them will be from a rural background just like yours. Exploit that connection and remind them of their old values. Encourage them to go out into the hills, let their minds wander, reconnect with nature, the seasons… reflect on what is important in life.'

Tom sighed, distracted by the song of the skylarks now ascending and falling like a gentle shower of rain above the lake. 'You make it sound so easy, brother.'

'You're genuine, Tom, they'll appreciate that.'

Partly reassured, Tom changed the subject. 'So tell me, how are things in Cumberland? D'you still see William Wordsworth?'

'Frequently, and he often asks after our family. I told him you'd read part of his Lucy poem at the funeral.' A frown settled on Jonathon's brow. 'I was surprised at his reaction.'

'Surprised? In what way?'

'He seemed unexpectedly touched, and said he considered that poem to be one of his best pieces of work. I dared to ask if Lucy was anyone special. He shook his head, with a noncommittal half-smile, and replied, "Just a northern lass."'

The following morning Tom left Ravendale, his possessions in a worn leather bag. Neighbours gathered outside their houses and cottages to wish him well, and he acknowledged a familiar whistle from Jos and Edward working in the field below Highburn. He made the final ascent to the top of the fells and stopped to take a long, last look at his old home. Swirling clouds cut off visibility as a raven emerged from the gloom.

He arrived early outside the Kings Arms where he was due to pick up the southbound coach. Settling himself on the bench, overhung with the ivy and woodbine growing up the inn wall, he looked along the Great North Road heading towards the Scottish border. Beyond the last habitation he could see a young couple, the man with a bag thrown over his shoulder, walking hand in hand. Perhaps the anvil at Gretna was their destination. Turning to the south, the rhythmic clank of trotting horses indicated a small party of soldiers, fading into the distance. His thoughts turned to Bonny Prince Charlie, marching through Shap in pursuit of the English throne. So many men and women, looking for a richer, more fulfilling way of life, must have taken their first leap into the dark on this very highway. Now it was his turn.

A couple of middle-aged men, in tattered clothes and with few obvious possessions, approached from over the rise. Tom shifted along the bench to make room for them. 'Where are you heading?' he asked.

'Goin' to try our luck in Manchester,' one of them replied, scratching a greasy head. 'We've heard there's good money to be made there. Glasgow was a bleedin' waste of time.' Part of the floating population, they had many tales to tell, and Tom listened intently to the incidents they had encountered travelling the country. Despite their often miserable experiences, he felt a buzz of excitement – his years in the wilderness were at last over.

With Jonathon's advice in mind, he formulated his first sermon as the coach swung and rattled along the potholed road to Lancaster, a dust cloud in its wake.

Chapter 21

November 1834

On this, his first foray into Lancashire, Tom was intrigued by the proximity of conspicuous wealth and overcrowded squalor. On the western edges of the manufacturing towns, approached by avenues of lime trees and surrounded by formal, well-tended gardens, stood some of the finest houses Tom could imagine. In the town centres factories, like prisons barricaded by iron gates, belched smoke onto the lowly dwellings of the workers clustered below.

An acrid fog swirled round as the coach clattered to a halt in front of a soot-blackened inn, the Old Bull. Stepping down onto the cobbled highway a bitter chill stole his breath, and a cacophony of bells bore down on his eardrums as scores of millhands spilled out onto the street. He drew back against a wall as a sea of white faces tramped past, with the rhythm of an army. Women swathed in grey shawls; girls chattering animatedly; children towed along by their mothers. A woman with large blue eyes set in a pallid complexion caught his attention. As she drew up her hood a lock of auburn hair strayed across her cheek. Probably recognising a stranger, she gave Tom a swift smile, before disappearing amongst the throng. Within five minutes, the street was empty, the mill gates locked.

Dazed by the experience, Tom stumbled into the inn and ordered a drink. Here he jostled with the men from the mill who had also made this their first stop. The smell of their bodies was unfamiliar; a rancid mix of oil and sweat. Some stood chatting in groups, while some of the older men sat alone. He listened to the conversations going on around him, but found the dialect hard to follow, the meaning sometimes obscure. These were the very people who might be worshipping in his church on Sunday, and would certainly be those expecting his pastoral care during times of distress. He had travelled less than a hundred miles, but it felt like a foreign land.

'I hear there's another mill being built south of the Irwell,' a robust, red-bearded young man said.

'Ach! We don't need any more bleedin' factories,' grumbled his companion.

'More machines, less labour,' protested another. 'It'll leave us all destitute.'

Tom downed his drink and weaved his way back to the counter. 'Where will I find the vicarage?' he asked. There was a shuffling of feet, and an uncomfortable silence descended as the men turned to stare at the new arrival. The landlord made some comment, drowned out with ribald laughter.

'It's the Reverend Anderson I'm looking for,' Tom added.

'Yer go left at top o' the hill. It's next to the church – as tha'd expect.' More merriment. 'And don't be put off by the butler.' His voice was heavy with irony.

Tom acknowledged the comment with an amiable nod and pushed his way through the door and out into the night. Here, to his amazement, gaslights illuminated the streets and even through the mist the tower of the church was distinguishable. On reaching his destination he nudged the main gate open with his shoulder, and a pair of Newfoundland dogs lolloped towards him, barking ferociously. Tom was easily able to placate them, and by the time he had reached George's cottage they were following him obediently, tails wagging.

'Hello, my dear friend,' said George, taking his bag and ushering him into the sitting room. 'So good to see you again.'

A fire crackled in the hearth and the room smelt headily of cloves and woodsmoke. Catherine glided out from the kitchen and put a sparkling glass of whisky straight into Tom's hand. Dressed modestly in fine green wool, she looked elegant, but gaunt. Gone was the youthful curve of her cheeks and the sparkle in her eyes. He kissed her formally, and sank thankfully into a leather chair.

'Your good health,' said George. Relaxed, they began to catch up on the intervening years.

'How d'you find Halesden after Oxford?' Tom asked.

George shook his well-groomed head with the self-confidence of a man whose destiny had been assured since childhood. 'Nothing can compare with a university city, or indeed academic life. All that tradition; the architecture, the gardens, the formality of life in hall, the sport, the taverns, the drink, the women available for bedding… I could go on and on.' He laughed heartily.

'You sound regretful you had to leave.'

'The time had come. I needed to earn a living, and with father's connections becoming a cleric seemed the obvious choice. Regretfully advancement is proving agonisingly slow.'

'So you're keen to move on from here?'

'I must warn you, Tom, this town is depressing. The clergy are not appreciated as they should be – it's the chapel that wields the power. And among the poor and ignorant there's an undercurrent of unrest that you feel could explode into violence at any moment.'

'So the position will be challenging?' said Tom with a wry smile.

Catherine threw a shovel of coal onto the fire; it blazed up, highlighting the flush on her cheeks. George waited until she had rejoined him on the sofa before continuing.

'To understand how life is lived here, Tom, you need to know something of the history. Mechanisation is coming, but until recent times the pace here has been slow. All the yarn is produced in the factories, and cotton has almost replaced wool in the manufacturing process. However, there are still a sizeable number of handloom weavers in this town – you'll have passed some of their cottages on your way here. They are still able to compete with the power-driven machines by specialising in delicate fabrics – silk, muslin and the like. For generations these men have been used to their independence, and are constantly in confrontation with the mill owners. I've been told there were serious riots just a few years back when scores of power looms were destroyed.'

'And they've had to summon the military more than once since we've lived here,' Catherine intervened. 'Once a mob gathers it can quickly escalate into an ugly situation, particularly on a Saturday night when the men are full of drink.' She got to her feet. 'Can I get you another whisky, Tom?'

Before Tom could reply, George motioned her to sit down and in a raised voice continued. 'The other situation which influences the culture is the number of women and girls in full-time employment – they make up more than half of the labour force. I can assure you it's a disgrace the way some of them neglect their husbands and families.'

The warmth of the room and liquor had penetrated through to Tom's bones, and he got up to remove his jacket. The hiatus gave him the opportunity to lighten the mood by changing the subject. 'D'you still find time for wrestling?' he asked.

'Not since I came down; but there is a reasonable social life. Hunting is a popular sport, and there are plenty of parties and rubbers of whist with so many wealthy merchants living locally. Catherine and I are usually included because we are related to the rector.'

Tom concluded from his comment that no invitations would be coming in his direction. He swirled the bronze liquid in his glass before turning to address Catherine directly.

'And how have you settled here?'

'Not so well,' she said ruefully. 'I'm not comfortable with the urban environment. I miss the fresh air, and the freedom to walk and ride alone. You have to understand, Tom, that it wouldn't be considered proper for me to take the dogs out on my own.' Her face looked sad. 'Perhaps, when you've time, I can show you some of the Pennines. The countryside is nearly as beautiful as the Lake District.'

'I should welcome that,' he said, flashing an easy smile.

Tom was woken by the intermittent clanging of factory bells, which gathered momentum as six o'clock drew near. As if answering a call to prayer the metronomic tramp of clogs on cobbles followed. Today he was to meet his potential employer, the Rector of Halesden, and he was determined to make a good impression.

Catherine escorted him over the small, neat lawn and pulled on the bell rope. A stout, ruddy-cheeked man of perhaps sixty years opened the door. Across his waistcoat dangled the gold chain of a hunter watch.

'Uncle, this is Thomas Shaw, a longstanding friend of ours from Bampton.'

Tom was ushered into the study, but had little opportunity to take in his surroundings as the Reverend Anderson seemed anxious to conclude their meeting in as short a time as possible.

'You'll be expected to wear your clerical clothes whenever you are out in the town. A clean tabard daily, and hair to be kept no longer than shoulder length. Facial hair is not encouraged at curate level and I recommend you buy yourself some new trousers with your first salary.'

Tom was taken aback by the tone of the conversation, and all the references to his appearance. 'Is there anything in particular I need to know about working in this benefice?' he asked.

'There's a lot of anger over steam power replacing labour. Messrs Hargreaves and Whitehead, they own Riding Mill in the centre of town, will expect you to subdue this by showing the lower orders the consequences of any belligerence in this life – and expressly in the life hereafter.' Reverend Anderson sniggered. 'Guide them towards obedience, that's all we ask. You can start by taking the service at St James' on Sunday.'

Tom waited in vain for any enquiry regarding his beliefs, opinions, qualifications or experience.

Charles Anderson rose to his feet. 'Now we need to find you somewhere to live. I have here two addresses where they have rooms to rent. You must visit them today and choose which suits you best. I strongly recommend

Mrs Southgate. Her property is away from the town centre so there will be less trouble at night. She is also a regular attendee at our church, and will take pride in seeing you are well turned out on a Sunday.' Reverend Anderson proffered his hand. 'I hope you'll settle in quickly, Thomas Shaw. I have more pressing matters to deal with these days, and need to be relieved of some of my responsibilities.'

In his first act of defiance, Tom chose the non-recommended accommodation. He wanted to immerse himself in the atmosphere of living in a manufacturing town, so he could feel and become part of it. The first-floor room he rented overlooked Riding Mill, and beyond he could glimpse the Pennines. Opposite was the tavern where he had taken a drink on his first night. Here the mail coach arrived with a great clatter in the early hours of the morning, and postilions heralded the arrival of private coaches throughout the day. Below his window, unshod children hung round the factory gates and mingled with the market stalls and newspaper sellers.

His landlady, an elderly widow, ran a poorly stocked draper's shop from her front room, selling calico, haberdashery and locally made woollen items. Her total disinterest in his position or wellbeing suited him well.

On his first Sunday morning Tom stood nervously by the side of the rector. St James's was a large church, very different from the homely chapel at Newton Rigg. Stylishly dressed men and women, accompanied by well-scrubbed children, occupied the front pews. Behind, and in the side aisles, sat an assortment of grey-attired humanity; the men's white mufflers their one concession to the Sabbath. Catherine's was the only familiar face he could pick out, her pale cerise cloak a jewel amongst the sombre garb of the other women. He was heartened to see her; pleased she had come to offer her support.

With three hundred pairs of eyes focused in his direction, he climbed the steps into the pulpit, and gripping the edges, inhaled deeply. 'My text today is taken from Psalm 121, *I will lift up mine eyes to the hills from whence cometh my help.*' As advised by his brother Tom made it personal, illustrating his theme with anecdotes of life in Westmorland. He took his imagery from the natural world and he kept the words simple. The children stopped wriggling in their seats as he told them stories of rearing lambs by hand. Childish laughter echoed through the cavernous building when he spoke of the lamb that nudged the sheepdog out of the way, so it could settle nearest to the fire.

He concluded, '*My help cometh from the Lord, which made heaven and earth*', and a loud whisper from a high young voice echoed round the nave: 'So who made the Lord then?'

Heads turned. A murmur of disapproval rose from those near the altar, and a ripple of laughter from those behind. Tom wasn't fazed. Interactivity was the way in the country churches and he was used to interruptions.

'A thoughtful question, lad, and one of the mysteries at the heart of our universe. A question I suspect some amongst you will never have thought about.' His eyes fleetingly scanned the front pews. 'But to answer it requires faith, and that isn't so easy to explain. Indeed, it's something that has baffled me since I was your age and continues to do so to this day. Maybe it's beyond human understanding.' With a gentle smile he announced the last hymn. When the congregation rose from their seats Tom recognised the boy's mother. It was the woman he had had a passing encounter with outside the mill when he first arrived in Halesden.

Hands were shaken, and compliments paid, as the rector and his new curate greeted the congregation on leaving church. 'I liked the sentiments and tone of your address, young man,' said Mr Hargreaves, proffering Tom his hand. 'I'd recommend more of a lesson on the consequences of sin – once you settle in. But get their trust first.'

Tom thanked him, and acting on impulse asked, 'May I visit your factory sometime soon? I'd like to gain a better understanding of the work your employees do.'

Benjamin Hargreaves looked taken aback by this request, but responded amiably. 'I see no reason why not. Call in and see my manager one morning next week.'

As the departing congregation pressed by, Tom saw the boy who had asked the question being hustled along by the father. He turned to the rector. 'Can you tell me anything about that family?'

'That's Betha Lewis and her children,' he sneered dismissively. 'The boy who spoke out of turn during the service is her youngest. Her husband was a handloom weaver, and used to be a sidesman at this church – until they transported him for machine-breaking, back in 1827. He was a clever man; self-taught with a good knowledge of history and the scriptures, but opinionated. That was his downfall.'

'So that's not the father?'

'No, no, that's her brother, Sean Kelly... another political agitator in danger of getting himself into trouble. He still works independently, but Betha and the older boy, I can't remember his name, are both employed at Riding Mill.'

The working conditions in the mill proved an eye-opener for Tom. His eardrums vibrated with the pounding and clatter of the machinery, and perspiration ran down his forehead from the oppressive heat and humidity in the spinning room. The wooden floors shone with the spillage of oil, polished in by the slippered feet of the women and girls who bent over the machines in loose calico shifts, with little evidence of undergarments.

'We're driving six thousand spindles here,' the manager told Tom with a satisfied smile.

'Why aren't the windows open to let the air circulate?' Tom asked as he tugged at his jacket, and wiped his upper lip with the back of his hand.

'Because the damp atmosphere is good for the yarn.' The manager's voice was sharp. 'If it becomes brittle it snaps. You'll find the worst accidents happen when the yarn breaks, and the children have to lean across the machinery to rejoin it.'

'But surely they turn the machinery off first?'

The manager walked briskly ahead, ignoring his direct question. 'It's our priority to protect our employees; that's why the women are wearing caps.'

Tom noticed one of the frames stood idle. 'Is it waiting to be repaired?'

'No, that's usually manned by one of our fastest operatives, but her daughter is ill. They say it might be measles, which will be grave news if it spreads. Any loss of production certainly won't please the partners.' His manner seemed flustered as he hurried Tom upstairs to where the men were operating the looms.

Tom made several attempts to get into conversation with the weavers but their responses were monosyllabic, their eyes never leaving their work. A young man with an Irish accent was more forthcoming, and responded to Tom's question about the ages of the children he had seen running back and forth to help the spinners.

'It's disgraceful, sir. Many of them are only eight or nine. They should be at school or outside in the fresh air, not stuck minding machines for ten hours a day.'

'That's not how their parents see it,' interrupted the manager sharply, and with a warning look. 'They rely on them as wage-earners; contributing to the family income.'

Tom shivered as he left the tropical atmosphere for the frosty air of the streets; his nostrils impregnated with the smell of oil and cotton. He made straight for the church for a quiet moment to make sense of it all. As he pushed open the heavy oak door he almost tripped over a young couple crouched down in the lobby. The woman was clutching a bundle of fraying blankets; and the man's arms circled her shoulders. They looked utterly dejected. The young man struggled to his feet to speak to Tom.

'Please, sir, cud ye give our boy a Christian burial? Ee's just six months t'day.'

Pushing up between the mean cobblestones flowered a golden dandelion. Tom bent down to pick it before stepping into another darkened room, where his nostrils were assaulted by the stench of death. A little girl lay on a thin palliasse, covered with a stained, fraying blanket. Her mother cowered in the corner, arms crossed over her swollen stomach. Tom squatted on an upturned box, and laid the bloom by the child's face. He explained how it had grown from a seed, wafted around on a windy day, and chosen to flower just outside her door. Gently he stroked her cheek and delivered the last rites. Once outside he paused to take several deep breaths before moving on to the next household, where a similar scenario was played out. A few days later, he was conducting a burial service for both families.

Never had Tom witnessed anything like this measles epidemic. Back in his rural homeland they were able to control contagious diseases by isolating those infected, but here the overcrowded households made it impossible. George and Catherine did what they could, but kept their distance by delivering comfort from the doorstep, unable to fully share the burden of the stricken families.

Each evening he returned exhausted to his lodgings. He ate his simple supper by the window in his room as he watched the workers swarm out of the mill. He took comfort from the daily routine. The rhythm of their feet triggered a distant memory of a packhorse trail coming down the Nan Bield Pass – the regular beat and scattering of loose stones. There was also the added attraction of a possible glimpse of Betha. On finishing his meal restlessness took him back out onto the streets, where he roamed until overcome by sleep.

Returning late one Saturday night two inebriated men fell out of the inn, brawling. Spying Tom, they changed tactics. 'Luk! 'Tis that new bloody parson. Let's get 'im.' Squaring up to Tom one of the men took a swing, and narrowly missed landing a punch on his jaw. Tom reacted instinctively by throwing his arms round him in a wrestling hold, and pinned him face down on the ground. He then turned on his companion and administered the same treatment. The rowdy band of customers who had poured out of the inn on hearing the commotion, to watch and cheer, stood quietly nonplussed. Tom dusted down his clothes, wished them all 'Gud neet', and nonchalantly crossed the street towards his lodgings, as though this was an everyday occurrence.

'Well done, Reverend! You've certainly shown 'em.' A Belfast voice called out from the crowd. Turning, Tom saw a sandy-haired man with a wide grin approaching.

'Should I know you?' he asked.

'Sure you should. I'm usually in church on Sunday, and it was our lad you answered when you overheard his comment in church a few weeks ago. I can tell you, that shook everyone too.' He proffered his hand. 'I'm Sean Kelly. I reckon that'll be the last time you're on the receiving end of any aggravation in this town.' He beamed. 'Drop in on us next time yer passing. The third cottage goin' up the hill. There's always a pot of something brewing.'

Tom thanked him and mounted the narrow stairs to his room.

A cloud of dust, churned up by the wheels of passing carts, hung in the air as he looked down on the lamplit street. The revellers were now taunting a poorly clad street minstrel, who was hoping to pick up a few coppers from the passers-by. The night had ended well. Tom felt he had turned a corner.

Chapter 22

Following the confrontation outside the tavern, Tom became a regular visitor at the Lewis household. Each time his mood brightened as he stepped through the stable door into the warmth of their living room. By the standards of their neighbours it was well furnished: an oak table, chairs, pictures and a brass hunting horn on the walls. On a shelf *The Age of Reason* and *The Rights of Man* perched alongside a well-thumbed Bible. In the half-cellar below the cottage young Sam, if not at school, was usually to be found helping his uncle.

Betha remained an enigma. One day, as she sat quietly knitting, Tom dared to ask, 'What happened to your Arthur?'

Her needles clicked away as she explained. 'We'd had a difficult year. I'd been unable to work because Sam was a sickly baby, and Arthur was slaving from dawn until dusk, for little reward. He was so incensed with the way our livelihood was being stolen he joined up with a group of Luddites and one night, unbeknown to me, they raided the mills over at Rossendale and destroyed the looms. The owners brought in the Rifle Corps, and the soldiers opened fire on the protesters. Arthur wasn't hurt, but they did kill four men and dozens were injured.' She shrugged. 'Arthur was arrested, put on trial and eventually transported to Van Diemen's Land.'

'D'you hear from him regularly?'

'We did during his first few years.' She put down her needles. 'He writes a good letter. But it's been a long while since he gained his freedom and I've heard nothing for over six months. He was trying to put aside some savings before he came home so may have moved to the mainland... or something may have gone disastrously wrong.'

'You must miss him.' Tom watched closely as she slid her wedding ring up and down with her thumb and forefinger before replying, in a matter-of-fact tone.

'I did, but I've got used to it. Yer have to... and my brother is a great support.'

The next time Tom called by the windows were blacked out. His eyes took a moment to adjust to the semi-darkness before alighting on Sam, who lay under a patchwork cover, with swollen eyes and a running nose. Sam had measles.

'Are you frightened?' Tom laid a hand gently on Betha's arm.

Averting her eyes, she mumbled, 'The Lord will decide. What will be will be.' Betha sometimes reminded him of Hannah; but she also had a granite resolve, which was reminiscent of Lucy.

'He's a strong, well-fed lad. I know he'll have the best of care.' Tom did his best to keep his voice light. On leaving their cottage, he headed off, on a whim, towards the open country to look for hazel bushes. Finding some suitable branches he cut a short length, and whittled the wood into a whistle. That evening he returned to the Lewis household.

'How is Sam?'

Betha's face was strained as she gestured to the bed

where he lay with a high fever and angry red rash. Tom walked over to the boy and sat down on the bed.

'Look, Sam, I've brought you a present. Sit up and see if you've enough breath to raise me a tune.'

Sam put the whistle to his lips and took a deep breath. A sweet musical sound filled the room, and a wide smile lit up his blotched face. Tom looked across at his mother to see her eyes mist with tears.

'Now you've to make me a promise, Sam, to get better as quickly as possible. Once you are back on your feet I will take you up into the hills, and show you the bushes which make the very best whistles.'

David, who was the same age as Hannah's Edward, would sometimes accompany Tom on his Saturday hill walks. During these excursions Tom was able to share the ways and mysteries of the countryside and one day, when out together, David brushed his bare arm against a patch of nettles.

'Blast these useless weeds!' He rubbed his elbow in irritation.

'Not always so useless,' said Tom. 'At home our mam used to boil up young nettle leaves and serve them with poached eggs – there's nothing we liked better. Next spring we'll nip out the tops and take them home for your mam to make you some nettle soup.' They continued on their walk and an inconspicuous little brown bird darted into the hedge ahead of them. 'Did you get a glimpse of that dunnock?' Tom asked his companion. 'She might look like a plain wee creature, but it's my guess there'll be a different father for each of the eggs in her nest this spring.'

A wide grin spread across David's face. 'She sounds like some of the women at our mill.'

During the troubled weeks of the epidemic Tom found time spent with Sean Kelly was also a welcome distraction.

'The working man has no voice,' Sean moaned as they stood side-by-side outside their cottage door. 'Look over there.' Tom followed his gaze towards the clusters of closely packed houses dwarfed by the red brick mill belching smoke. 'That used t'be good agricultural land; now it's ramshackle homes. No gardens for a pig or a few vegetables, no open spaces for the kiddies to play.'

After downing a few ales Sean's anger would surface. 'It's because ordinary folk aren't represented in parliament that we can't challenge the corn laws, or the working conditions of the young – do they realise in London how many miles our child piecers walk each day? I'd like to lynch the lot of 'em.'

Tom empathised with his views, but was aware that changes would need careful managing. 'Remember what happened to Arthur,' he would caution. 'You cannot use violence; it won't work as a bargaining tool. If you want reform, you must negotiate. You've plenty of Irish blarney; use that to your advantage.'

'I think you could use it to even better effect than me, Reverend,' Sean would reply with a wink.

By the time the spring arrived, the measles outbreak had run its course. Sam had made a complete recovery and there were no more fatalities. It was as though the nightmare had never happened – except for the forty-three newly dug graves huddled together in the churchyard, and the families who now mourned the loss of a child.

Catherine, with the blessing of her uncle, organised a Saturday jaunt for George, Tom and herself to ride out to the Eastern Pennines.

Seated on their hired thoroughbred horses, George and Catherine trotted ahead. Catherine's elegant attire and upright carriage complemented that of her immaculate brother, and Tom chuckled to himself as he followed behind in his checked linen shirt, patched jacket and worn boots. They cantered for a while and then, as the ground grew steeper, slackened their pace to a walk.

'My mount is getting restless,' said George. 'I'm going on ahead.'

Tom longed to join him. To have the wind pounding in his ears, and the freedom of speeding across open moorland into the unknown would have provided the excitement he was missing – but he knew this was not the purpose of the outing. He dismounted and offered Catherine his hand as she stepped down onto the grassy sward. A clear, expansive view stretched towards the Scottish border, but to the south, only the tower of the church floated above the smoky gloom.

'These bloody mills!' he exclaimed in a moment's exasperation.

'You look tired,' Catherine said soothingly as she searched his face. He removed his jacket for her to sit down.

'I'm sorry,' he said. 'It's the aftermath of the measles epidemic… it's harrowing, first visiting and then burying sick children.'

'You're becoming too immersed in their lives, Tom,' she said, carefully pulling the fingers of each glove before removing it. 'The clergy need to keep their parishioners at a respectful distance. It's their spiritual needs you're paid to take care of, and most of that can be achieved at the Sunday services. You've certainly increased the size of the congregation since you arrived,' she added approvingly.

'I sometimes wonder if that's because the epidemic has heightened their fear of death, or because they want to see the wrestling parson.' He threw her a playful look.

'You underestimate yourself, Tom. Whatever the reason you're gaining the respect of the workers.'

'But not the regard of their masters?'

'Well, no!' She raised an eyebrow.

'You'll remember how back in Westmorland the priest joined his parishioners for meals, lodged with them, helped them salve their sheep... he was at the centre of the community, respected by landowners and labourers alike. Here it's so different, there's such a divide.'

'I know, the culture's not the same.' She touched his arm self-consciously. 'But don't get too dispirited.'

Tom studied her anxious face; her wind-whipped cheeks an antidote to the grey desolation of the world he had inhabited of late. 'You're right, Catherine, how can I get disheartened on a perfect day like this?' He gestured towards the northern horizon, *'With a clear blue sky, and the mountain dancing with lambs.'*

She gave him an admiring look. 'That's the perfect description, Tom.'

'I think it may be Wordsworth's, not mine.' He laughed.

'I've noticed how you like quoting him in your sermons.'

'That's because I think the poets often say it best; the lyrical language is more memorable.'

Catherine's face lit up. 'Do you remember giving a robust defence of William Wordsworth when you first came to dine with my parents? I was just a child and thought you were so brave challenging Father.'

Tom remembered the occasion very well, and how his defence had been on behalf of Lucy rather than the poet.

For a brief, dreamy moment he was back in the past with his family. Catherine broke the spell.

'Listen! Was that the cuckoo?' Rising up from a nearby clump of trees came the familiar double note, followed by the pause that made them both freeze, their ears alert to catch the sound again.

'*The wandering voice!*' said Tom.

'And here comes our wanderer,' Catherine added as George came galloping across the open moor towards them.

As the summer progressed, Tom continued to gain the trust of the townsfolk. They sought his advice over disputes with their employers, and he drafted or wrote letters on their behalf to their landlords. He asked permission to start a Sunday school for the children, but his request was refused.

He frequented the free library, managed by the Methodists, where he came across the radical newspaper, the *Northern Star*, and its campaign for a People's Charter. Each week he collected the out-of-date newspapers from the vicarage, which he read in the evenings, sharing the light from the street lantern outside his window with the fluttering moths. Late into the night, curled up under his thin blankets, he planned his sermons to introduce references to the political issues of the day.

Chapter 23

Ravendale, June 1838

The highlight of Tom's year was the annual visit home to his family. He stepped off the coach at Shap and stood by the side of the road, drawing in the crisp clear air. His whole body and soul felt reenergised at the thought of being reunited with his father and mother, brothers and sisters. He had so much to tell them all.

On the second day, he headed out to visit the Teasdales. He crossed the beck by the stepping-stones, and swung his long limbs through the black, boggy wasteland to their farm. Hannah was alone.

'Jos and Edward have gone t'bring down the ewes for washing and clipping,' she said. 'They should be back within the hour. Stop and tek a bite t'eat with us.'

Tom settled himself on the window seat, and watched while Hannah kneaded some oatmeal dough. He thought how comely she looked; her sleeves rolled up revealing freckled arms, her face pink with the exertion.

'How have ee all bin keepin'?' he asked, slipping back into the vernacular.

'Edward's well. Jos spends most of his time out on the hills; if he has worries he doesna share them with us.'

'Different from his da then?'

Hannah looked up, frowning. 'What d'yer mean?'

'As I remember Edmond used to be cursing much of the time, and could be quite brutal with his sons.'

Hannah shrugged her shoulders as she slapped and pummelled. 'I know it's no excuse but it was that fire and then t'drink with him. Jos has nivver laid a finger on me.'

'I'm sure he hasn't,' Tom said quickly. 'Does he still go out celebrating with the miners up at the quarry?'

'Nah, he only drinks at home these days. He doesn't want to influence the boy.'

'He gets on well with Edward then?'

Her eyes sparkled. 'Aye, ee's everything to him,' she replied in a fond tone.

'Is he still going to school?'

'Nah, Jos says there's no point. Anyway we can't afford the fees.' In days past Tom had offered to help support Edward at the grammar school, but he sensed Hannah's loyalty to Jos had deepened over the years. There was nothing to be gained by suggesting it now.

Hannah fed two loaves into the bread oven, flicked back a loose strand of hair from her damp forehead, and wiped the flour from her hands on her apron. Tom wondered, not for the first time, why no other children had come along. Hannah would have blossomed rearing a large family.

'Is Simeon still doing well up at the castle?'

'Aye, he travels a lot with Sir William. We can hardly understand him now; he talks that grand.' She laughed.

'And how about your brothers?'

'They're all married with their own bairns. Lance moved to Manchester and married a local lass. Mark is working on a farm t'other side of Penrith. I nivver hear anything of them. Mebbe they'll turn up one of these days.' They both looked towards the window as the echo of bleating sheep could be heard approaching from over the skyline.

'I'll stroll up to meet them,' said Tom. No sooner had he stepped outside than Jos appeared in the yard ahead of the flock. He dipped his hands in the water butt and shook them dry.

'We've been expecting yer,' said Jos. 'I've left Edward t'settle the flock in the top field. Ee'll be along shortly.'

'Hannah's looking well,' said Tom by way of conversation.

'Aye, she's a good lass. Spends too much time with her prayers for my liking, but I suppose that's not a bad thing.'

'I'm not in a position to argue with that,' Tom laughed. 'How are the sheep?'

'I'll get to count them when we finally bring them into the home intake; after we've had summat to eat.'

They chatted over laver bread and stewed mutton, but Tom was unable to get Jos or Edward to speak openly about how they were coping economically. It was very different from the community back in Halesden, who were always so vocal in communicating their concerns and perceived injustices.

Dawdling back to Ravendale Head, Tom paused to watch the next generation of children running down the track on their way home from school. Two little girls, slim-bodied with flawless peachy skin, hung back. Tom recognised them as Luke Yarker's daughters. Their father stepped through the oak door, turned the iron key and then disappeared into the chapel porch. Tom guessed the key would be hidden under the loose stone behind the second wooden pew – where it had been kept for generations.

'How's it going, Luke?' he called out. 'Many in school today?'

A wide grin spread across Luke's face. 'Good to see you, Tom.' Luke marched over to shake his hand. 'Not s'many as I'd like. To be truthful I'm not sure how much longer I can keep going as schoolmaster here.'

'Your girls look bonny.'

'Aye, they never miss a day of school and both can read fluently,' he said with quiet pride. 'I'm glad to see you, Tom. I've been meaning to write for some time. Agnes and I were wondering if there were any opportunities for me in Halesden. Agnes thought she might find herself a job too, perhaps at one of the mills. It would help with the girls' education.'

'My influence isn't worth courting at the moment,' said Tom with a wry smile. 'Come back to the farm with me and I'll update you on the urban way of living.'

The friends strode leisurely down the lane, while the girls skipped along singing one of their playground rhymes. Chaffinches and robins hopped from bush to stunted tree, and rooks cawed from their colony in a clump of oak. From beyond the enclosing walls, a lamb bleated for its mother. Tom noticed with concern how the stonework had bellied, and in some places collapsed. Nothing in nature had changed, but man's influence was beginning to wane.

With tankards in hand they drifted out into the garden. Here Tom launched into an account of how the youngsters fared in Halesden. 'They allow children to mind the machines – some are as young as eight, though the managers deny it. I know our youngsters have always helped out with spinning and weaving at home, but the difference in the factories is the conditions. The heat, the damp, the noise and the dangers from the vibrating machinery – it's brutal.'

'But why d'they need to employ bairns? asked Luke.

'Aren't there enough men and women out there looking for work?'

'Trade is booming. Everything and everybody sacrificed for the sake of the mills.'

'So their mothers work too?'

'Just as soon as they can farm out their babies, and when they get home of an evening they're too tired to cook and care for their families properly. The whole system is dehumanising, and the greatest injustice is that schooling is such a low priority. The present urban generation won't have the advantages we had living here.'

'What about the mill owners – d'you have dealings with them?

'Occasionally... at the lychgate. Most are so focused on making money they fail to provide the basic amenities for their workers. The mortality rate amongst the children is alarmingly high, something I experienced shortly after I arrived in Lancashire with a measles epidemic. You wouldn't believe how many babies and children I buried in my first few months... I just couldn't get used to it.'

Luke nodded his head in sympathy. 'You're painting a dismal picture, Tom.'

'You're right, and perhaps I'm blinkered.' Tom swallowed a long draught while he gathered his thoughts. 'It's such a contrast from the world I knew here, but I have to confess there is another side – an exhilarating undercurrent, as though we are on the cusp of some major changes. You can sense the tension in the taverns and the clamour at the public meetings in the town square. The workers are beginning to fight back. They want more control over the way they live and I find the mood exciting.'

'Does that influence your role in the church?'

Tom's eyes narrowed. 'I suppose it does. I cannot

explain the feeling of power to have five hundred men and women listening to your every word. I feel alive in a way I never could here in Westmorland. The rector and benefactors expect me to preach from their edited version of the Bible, but that is something I feel I must challenge.'

'So that's what you meant when you said you were out of favour?' Luke grinned.

'I have a stubborn streak,' Tom acknowledged.

'Aye, I remember. How does George react to all this?'

'Deep down I don't think he approves of the system, but he wants to progress within the church and it is difficult for him, being family.'

Raggy, Rock's great-grandson, nuzzled against Tom's arm and placed a white paw on his knee.

'And is there a woman in your life?' asked Luke.

Tom stroked the dog's soft head before replying hesitantly. 'Catherine Bland is still without a suitor... and there's another – but she's not available. Her husband's in exile for his involvement with the rioting back in '27. Her family have made me very welcome.'

Luke nodded, acknowledging the confidence. 'Just be true to yourself, Tom. Anything else would be hypocritical.'

Tom drew a deep breath. To have this approval from a trusted friend was just the support he needed. As the ale frothed into their tankards he reflected on the irreplaceable value of childhood friendships, which bound as tightly as the iron bands on the barrel from which he had drawn the ale.

It was with a renewed sense of purpose that he returned to Halesden to continue his ministry.

Chapter 24

With a clanking of pistons the organ spluttered into life. The muffled sound echoed and re-echoed round the cavernous building, and bore into Catherine's aching head. The choir stalls were full and in front of the altar, waiting for the congregation to settle, stood the portly figure of her uncle in his embroidered gold and rose vestment. By his side stood the much taller figure of Tom in a black cassock and starched white tabard. His dark hair, now flecked with silver, tied back with a thin strip of black ribbon.

Glancing over her shoulder, she saw a number of folks standing at the back. Tom was gaining an impressive following. There was something in his conversational style, brought from the country pulpit, which demanded attention. Elderly weavers nodded their heads in approval; children sat wide-eyed and attentive, mesmerised by his simple tales; young women admired his physical appearance and soft dale voice.

She placed her prayer book carefully on the shelf of the pew, and peeled off her brown leather gloves to lie alongside. She was impressed by Tom's commitment and passion, but she knew her uncle was not. On several occasions recently she had overheard him having a dressing-down at the vicarage for using the pulpit as a political stage. She feared the response to today's sermon, and her stomach muscles tightened involuntarily. She loosened her belt.

Tom's knuckles whitened as he grabbed the carved edges of the pulpit, and glanced casually round the congregation. Catherine listened in dismay as he announced the text for his sermon. *'It is easier for a camel to go through the eye of a needle than for a rich man to enter the kingdom of God.'* An audible whisper breezed through the church. Those in the front pews shifted uncomfortably and Lord Beaumont's veined cheeks glowed, the colour of ripe plums. Catherine bent her head and closed her eyes.

'You've gone too far today,' Catherine heard her uncle growl under his breath as he stormed past Tom, pushing his wife ahead of him. 'I'll see you in my study first thing tomorrow morning.' She hung back, hoping for the chance of a word, but as always a gaggle of drab-shawled women clustered around him like hens round the rooster. She slipped away to face the onslaught back at the vicarage.

'He has great communication skills, Uncle, you cannot deny him that,' she heard George plead as she joined them in the panelled dining room. 'Your church is full to capacity every Sunday. That must impress the bishop.'

'But at what cost, damn it?! I need to safeguard my reputation locally. I'm not going to lose it for the sake of some country bumpkin with a mission.'

'But they listen, they trust what he says. You'll be able to use that to your advantage when the time is right.'

Charles Anderson marched across the Persian carpet to pour Catherine a sherry. The sun, striking the cut-glass decanter, made her head swim. 'The blasted man sounds like a Non-conformist,' continued her uncle. 'That doesn't impress the likes of the Earl of Beaulieu, Lord Beaumont or indeed Benjamin Hargreaves and the other cotton barons. I was in a position to scrutinise their faces in church today; they were appalled. They're our benefactors and we are their representatives. They expect us to exercise control over the town; not humiliate them with talk of misuse of wealth.'

'So what will you say to him, Uncle? Catherine asked tentatively.

'Say to him! Tell him, you mean. Tom Shaw has to go. I can't face this sort of disruption, not at my time of life.'

Catherine moistened her lips before proceeding. 'Please remember, Uncle, that Tom shoulders most of the responsibility for this parish, so you are free to enjoy your bridge and other pleasures. It might not be so easy with a successor. They might not be as competent or prepared to work so hard.'

'That's enough, Madam,' snapped Charles Anderson. 'Whilst you're under my roof you won't question my decisions.'

Catherine's voice faltered. 'Will he be offered another living locally?

'Not if I have anything to do with it.' Charles Anderson frowned. 'Your so-called friend has betrayed my trust.'

Catherine found the food on her plate cloyingly tasteless, and the meat tough. She missed the flavours and succulence of the meals produced back in her Westmorland home. Today Cook had excelled herself in providing an unpalatable meal. She shrivelled under her aunt's gaze as she sent each plate back to the kitchen, untouched.

A long silence ensued until George cleared his throat and said, 'One of our parishioners was telling me that

Andrew Gasson is creating a community for his workers at Clattonbury, based on the progressive ideas of Robert Owen. The new church they have been building is nearly finished.'

'That sounds an interesting project,' said Mrs Anderson, turning to her husband with an encouraging smile. 'Perhaps you could put Tom's name forward – to be his first curate.'

Catherine noticed George's shoulders relax as he added, 'What a good idea, Aunt. The village is many miles from here, and in a different diocese. You would no longer have to concern yourself with the effect on your patrons.'

Heartened by this unexpected turn in the conversation Catherine ventured, 'And it would protect you from any backlash from the local people, Uncle. There might be repercussions if you sacked him.'

Charles Anderson grunted by way of reply, folded his napkin and stomped out of the room.

On Sunday evenings Tom relaxed with George and Catherine, but after the debacle over his sermon he knew he had some explaining to do. He scanned their serious faces as he joined them at the supper table.

'I assume I'm in deep water?'

'Up to your ears!' replied George. 'Why d'you do it, Tom? He gave Tom a withering look. 'You must've known you were putting your employment in jeopardy with such a controversial sermon.'

Tom picked up and played with the handle of his knife, twisting it uneasily in his fingers as he composed a response. 'I value your concern, George, but I get so angry at the cant I'm expected to deliver each Sunday. It's not just the masses who should be held to account for their behaviour.'

George drew back his chair, scraping it noisily on the

stone floor. 'You take it all too seriously. They'll get their reward in eternity, that's all they need to be told.'

Catherine's cheeks glowed and her voice was unsteady as she added, 'Keep the faith, Tom – make that your mission.'

'Faith!' Tom exhaled loudly and sunk his forehead in cupped hands. 'The very word haunts me. How can I make a robust case to persuade others when I'm not confident I can distinguish between belief and imagination? I took holy orders because I needed to make a living – not because I had a vocation.' He took a slow draught of warm ale from his glass and looked accusingly at George. 'And I reckon it was the same for you.'

George tapped his index finger on the table, but let the comment pass unanswered.

Tom felt overwhelmed by a deep, unrelenting weariness which gnawed at his whole being. He rose abruptly from the table and thanked them both for their hospitality. 'Wish me luck tomorrow,' he said breezily as he let his hand fall lightly on Catherine's shoulder before stepping out into the peace of a starlit night.

The following morning, at one minute to nine, Tom followed Catherine along the panelled corridor to Charles Anderson's study. His eye was unavoidably drawn to her trim, silk-clad rear. The situation brought to mind Hannah's translucent dirndl skirt with her apple bottom rolling down the lane towards Ravendale Head so many years ago. He almost laughed aloud at the ludicrous comparison, but recalling the incident re-energised him, and strengthened his resolve. As Catherine knocked hesitantly on the door, the long case clock in the hall rumbled into action and struck the hour.

'Sit down,' Reverend Anderson ordered sharply. 'I

cannot stress too strongly how disappointed I am in the way you have taken advantage of my generosity in giving you a position here. The church's patrons and I – who, let me remind you, pay your salary – expect you to follow our dictate. Obedience to our authority is essential. You are paid to subdue, not inflame political differences in the community – and pick your texts accordingly. In this regard you seem to take pleasure in letting me down.'

Tom took a deep breath and linked his hands calmly in his lap. 'I fully understand what you are saying, sir, but that conflicts with my interpretation of my clerical duty, which is to preach the word of God as it applies to all our parishioners; including those occupying the allocated pews. I believe the scriptures are intended to guide people's lives, not shield them from the truth or frighten them into submission.'

'Damn it, man – are you defying me?' The rector thrummed his fingers on the heavy oak desk.

'Only in so far as I'm not prepared to selectively choose the texts I use when preaching.'

Charles Anderson's eyes blazed. 'I can take no more of this,' he said. 'If that is your final word I will inform our patrons you will be leaving your post before Michaelmas. I know there are many young men who will be thankful to be offered such a rewarding opportunity.' He rose stiffly from the leather armchair, and with an angry, dismissive gesture waved Tom out of the room.

The parishioners at St James's ran a rota for cleaning the church, and it was Betha's duty, on Friday evenings, to dust and polish in preparation for the ladies of the Altar Guild who would attend to the flowers. Her routine was to go straight from the mill so she could be home by seven o'clock to feed her family. Tom made it his habit to be occupied in the church at the same time, sorting the hymn sheets or checking readings from the Bible displayed on the lectern. It was an hour he always relished, and today he was hoping to share his concerns with Betha over the impending loss of his employment.

They sat on the front pew, knees almost touching, while she recounted some crisis that had occurred that day at work. Preoccupied with his own problems, he was barely aware of what she was saying. The tang of beeswax was overpowering, and as he fumbled with his ordination ring he was acutely conscious of how close her face was to his, until Betha stopped in mid-sentence.

'Did yer hear something?' she whispered. They froze. The creaking of roof timbers, the fluttering of a bird in the belfry; then a soft moan emanating from the back of the nave.

'But there's only you and me here,' said Tom. 'I've been around for an hour or more. I'd have noticed if anyone else had been about.'

'It sounded like a sob,' said Betha. She walked slowly down the centre aisle, glancing to left and right. At the very back, crouching between the pews and hugging her knees, was a prepubescent girl. Betha bent down. ''Ello, Molly. What're you doing here?' Tears streaked the child's grimy cheeks as she pushed aside a greasy lock of hair. Betha gathered her up in her arms and sat her upright on the bench.

Tom approached hesitantly. 'D'you know who she is?'

'Aye. It's little Molly Bennett. She works at our mill along with her mother and older sisters; though I don't think she was at work today.'

Molly's sobs subsided to a whimper.

'What's wrong, dear?' Betha asked.

Molly snivelled for a while. Finally, her words tumbled out. 'It's mi da, ee's always 'urting me… after ee's been out drinking.' She sniffed. 'Nearly every week ee tries it on.'

Betha exchanged a glance of mutual understanding with Tom.

Too close to his own guilty secret, this was a situation for which Tom had no answer, no comforting words. He felt numb as he struggled to say, 'Does he do the same to your sisters?'

'I dunno.'

'Have you asked them?'

'No, ee said ee would belt me within an inch of my life if I told anyone.'

'I tell you what, Molly,' Betha said cheerfully. 'I could do with some help around the house – my boys run me ragged. Would yer like me to ask yer mam if you can come and live with us for a while? It'll help her having one less mouth to feed, and I could do with the support.'

Molly lifted her tearstained face. 'Oh, thank yer, Mrs,' she mumbled.

'Just let me get my shawl and we can sort this out right away.'

Tom watched in admiration as Betha walked hand in hand with her young charge, down the winding path towards the town. Just before they disappeared from view she turned and gave him a friendly wave.

The incident shook Tom. He had been completely bereft of ideas as to how he could help the abused child, but Betha had immediately risen to the occasion. He respected her calm response and pragmatic solution. She really was a special woman.

The July heat was unusually intense when Tom and Catherine set off on a pastoral visit to an elderly widow, who lived alone on the edge of the town. The woodland track was littered with debris and Catherine, usually so in control, was frustrated by the brambles which spread their tentacles across the path. Some caught at her skirts; others pulled at her carefully arranged hair, leaving a streak of dried blood on her cheek and dark stains under her armpits. There was a nervous ring to her voice as she asked, 'Have you planned your sermon for Sunday, Tom?'

'I was thinking perhaps the story of the widow's mite?' He cast her a mischievous glance.

Catherine sucked in her breath in alarm. 'Tom, you mustn't! You need to lie low for a while. I think Uncle may be having second thoughts.'

'Second thoughts? What d'you mean?'

'George has suggested that he should put your name forward to the proprietor out at Long Mill, on the river at Clattonbury. They are looking for a priest to take charge of the church that has just been built.'

Tom's eyes opened wide – this was an interesting proposition. He had heard inspiring reports of Andrew Gasson and his model village. 'I was just teasing.' His voice softened. 'It was good of George to suggest me. Your family have always been very kind.'

'You're a good man, Tom,' she said, sneaking a sideways look. 'Though I still haven't worked out what drives you.'

'You don't really know me, Catherine,' Tom said. 'But I can promise you, I'm not always the honourable man you choose to see.'

'I'm not sure I understand what you mean.' Her voice sounded self-conscious. 'But I do know you could fit in anywhere; especially with the right wife to guide you.'

Tom held back before responding, taking time to formulate a careful reply. A pair of yaffles rose squawking from the meadow grass, and provided the distraction he needed.

'I'm sorry, Catherine, but I have no wish to "fit in", and I certainly have no intention of taking a wife. If I married one of the grey-shawled women at our church I wouldn't have enough money to support her, or a family. If I married someone with their own income, I couldn't supply the lifestyle they expected. There is only one woman who could have worked alongside me, and that was my sister Lucy. Like you and George, we understood each other. No one else could adapt to my way of living. I couldn't make them happy.'

'You could make me happy,' Catherine blurted out, a wave of colour sweeping over her cheeks. They both flinched as a startled rabbit darted across their path. 'If we were ever to marry my dowry could support us both.'

Again Tom hesitated. He was aware he hadn't always played fair with Catherine, and with her loss of composure regretted that the situation had finally come to a head.

'You're an exceptional woman, Catherine, but I know I wouldn't be a good partner for you, and your family wouldn't approve.' Almost apologetically, he laid a hand on hers.

'It's worked for Christopher and Alice,' she said defiantly. This was the first time her brother's name had been mentioned during Tom's time at Halesden. He was interested to hear more, and welcomed a diversion in the line of conversation.

'Tell me about them,' he said. 'I'd heard they'd eloped to Canada. Are they still there?'

'Yes, Christopher is farming on the west coast, near

Vancouver, and they have a young family. I receive a letter every Christmas and pass it on to Mother. Father won't let us mention his name.'

'I'm pleased it's been a successful union,' said Tom. 'Alice was a smart girl. The pioneering life will have suited her talents well. And to think, a new branch of the Bland family in Canada – that is something to celebrate.'

They strolled on until Catherine said hesitantly, 'It could be the same for us.' For years Tom had been flattered by Catherine's attention, and knew what he was about to say would be hurtful.

'No,' he said decisively. 'Our backgrounds are too diverse. It would be an insurmountable divide, and I have a selfish streak… you deserve better.'

'So I'm rejected.' Her voice was flat.

'It's best that way; for both of us.'

Catherine turned her head away, but he saw her dab her cheek with the back of her hand. He felt genuinely sorry that he was unable to return her affection.

Chapter 25

Andrew Gasson perched on a fallen log, his back supported by the trunk of a leaning apple tree. Spreading before him was a rough lawn, and beyond bubbled the River Ribble. On its bank rotated the three wheels which drove the mechanisation at the mill.

Andrew was the son of a French mother and Scottish father. He had been raised in Selkirk, and brought up as a Presbyterian. Having proved himself gifted at the local charity school he left home at fourteen to seek his fortune in the manufacturing industry, finally settling in Preston. Appointed, at a young age, as a junior manager in one of the largest mills in the town, he had been mentored by of one of the owners, an advocate of the New Lanark approach. This philanthropist now financed the current venture at Clattonbury. A single man, Andrew lived alone on the fringe of the new housing development. The church, school and community facilities were the final editions to the scheme he was overseeing.

The visitor he was expecting today was Tom Shaw, who had been recommended by the rector at Halesden for the post of vicar in the newly built church. Upon asking around, his interviewee had been described variously as a man of compassion, or an outspoken mischief-maker. Andrew looked forward to their encounter. On hearing Tom's voice he walked over to greet him.

'Thank you for coming.' He studied Tom's open, smiling face as he shook his hand. 'I've had plenty of reports about you... some of them good!'

'That will no doubt depend on who you've been talking to, sir.' Tom responded confidently to the humour.

'I've certainly been told of your commitment to pastoral work, and how you are a charismatic preacher filling St James's church to capacity. What's your secret?'

'There's no secret. I focus on the positive and aim to keep the message simple, so even the children can understand.' Tom was momentarily distracted by a pair of sparrows squabbling loudly in a nearby hazel tree. *'Not even a sparrow, worth only half a penny, can fall to the ground without your Father knowing,'* he added with a half-smile.

Andrew laughed heartily, enjoying the aptness of the quote, and ushered Tom to join him on the makeshift seat.

'I've also heard encouraging reports as to how you run the community here at Long Mill,' Tom continued. 'I should be interested to hear your philosophy.'

Feeling relaxed, with the warm sun playing on his back, Andrew folded his arms and began. 'Let me explain. The population of this village is around a thousand, and most of employable age work at our mill. We see their welfare as paramount to the success of the business. We are fortunate in our location near a supply of fast-running water.' He gestured to the river at the bottom of the garden. 'And we've recently added steam engines to use during the dry season. Our production of yarn and woven materials is thriving, and we want our employees to benefit from our success as well as our investors. Most of our workers come from within twenty miles of here, from rural Lancashire or Yorkshire. It suits them well. The houses belong to the company and we charge a fair rent.' He paused as the bell from the factory clanged loudly, announcing the workers' midday break. 'It's still far from perfect: overcrowding where there are large families, and the standard of cleanliness in many of the households is poor. With education I hope we can improve on that. Because of the isolated situation of the factory we aim to provide as much as we can for our employees. Our shop stocks all the essentials at little over cost price.'

'And what do they do for recreation?' Tom asked.

'You'll observe there's no tavern in the village.' He gave Tom a meaningful look. 'We plan a community room for entertainment, and the school will double as an educational institute for the adults. We encourage our employees to grow some of their own food in allotments on the edge of the village, and to take their children out into the countryside at every opportunity. If they want more they have to travel to Halesden or Burnley.' He sat back and turned to face his visitor. 'Now it's your turn. Tell me about yourself and what you can bring to our community.'

Andrew listened attentively as Tom gave a detailed account of his upbringing, experience as a priest and burgeoning political interests.

'I've witnessed the injustices resulting from the way this country is run from a rural perspective, and more recently in an industrial town. It doesn't have to be this way. It's time for change, and in my opinion the only way forward is for all working men to have representation in parliament.'

'I agree,' Andrew responded without hesitation. 'It's a feudal system. The demands of the Chartists seem fair and reasonable, but it'll be a long fight. I don't see the aristocracy and landowners giving up their privileged position easily.' He shook his head.

Having completed his potted biography, Tom raised the

question of education. 'You say you are concerned for the welfare and schooling of the children. I should like to hear more of your plans.'

'You won't find any children under the age of eleven working in this mill.' Andrew broke into a smile. 'And you're right; I want to set up a proper school as soon as possible so all our youngsters learn to read and write. I will be looking for a suitable master, someone the vicar who is appointed can work alongside.'

'May I suggest a possible candidate?'

'I should be interested to hear of anyone you could recommend.'

'A friend of mine, who is the only master in the local school back in Westmorland, is looking for a more challenging position. We were educated at the same grammar school, which has an excellent reputation. His wife and two young daughters are also literate, and could help with the younger children.'

Andrew turned to face Tom. 'I think we could work well together, Tom Shaw. If this is something you would like to take on I shall be pleased to recommend you to our patron as our first parish priest. But before you make any decisions you must spend some time looking round the village, and talking to the residents.'

Nelson Street, Victoria Street, Waterloo Square – the patriotic names amused Tom as with rising enthusiasm he paced up and down the neatly planned pathways. Two hundred or more back-to-back houses were clustered together in blocks, served by communal water pumps and privies. A group of elderly women were chattering animatedly in the central square as they drew water. With their sombre, dark-toned shawls they reminded him of the colony of rooks who resided near the chapel at Ravendale. They responded cheerfully to his greeting before returning to their huddle.

Hearing the shrieks of children he wandered the short distance down to the river where some youngsters were playing in the shallows, throwing sticks and splashing each other with the cooling water.

'Caught any fish today?' Tom called out.

'No, mister,' replied a tousle-headed lad. 'I can see 'em, but they always swim away.'

Tom smiled at the boy. 'Maybe I can teach you how to hook them – someday soon.' He walked jauntily back to the mill, feeling more optimistic than he had for many months.

'Thank you, Mr Gasson. I should be honoured to serve the community here in Clattonbury. Please will you put my name forward to your sponsor?'

'That's good!' Andrew Gasson slapped his thigh enthusiastically. 'Now you must call me Andrew, and as soon as you return to Halesden send a letter to your old school friend inviting him to come for an interview. I will, of course, cover the cost of his travelling expenses.'

That evening Tom dispatched a letter to Luke Yarker, and by the end of August the friends had been offered, and accepted, the vacancies. A few weeks later they moved into adjoining cottages close to the newly built church.

Tom was welcomed at his first service by a full congregation, and the following day a host of well-scrubbed faces greeted him when he took the morning prayers at school. Luke had grouped the children round tables, recreating the informality of the dale school. Rebecca and Anne sat proudly with the youngest children, the older girls were clustered around Agnes, and the boys sat with Luke in their midst. Thus daily life at Clattonbury continued to run smoothly, giving Tom and Luke an opportunity to establish themselves in the village.

Elsewhere told a different story. An abrupt downturn in the economy was causing distress as short-time and unemployment hit Manchester, and rapidly spread east towards the Yorkshire border. One Friday evening Tom made his regular trip into Halesden, and was accosted by Sean the minute he set foot in the tavern.

'Tom, so glad you're here. We've just heard, there's to be a mass meeting up on Kersal Moor on Monday to promote the Charter.'

Tom acknowledged his comment with a friendly wave and brushed past him to order a drink from the landlord.

'There'll be speakers coming from all over the country,' Sean continued excitedly as he followed in Tom's wake, 'from London to Scotland. We're organising a party of supporters from here. You've got to come along, Tom.'

'It sounds interesting. I'll discuss it with Andrew and see if Luke can get away from school for a few hours too.'

'It's an evening meeting,' Sean enthused, 'so anyone living nearby can go after they've finished their shifts. They're talking of thousands, maybe a hundred thousand supporters attending.'

Tom could not resist a smile at Sean's eagerness. 'I'll do my best to be there. We'll catch up with you all somewhere along the road.'

Kersal Moor loomed ahead. 'Did you ever imagine we'd be involved in something like this?' said Tom, as he and Luke stood back to absorb the scene.

From north, south, east and west they came: men, women and children, lit by the light of a waxing moon and thousands of torches. Like ants bustling back to the colony, scores became hundreds and hundreds thousands as the columns snaked their way upwards, through the bracken and past the rocky outcrops. Some lines moved to the pulsating beat of drums, others to the rhythm of song. Banners of purple and green silk, bearing the inscriptions *Universal Suffrage* and *Vote by Ballot*, fluttered in the light breeze.

'It's as if all the workers in England have been gathered together,' Luke said. 'How did they orchestrate such an immense assembly?'

Half-a-dozen men, their faces streaked with grime and sweat, pushed by carrying skull and crossbone placards, eerily illuminated by the light of their torches. The two friends hung back, and standing where they were on the perimeter Tom sighted a few horsemen, muskets laid across their saddles, keeping to the shadows as they circled the throng.

On a flat plateau, where horse racing was usually held, a party atmosphere prevailed. Bonfires blazed and the smell of roasted salt pork, mixed with woodsmoke, wafted through the still air. Ale and cider flowed freely, little groups of musicians played popular tunes and children danced.

'We need to look for Sean and the others,' said Luke. 'They'll have made for the table rock. The speeches will be starting from there.'

Tom found the atmosphere electrifying as speaker after speaker picked up the loudhailer and presented their case. Some railed against the mill owners, parliament and even the young Queen Victoria for the sufferings of the working man. Some read inflammatory articles from the radical press, while others favoured a softer approach in the fight for democracy. Yet others addressed the practical aspects: electing delegates to the convention, collecting signatures for a petition and raising money to fund the campaign.

Finally it was a passionate Irishman, Feargus O'Connor, who set the meeting alight with a scintillating speech. Tall and striking in a blue frock coat, he had the demeanour of a gentleman and the eloquence of a professional orator as he meticulously explained the main points of the Charter: votes for all adult males and secret ballots. To a background of thunderous cheers, which echoed and re-echoed round the distant hills, he dedicated his life to the liberation of the working man. He stirred the crowd into hysteria as he proclaimed, 'Today is the day the Chartist movement has been born.' Horns hooted, men and women embraced each other and a silent tear ran down the cheeks of an old man standing at Tom's side. Sean threw his arms around Tom, overcome with the emotion of the moment and the appeal of his fellow Irishman.

'Our day is coming, Tom. Next time I'll be on that platform and you should be too.'

It was close to midnight as the crowd melted away; the silence and red glow of the torches on the downward tracks highlighting the clandestine nature of the gathering.

'How many folks d'you think were there?' Luke addressed Sean.

'Oh man, they're saying it could be over two hundred thousand. That's equivalent to the whole population of Manchester.'

Tom could identify with Sean's elation as he recalled a distant conversation at Ambleside, when his brother and William Wordsworth had debated the French Revolution.

Four months later, Tom was attending to some correspondence in the vestry when a rider appeared at the church door.

'Mr Shaw? Are you the Reverend Thomas Shaw?'

Tom assented.

The carrier drew an official sealed envelope from the bag slung across his chest. 'I have a letter here that needs to be signed for.'

Tom pulled off the seal and read:

You are subpoenaed to appear on the 1st February 1839 to give testimony at this court, in defence of Joseph Teasdale of Highburn.

The writ came from the county court at Appleby.

Chapter 26

May 1839

'Stand still, man!' the prison warder snapped at Jos Teasdale as he handcuffed him to Daniel Sarginson, a young slate miner from Whitehaven. It was an hour before dawn, and the streets were quiet as the two prisoners were escorted to the Cathedral Square. Jos could hear the tossing and jangling of reins and the scraping of hooves on the cobbles as they drew near to the waiting stagecoach. He slapped his free hand against his thigh for warmth as their canvas bags, containing a few personal possessions, were thrown in with the luggage of the other passengers. He didn't want to lose sight of his violin. On seeing the shorn heads and prison garb, a low gasp of horror rose from the coach as the pair mounted the steps to the outside seats.

'Where are we mekin for?' Daniel asked the guards through chattering teeth.

'We're bound for London, so along Watling Street and to the Thames docks.'

'And after that?'

'Australia, of course. In the meantime we'll be travelling day and night, just stopping to change the horses.' Dan gave Tom a wink.

'Is London where the ships sail from?' he asked.

'More likely one of the Medway ports, but you'll have to start your sentence on a prison hulk.'

The road was empty as they cantered over Shap. Jos focused his gaze on the uplands to the west, trying to identify some feature, anything to link him with home. This would be the last sight of his birthplace for many years, and he was painfully aware he might never see these mountains again. Despite the biting cold, and his fears for the future, he began to enjoy the journey after the weeks of incarceration in Carlisle Gaol. The guards were friendly enough, the weather fair, and for someone who had never been further south than Kendal the changes in the landscape over the next three hundred miles were a revelation. Three days later they were speeding through the outskirts of London.

On leaving the city the River Thames opened out, bordered by flat, muddy marshes spreading far inland. Sloops and barges plied up and down, and where the water ran deep, magnificent sailing ships glided by, ropes clanking noisily against the masts.

Jos twitched his nose and turned to his companion. 'What can I smell, Dan? It's powerful.'

'Seaweed,' Daniel laughed. 'And listen to those birds squealing overhead – they're seagulls. There used t'be hundreds of them circling the fishing boats at Whitehaven. We canna be far from the coast.'

The coach rattled on, eventually pulling up at some docks where, in the filth-strewn estuary mud, rested a prison hulk. Covered in barnacles, its sagging chains stretched out across the detritus sluiced down from the city.

'This is it, lads – Sheerness and the end of your journey. You'll be holed up here till there's a convict ship available.

Then, if you're lucky, off to the New World.' The older warder slapped Dan on the back in a friendly gesture.

'How long will we have to wait?' Jos asked.

'I canna say; some prisoners are detained for months, even years. Others never leave the port... except in a canvas bag.' He laughed.

'How d'they choose who'll go?'

'It's a bit of a lottery. The companies that charter the ships are paid a bonus for each convict they land safe and well, so they need to be confident the men they select will survive the journey. You two look strong and healthy, much fitter than most of those huddled down there.' He nodded in the direction of the quay.

'On t'other hand,' said his companion, 'they like to hang on to those with practical skills. They're of more use to the working parties.'

'It's my guess you'll both be on yer way before too long,' the older guard added encouragingly. 'But hang on tight to yer possessions. Remember yer among thieves now!'

With this parting shot they were handed over to the authorities where, in a cramped office on a compound circled by dogs, their particulars were noted and handcuffs replaced with leg irons. Corralled alongside the cattle waiting for their final journey to Smithfield they shuffled out like caged beasts, to join the masses assembled on the wharf.

Never had Jos witnessed so much noise and bustle as was to be found on the slimy, cobbled quayside. Passengers jostled each other as they boarded the Atlantic packets on their regular schedules. Wives and families wept as they waved their loved ones goodbye. Men in uniform milled around; some smart and eager, mustering for service with the East India Company; some shouting and brawling, the worse for wear from the rum that flowed freely. Yet others, on the final journey home from foreign parts, hobbled on crutches, wounds bound with soiled, bloodstained bandages. Women from the brothels mingled with the throng, and mangy dogs slunk around scavenging for food. A stench of unwashed humanity, animal excrement and gutted fish hung in the air. Sickened, Jos lifted his head towards the chilly wind that cut across from the east. Now he could smell the salty tang of the sea.

Absorbed but wary, Jos stood close to Daniel, alert to the snatches of conversation going on about him. Mostly Londoners, the accents and slang were difficult to follow, but he soon gleaned that life on the hulks was grim. More encouraging was the gossip that conditions aboard the convict ships had improved from the hellholes of the early days, and with good behaviour most men gained their freedom after three years. Most heartening was the inference that opportunities for free men abounded in Australia.

Having suffered the enforced break with home he now wanted to sample life on the other side of the world, and to regain his liberty. The prison guards had told him that running livestock was a valued occupation, and there wasn't much he didn't know about sheep. This could be the greatest opportunity of his life. If all went well he might eventually bring out Hannah and his boy to join him.

'I hope we're moved on quickly,' he confided to Daniel.

There was a sparkle in his young companion's pale blue eyes when he replied. 'Aye, me too, I canna wait to get going.'

They were not disappointed. Within six weeks both men were allocated to the same ship, the *Edenvale*, a sound vessel on her third voyage to Port Jackson.

Chapter 27

Two hundred and fifty convicts were mustered on the quay waiting to board the *Edenvale*. Jos and Daniel had taken their place ahead of a large Welsh-speaking contingent when Dan, hampered by his shackles, trod on the foot of an ill-kempt bear of a man standing behind him. This brought forth a deluge of confrontational abuse. Jos recognised the language immediately, and stepped in with a few well-chosen words learnt long ago from Alice.

'Boy, that put you in your place, Isaac Evans,' said one of his group, laughing heartily. There was no retaliation from Evans but Jos felt uneasy; a long incarceration stretched ahead.

First the free settlers, many poorly clad, threaded their way between the rain barrels on deck, each clutching an assortment of bags, cooking utensils and household items. The convicts followed, dragging their way up the gangplank before dropping down into the overcrowded, stuffy between-decks area. From below, penned in the cargo hold, Jos could hear the cries of distress from the sheep, pigs and hens which were to provide fresh meat on the voyage. Once the last prisoner descended, the iron rungs the heavy hatch clanged shut.

Jos lay in his hammock, wrestling claustrophobia. The low beams pressed down on his head, as if he was once again submerged in the shadowy, subterranean tunnels under Harter Fell. The timbers on the ship creaked and groaned, and he wondered how he could endure the next four months; longer if they encountered problems. He pulled the thin blanket over his head, and tried to mask the putrescent reek by recalling the scent of damp peat and newly mown hay. His violin case lay close to his chest. To obliterate the constant groans of his fellow prisoners he pressed his fingers in his ears and sang silently. *While Shepherds Watched Their Flocks by Night* spun round in his brain like a never-ending carousel.

The *Edenvale* rode gently at anchor for a few hours, awaiting favourable winds. Finally the ship's bell clanged. Captain Stoke read an extract from the Bible and all decks joined in reciting the Lord's Prayer. From the prison deck the hushed singing of a Welsh hymn added to the poignancy of the moment. The mooring ropes were cast off; a tug towed them out of the Medway, and the fully rigged ship slipped through the gloom into the open sea. It was three o' clock on 15th May 1839. Through obstructed portholes, the convicts watched the white cliffs gradually fade from view.

The early stages of the voyage went smoothly, with seasickness abating as the travellers got used to the motion of the ship. Once out of sight of land the leg irons were removed, and each convict was allowed a twice-daily hour on deck for fresh air and exercise. The ship's surgeon established a routine below decks, so prisoners maintained their personal cleanliness and that of their quarters. The master ensured there was no brutality from drunken officers by meticulously monitoring the rum distribution to the crew.

Jos was the first to sign on when the chaplain, Father

Gardiner, offered religious instruction and classes in reading and writing. In this he was helped by some of the wives of the free settlers who had been sponsored by their churches. Each day, weather permitting, a select group gathered round the scrubbed table in the mess area for three hours' tuition. Jos knew this was just the project he needed to get him through the coming weeks, and he set himself the goal of being able to write fluently by the time they reached Sydney. However, this dedication to study didn't endear him to Isaac Evans, who mocked him persistently as 'the professor'.

At dusk the iron bolts were drawn and Jos would brandish his fiddle, accompanying the singing of sea shanties and regional folk songs; the unfamiliar language of the Welsh always in the ascendancy. Once darkness fully descended the guards patrolled, swinging their oil lamps into the darkest corners of the deck. Rats scuttled about; men snored; some screamed out in torment while others quietly moaned. Jos, hands behind his head, found these never-ending nights the toughest time as he lay in his hammock waiting for the distant dawn.

He thought about his wife and son and relived the tasks they needed to perform, willing them to have a good season lambing. He revised his lesson of the day, mentally seeing the words, joining the letters with his index finger, constructing sentences.

After midnight, when sleep still eluded him, it was the memory of Lucy and the events that had taken place twenty-three years earlier that haunted him. He cursed himself for misjudging the situation when they visited the eagles' nest, and recalled the dark days when she had distanced herself from him, shutting him out whenever they were in each other's company. It was only when he remembered that magical Christmas night when they had made music together, and she had pressed her lips against his under the mistletoe, that he relaxed. In his imagination it felt so real. The sweet scent of woodsmoke mingled with her warm breath; the clashing of their teeth; the erectness of her nipples beneath her light wool dress – and the gentle swelling in her belly.

Time after time he replayed the scene when he had confronted her coffin. A room scented with evergreen and dried lavender, watched over by her family. Despite their closeness he was the only one to know her deepest secret, how she was part of his life too. Beneath the polished wood he saw a marble angel carrying an infant – his child. He pictured a beautiful girl, the image of her mother. Each July he counted another year. This summer she would have been twenty-four, the same age as his companion Daniel.

He tried to make sense of why he and Tom, who had once embraced as brothers, had become so estranged in the intervening years. The distancing started after the clipping in the summer of 1815. Jos remembered teasing him for being drunk – but there was something else, something he had never resolved; though he suspected it involved Lucy. He now recognised it was in retaliation to Tom's attitude that he had befriended the gang at the quarry. He had envied Tom his loving family, his education, his friendship with George... but most of all, the relationship he had with his sister and his promise to her of a future together beyond the fells.

It was often first light before he sank into the welcoming downy nest of oblivion.

On reaching the equator the steamy heat became unbearable, and for days on end the *Edenvale* was becalmed. Tedium bore down on the whole company, with the clanging of the watch-bell the only signal of the passing of the hours. Jos stretched out naked in his narrow hammock. The scratching of flesh could be heard throughout the ship as passengers and prisoners alike were tormented with a plague of fleas. Jos pressed his palms tight to his ears as a demented prisoner rattled the iron bars on the hatch, hour after hour.

Energy and motivation dropped, so the quality of food and ship board cleanliness suffered. Fresh water was rationed as the rain barrels emptied and tempers flared with angry confrontations over the allocation of water. The warders retaliated with punishments, including denial of the daily exercise time, and several convicts had their shackles replaced. One belligerent Yorkshireman received a flogging from a frustrated guard.

Father Gardiner did his best to calm the situation by leading twice-daily prayer sessions, imploring God to lead them out of the doldrums, but his words fell on deaf ears. The master's concern was over mutiny or suicide; he couldn't afford to lose a man overboard. Jos's unease was for Daniel, who sat holding his knees to his chest, silent and withdrawn.

During his allotted time on deck Jos would hang over the handrail looking down into the bottomless blue ocean. Sometimes porpoises played in their wake or whales would swim close by spouting water, but for days even they had vanished. The boundless sea was an unbroken sheet of smoky blue glass.

Daniel came up and rested his hands on the rail next to Jos. His languid voice cut into his thoughts. ''Aven't ee seen enough? Sea, sea and more bloody sea.'

'Yer reet lad, but I can find another world beneath this

ocean, a distant land which reminds me of home. Focus your eyes, Dan, look deep, deep down…'

Words from *The Brothers*, recited long ago by Tom, flooded back. He repeated them to Daniel.

> '…*he, in those hours*
> *Of tiresome indolence would often hang*
> *Over the vessel's side, and gaze and gaze,*
> *And, while the broad green wave and sparkling foam*
> *Flash'd round him images and hues…*
> *Below him, in the bosom of the deep*
> *Saw mountains, saw the forms of sheep that graz'd*
> *On verdant hills, with dwellings among trees,*
> *And Shepherds clad in the same country grey*
> *Which he himself had worn.'*[9]

As a young man Jos had thrilled to the rhythm of the phrases and the pace and pitch of Tom's voice, but had little sense of the meaning. Never once did he think he might be in his current situation. He closed his eyes, semi-disorientated; lost between the words in his head and the shifting ocean below. Now he understood. Shaking himself back to reality he put a comforting arm round the broad, bare shoulders of his young companion.

'Think of home, Dan – we're goin' to be alreet. I just hope you can sense it too.'

Together they climbed back down the ladder to find, not for the first time, Isaac Evans leaning over Jos's hammock and tampering with his bag.

'What do ee think yer doing?' Jos shouted.

'Just checking to see if you've got a copy of Chaucer hidden away. I hear there are some juicy bits you cud read to us.' Evans winked at his comrades. Jos raised his fists in a gesture of defiance, but feeling Dan's restraining hand on his arm, resisted the temptation to take a swing at the Welshman.

That night Daniel spoke up for the first time in days. 'Give us a song, Jos, let's have a hymn.' There was a grumble from some quarters, but Jos took out his fiddle and lifted his bow to the tune of *Rock of Ages*. A low-pitched, melodious voice started up, resonating round the dark interior, and one by one the convicts joined in until the whole of the lower deck were singing or humming in harmony. The captain, chaplain and free settlers on the upper deck were in the middle of their meal when the melody drifted up. They stopped, mid-conversation, to listen. Spontaneous clapping broke out at the end.

The following morning a westerly wind blew up and the temperature dropped.

With the wind billowing its sails, and gulls screeching in its wake, the *Edenvale* made good time to the Cape. Here they dropped anchor to take on fresh water, vegetables and meat for the last leg of the journey. The monotony of life on board ship was at last in sight, and with the enhanced diet, the health and mental state of all those on board improved markedly. The guards overlooked the boisterous games held on deck during exercise time, and laughter replaced the melancholia of the last few weeks.

Jos was unendingly grateful to the chaplain and his helpers. He would arrive in Australia equipped for the future in a way he couldn't have dreamed of when he set out from Carlisle a few months previously. The general camaraderie between the upper and lower decks gave him the opportunity to thank Father Gardiner, and in return receive his blessing.

When Port Jackson came into view, the leg irons were replaced in readiness for disembarkation. Cross tides and winds battered the ship as it passed between the Heads, but once within the protective walls of the natural harbour of Sydney Bay the water was as calm as Hallswater on a summer's day. Captain Stoke dropped anchor to wait for health clearance from the colony's medical officer before proceeding to one of the wharves, where the free settlers disembarked. Finally the human freight was lowered into rowing boats and transported to the penal colony, which lay behind a sandy beach, well away from the growing town. As Jos and Daniel landed, a flock of cackling white cockatoos, followed by a pink and grey cloud of galahs, took flight into the trees guarding the settlement.

'Man, just look at those birds!' said Daniel in high spirits. 'This is another world.'

Jos picked up a stick and scratched in the loose sand, *Welcome to Australia*.

'Why did you do that?' asked one of the guards, mystified.

'Because I can.' He grinned knowingly at Dan.

Herded onto the beach, the convicts were dispatched into the salt water for a thorough cleansing. The fine sand shifted and sucked at Jos's toes as he stood unsteadily on the waterline, watching the gentle rhythm of the waves. He was grateful he had learnt to swim in the pools at Ravendale as he relaxed on his back, dragging his shackled leg. The water was icy cold, but to feel the push and gentle tug of the retreating surf calmed his senses, invigorated his skin and swept through his close-cropped hair. At last he was free of the foul smells which had enveloped him for months. Overjoyed, tears pricked his eyes before mingling with the salty water.

The men rubbed themselves dry with their shirts and were formally turned over into the custody of the governor of the colony. From here they were placed in camps to await their final settlement. Those who were literate were given paper and ink to write home. With suppressed excitement Jos carefully penned his first ever letter.

Sydney, 3rd September 1839

My dear Wife,

I have a smile on my face as I imagine Edward reading you this letter. I trust it will come as a pleasant surprise that I am now able to write to you, thanks to an inspirational chaplain on our outward-bound journey.

I hope you and Edward are well, and managing to survive on the income from our sheep. I'm truly sorry not to be there to support you both.

We arrived safely in Sydney Cove a few days ago with the full complement of convicts, which is a credit to both the master and surgeon. The journey took longer than expected but we were spared any great storms or infection on board. I was lucky to have a young companion from Whitehaven, who has been like a second son.

It is early spring here, and what an amazing country this is. Miles of closely packed gum trees with a distinctive aromatic smell. Some have red trunks and some silver that glow after dark. Others look like unshorn sheep, the bark falling off in long strips and lying in curls on the ground. Flocks of brightly coloured birds cackle and squawk overhead. Animals, the size of deer, bounce along at considerable speed on two back legs. Naked natives carry spears and play hide and seek with the white settlers. I've also heard tell of snakes and spiders whose venom is so toxic they can kill with a single nip.

I am waiting allocation to a settlement and hope to be assigned to a private sheep farmer. I should like Daniel to come with me. He is strong and willing, but as an experienced miner I fear he will be sent to the coalfields north of Sydney. There was a sizable contingent of Welsh miners on our vessel, who reminded me of Alice and her brothers. We enjoyed some rousing musical evenings together and I hope some of them will look after him.

I will now knuckle down to whatever is thrown at me, and count the days until we can all be together again.

Jos

Decontaminated, and in clean prison uniform, the convicts mustered outside the office of the governor general. Depending on their age, fitness and experience some expected to be assigned to government projects, and others to be employed by free settlers who would take responsibility for their conduct. First to be given posts were those with mining skills, which included most of the Welsh contingent and Daniel.

'Looks like I'll have t'learn their language now,' he said ruefully to Jos. They held each other close, neither able to trust themselves with words.

'Come on, you stragglers,' called out one of the guards. Daniel slung his bag across his shoulders and, towering over his companions, joined the contingent making for the

Newcastle coalfields. Jos watched him disappear beyond the compound gates before bending down to retrieve his own luggage. His fiddle had vanished.

Distraught, he looked frantically about – it had to be Isaac. 'Thief, thief!' he shouted as he hobbled after the retreating group. 'That bastard Evans has swiped my fiddle.'

Mayhem ensued. Government officials shouted and prison guards raced after the escaping prisoner. A shot rang out, but Jos carried on regardless through the compound gates. Daniel had heard his distressed shouts, and pushed his way to the front to find Isaac Evans with a violin case slung over his shoulder and a smug grin on his pocked face. He threw a punch, but Isaac, a far weightier man, retaliated, laying him flat. When Jos panted up Isaac tossed the fiddle onto the ground and took one big jump.

'Not much use to you now, you self-righteous bugger.' A cackling laugh and a string of Welsh expletives followed.

All eyes focused on Jos as he dropped to his knees and shook the worn leather case. Inside rattled the broken pieces of his violin.

'Back in line, there's nowt to see,' ordered one of the prison guards. Jos looked up to see Daniel reeling unsteadily, blood pouring from his nose onto his spotless shirt.

'Thanks, Dan. You've been a true friend. Tek good care of yerself, and I'll come and find you once I get my freedom.' He watched despondently as the party regrouped and carried on down the dirt track. With the case under his arm he returned slowly to the compound to face the consequences.

No action was taken following Jos's misconduct, and when his turn came he was assigned to a Scottish master,

Donald Stewart, who owned a station of one thousand acres, four days' journey west of Port Jackson. In return for his labour he was to receive his lodgings, provisions to make his own meals, and a small allowance for clothes and personal items.

He set off the following morning under escort, bound for the Blue Mountains.

Chapter 28

A lone at last. Jos pulled off his dusty boots and sank down on the canvas bedstead to take stock of his surroundings: bark walls, a roof laced with cobwebs and an earth floor. In the corner a three-legged stool and a shelf with a tin mug, plate and eating irons. Ahead, an open door. Beyond stretched an unfenced land of golden wattle, termite mounds and aromatic eucalyptus. It felt close to paradise.

He unstrapped the fiddle case and fingered the pieces of broken wood. Panic welled up as he fumbled to sort the pieces: the shattered scroll, once lovingly carved and decorated by his grandfather; the snapped pegs; the broken bridge. He pushed the bits back and forth, playing with them like an unsolvable jigsaw. Exasperated, he ripped away the lining of the case and retrieved the commonplace book he had brought ten thousand miles. This was the first time he had handled it since leaving Highburn and now, by the light of a bright moon and to a chorus of cicadas, he searched every page. The paper had survived the journey, and the trampling.

Long before sunrise he slipped out of the hut. A dog growled up at the homestead and he stiffened, waiting for it to settle before creeping along to the pile of stones and rocks he had noticed when they arrived on the bullock dray. He picked out two large, flat stones and returned to his hut.

Here he worked for an hour, using the knife and spoon to scrape a hole in the beaten earth. Satisfied, he buried the package between the guarding stones; repeating Lucy's care with the slates in Westmorland. He trod the earth back into shape and replaced the bed. He was ready to restart his life, determined to learn as quickly as he could how best to flourish in this alien environment.

Jos had been told by the officials in Sydney that the assigned property stood on the edge of virgin country. The owners, Donald and Flora Stewart, ran a sheep farm and had emigrated from Stirling in the early '30s. On this, his first morning, he walked confidently towards their homestead. The run spread west and north, and was unfenced apart from two paddocks surrounded by moveable hurdles for penning the sheep. An irregular line of vegetation suggested a creek ran along the southern boundary. Beyond the house stood a roughly constructed woolshed, open on two sides to the elements; a fence protecting an assortment of fruit trees and a dusty ploughed field standing ready for planting. A sweet smell drifted from some bushes near the house, and birds could be heard tinkling like bells blowing in the wind. In front of the porch a little girl was playing with a tame kangaroo. As Jos approached the front door opened, and a woman with sparkling eyes and a crisp pinafore tied tightly round a slim waist walked towards him.

'I'm Flora,' she said in a soft Scottish accent. 'Welcome to Toomara.'

Jos shook her small proffered hand. 'What's the name of that flower?' he asked. 'The one with the sweet scent.'

Flora turned and stroked a glossy leaf on the bush beside her. 'Frangipani,' she said with a knowing smile. 'It's a wonderful perfume to sleep with under the stars.'

'Glad to see you're about early,' a friendly voice called

out. Jos turned to face his new boss. A tall, lean figure, about fifty years of age, with a young dog bouncing at his side and a rifle slung over his shoulder. 'Take this.' He threw Jos the gun. 'I hope you know how to use it.'

'What's it for?' Jos asked, unable to disguise his surprise.

'We're plagued with dingoes and you canna trust the Aborigines. Keep it close by you at all times.'

'Right!' Jos wondered if he'd had a lucky escape with his early morning wanderings.

'We run eight hundred head of sheep here,' Mr Stewart continued. 'You'll be working with Rusty, an Aboriginal boy from the local tribe. He can be trusted and knows every inch of the terrain. You've come to us with good credentials as a shepherd, so I need you to take this dog and see how quickly you can knock him into shape for guarding the flock.'

'What's his name?' Jos asked.

'We've been calling him Clyde.'

In a calm, low voice Jos called the collie, who bounded across, ears erect. He raised a flattened palm and the dog dropped down on his haunches into a sitting position. Jos fondled his silky head. While he appreciated that close supervision could no longer be possible in this wild, open domain, Jos was heartened by the trust that was already being placed in him.

From beyond the woolshed a young black man approached; bare-footed, wearing a loincloth and with a dilly bag over his shoulder.

'This is Rusty, he'll show you the ropes,' said the boss by way of introduction. 'He speaks very little English, but is a quick learner and appears to be loyal to our family.'

Jos shook hands with his Aboriginal colleague, who responded with a show of perfect, pearly teeth.

'*Orana*. Come.' Rusty beckoned.

Jos followed in his wake as they shepherded the flock to fresh pasture. Alert to every movement or subtle change in the landscape, Jos was at a loss as to how his companion could find a way through what looked like hectares of identical trees. Only the sun served as a constant guide. The temperature rose steadily as the morning progressed, so when the track diverted through a small area of rainforest bordering the creek he welcomed the cool, moist atmosphere. Water dripped on his head, and fern fronds brushed his face.

After a few hours of plodding along in silence Rusty halted the sheep where the grass was plentiful. Jos estimated they had travelled about two miles.

'*Maji*?' Rusty said, gathering together a few sticks. Jos joined him in collecting brushwood and bending down, noticed a lump, the colour and size of a damson, attached to his arm.

'What's this?' He looked towards Rusty and tapped his forearm with his finger.

'Leech,' said Rusty. A broad grin spread across his face as he pulled it off and stamped on it with his bare foot. Blood splattered up Jos' leg and spurted across the dry earth. Jos wondered how long it had been there; he hadn't felt a thing.

On the return journey they ambled over higher ground, the flock quietly feeding as they progressed. Now relaxed in each other's company Jos took the opportunity to bond with Clyde, while Rusty diverted on short detours. Each time he returned to show Jos the contents of his bag: assorted roots and wriggling grubs. He patted his stomach and grinned. Arriving back at sundown they counted the sheep into the paddock.

Later, resting in his hut and listening to the clamour of

the birds, Jos scrutinised his arms and legs, which were red with insect bites. This would be the pattern of his days for the next few years. He wondered how he would cope with the boredom of such intense shepherding, and reflected on the benefits of the hefting system back on the fells at home. Ewes who, through generations of breeding, had taught their lambs to remain in families, without physical boundaries.

Shearing began six weeks after Jos's arrival and, as at home, drew in all the family and any neighbours who were available. Donald Stewart took charge of the shearing shed, helped by Angus, a wiry, red-haired Scot who had been with the Stewarts since he first arrived in Australia as a convict. Now a free man, Angus had chosen to remain with his assigned boss, taking on responsibility for the safety of the flock overnight. Jos had barely spoken to him, having seen him only briefly and usually after dark when he drifted around the station like a predatory ghost.

On his way to the shearing shed Jos passed a manmade pool created by damming the creek. This was to serve for washing the sheep. Three young Aboriginal men sat dangling their feet in the muddy water, waiting for the action to start.

For the first time in many months Jos started to whistle. Having honed his skills over many years he knew he was a competent shearer, and a buzz of excitement swept through him on hearing the sharpening of the scissors. Tarpaulins were laid on the ground to catch the fleeces, and under the eye of his boss he took control of his first whether. He cut the coat close, and in one piece. No nicks to the skin and at great speed.

'You seem to have got the hang of it!' Mr Stewart said dryly.

Jos acknowledged the comment as he wiped away the sweat from his brow with the back of his hand. By the end of the day he had sheared nearly double the number achieved by his colleagues. Donald Stewart was delighted, but Jos was aware he was not making a friend of Angus.

The clip was a turning point. Jos fenced off an area of garden where he planted vegetables and tobacco, he cared for his hut in the manner Hannah would have approved, and Clyde curled up each night outside his open door. Toomara began to feel like a home. Sometimes Flora walked by with the children and would stop for a chat. Catriona and Moira would sit cross-legged on the dry earth, their faces alive with interest as they listened to tales of life back in the old country. One day Jos told Flora the story of his shattered fiddle. A week later, half-walking, half-running, an excited Catriona arrived at his hut. In her arms was a once-loved violin that her mother had bought for Jos from one of the Scottish migrants in town.

On quiet evenings Jos now sat outside his hut, playing for his own amusement or that of the children. Sometimes, when the sun had dipped over the horizon, he saw the whites of the eyes of the Aborigines sitting silently between the trees just beyond the screen of vegetation. On celebration days those from the neighbouring stations congregated, and Jos was requested to provide some of the musical accompaniment.

One day he ventured to ask, 'Boss, could you invite Rusty and his family to come to one of your revelries?'

Donald hesitated. 'I'll need to think about that.'

At the next party, arranged to celebrate Flora's birthday, a large gathering were seated round the campfire, drinking and eating. A distant drone vibrating through the air caught their attention; primal and hypnotic, like a constant rumble of thunder. Some of the settlers glanced about them nervously, and one young man bent down and picked up his gun. Donald Stewart laid a restraining hand on Jos's arm as through the trees emerged a smiling Rusty and some of the young men from his family. With their bodies decorated with colourful clays and ochres they danced, blew their didgeridoos and banged clapsticks. The children jumped up spontaneously to join in, and soon the whole party were clapping and beating time with their feet. Jos watched Flora's reaction. Her eyes sparkled animatedly.

Jos respected Rusty, aware they could share knowledge which would be beneficial to them both. On their long sojourns Jos taught him many English words and also guided him in the art of shearing, a skill he knew he would find useful for earning money. He felt fearful for his newfound friend and colleague, whose culture and customs were more under threat than his own.

In return Rusty identified the venomous snakes and poisonous spiders concealed beneath the trunks of fallen trees, and under the wattle and banksia bushes. He pointed out the signs used by the Aborigines to navigate through the open country, and introduced Jos to the best sources of medicinal plants and wild food. Once, when Jos was concerned to see smoke on the horizon, Rusty explained.

'My people burn leaf litter. Make plants grow… stop big fires. It good thing, when wind right.'

Jos shrugged his shoulders in amazement; this was just how they controlled the heather on the fells ten thousand miles away. 'You really know how to manage your environment,' he said in admiration.

'We got hang of it!' Rusty replied with a cheeky grin.

Eager to master new skills, Jos volunteered to help his

boss build a new store for the animal feed. They worked together, stripping the thick, fibrous bark from the largest-girthed gum trees, and spreading the sheets out to dry in the sun. Together they trekked through the bush to select a suitable row of trees for felling.

'Make the undercut here and a back-cut there; you must be accurate – and don't cut too deep.'

Jos followed his orders, moving steadily from tree to tree.

'Now stand well back... behind me!'

Jos watched in awe as his master took his axe to the first tree. A slow wrenching sound, then a crack and thunderous crash as the tree toppled towards the next one with the incision. The eucalyptus fell like a row of dominoes. They sawed the wood, built a timber frame, and with the help of Rusty overlapped the dried bark to create walls and a roof impervious to the rain.

While they worked together Donald, normally a man of few words, pieced together the story of his life in Scotland, his motivation in moving to Australia, and the potential pitfalls white men encounter in the bush.

'The greatest danger, Jos, is getting lost. Always mark your track when you cover new territory. Build cairns like you did back in Westmorland, or score the trees. You won't have any need when you're with Rusty, but it's a different matter when you're travelling on your own.'

On warm evenings Jos lay on the coarse grass outside his hut, watching the sky darken; his senses attuned to the mysteries of the night. He stared up into the velvety void, with its millions of twinkling stars, and experienced an overwhelming powerful gravitational pull to the other side of the world. He imagined himself linked by this diamond-studded road to his old home, where the morning light would just be breaking through. He envisaged Edward, Meg bouncing at his side, striding off towards the fells, his lunch pack on his back. Back at their humble farmhouse he pictured reliable, sturdy Hannah struggling with a heavy basket of peat or pail of icy water. He hoped she was well fed and content. He often wrestled with his conscience over the real reason for marrying her.

The shadows could play tricks. Sometimes he fancied he saw movement among the trees, heard the crack of a twig or rustle of leaves. His eyes and body ached with the tension of watching and listening. Maybe it was an Aborigine from a distant tribe slinking past with his spear; maybe it was a wallaby or possum; maybe, and this was what Jos suspected, maybe it was Angus skulking around. Clyde's bark was usually a signal of danger but he was used to Angus, who would feed him the leftovers from his evening meal. It was the dog's indifference to whom or what was prowling through the undergrowth that raised Jos's suspicions. When daylight came he would hunt for footprints in the dust – but found nothing. Sometimes, when he returned to his hut, he sensed the leather bag in which he kept his personal possessions had been tampered with; but nothing was ever missing, and the money he had saved and stowed away remained intact. One quiet night he unearthed his precious package and buried it at a deeper level, using the working tools he now possessed.

Chapter 29

Donald Stewart was a generous employer who valued the services of his assignee, and paid Jos well over the nominated rate. Focused on the future, Jos saved every penny he earned to provide for his family. He never asked for a day off or went into town in search of pleasure.

In the spring he had helped the Stewarts raise a good crop of lambs, but by midsummer three months without rain had turned the grass to parched hay, and the creek to a string of stagnant pools. Grazing was now hard to find.

The undergrowth snapped and crackled as the shepherds trudged on with the flock. Even the birds had fallen silent. Jos sensed unease in Rusty as, unusually quiet, he kept stopping and listening, framing his eyes as he scanned the horizon.

'Is summat wrong?' Jos asked.

'*Warroo*; rising wind come from centre. See wisp of smoke on horizon? Right conditions for big fire.' He shook his head, and called his dog Muna to his side as though seeking assurance from the animal. 'Look! Beyond far ridge.'

A sudden blast of hot wind created eddies of dry dust and blew the hat off Jos's head. Far, far away, in the limitless blue sky, he saw a thin, grey curl of smoke.

'Aborigines?' he asked, concentrating on keeping his voice steady as he tried to hide any anxiety.

'No!' snapped Rusty. 'A spark could carry miles in this wind. Signs are bad.'

They pressed on in silence; two sets of eyes fixed on the horizon and the sullen grey cloud now spreading like a cancer across the heavens. The wind blew hotter and hotter, yet despite the heat Jos felt the chill of fear.

'Let's turn the flock and get back to the station,' he said. 'We might be needed to help the family protect their home.'

'*Bellombi*! No time.' Rusty laid a restraining ebony hand on his arm. 'Boss know how to defend property. We no chance return before fire arrives. Best we can do for Boss is save sheep. We go south.'

'But the fire must still be miles away. It might not even come in this direction.'

Rusty climbed on the top of an anthill and stood motionless for several minutes; listening, concentrating and observing the sway of the trees.

'It come. Faster than dingo. It come this direction.' As he spoke the smoke began to block out the sun and the light to fade dramatically.

'Wind's changing... blow towards mountains,' said Rusty. 'Need to get sheep other side of water. Safer there.'

Jos cast his eye along the steep sides of the creek. Crossing would be impossible for the flock. The sheep were now showing signs of anxiety; bleating and running in circles. His nostrils picked up the smell of burning wool as the first flecks of ash fluttered down on the backs of the animals.

'Move!' said Rusty. 'Turn sheep... I think bridge downstream.' The dogs responded obediently to his instructions, so they regained control of the flock and shepherded them as speedily as they could.

Jos was in unfamiliar territory, but Rusty's instincts proved right. Through the smoke appeared a wide dammed-up bridge over some shallows, with a deep pool on one side. As they crossed Jos pulled off his shirt and neckerchief and drew them through the muddy waters. He handed the scarf to Rusty to tie round his nose and mouth. The smoke was now so thick they could barely see where they were going, but the dogs held their nerve and the flock were ushered across to the far bank. Rusty ordered the dogs to chase them away and the sheep, coughing and terrified, scattered.

'Get down in water with dogs,' Rusty shouted, pushing Jos's shoulders. With their bodies submerged, the two men and their dogs dipped their heads as the fire roared past like a wild beast. Burning chunks of wood shot up into the sky and hot embers sizzled in the water. The heat was intense, the crackling deafening and the smoke choking – but the wind kept its course and the creek held as a firebreak. The flames passed a hundred yards north of where they sheltered. The raging inferno had moved on as quickly as it had arrived.

Gasping for breath they raised their heads and watched the smoke clear, funnelled east by the wind. What remained was a blackened panorama for as far as the eye could see. No movement, no birdsong, just a lifeless wasteland of skeleton gum trees and smouldering embers.

Once safe they clambered out of the murky water and mustered the flock, knocking off any smouldering ashes lying on their backs. Apart from the distress, they seemed to have survived the ordeal.

'We'll need to keep the sheep this side of the creek,' said

Jos. 'D'you have any idea how far it is to the next station?'

'You stay with *jumbuck*,' said Rusty. 'I track, find somewhere to use as a gathering pen.'

Despite the long drought there was grass stretching south of the creek untouched by the fire, and Jos was relieved to see the flock settling and beginning to feed. He pulled off his boots.

'You take these,' he said, 'and leave Muna with me.' With the immediate crisis over his concern was now for those back at Toomara. He sank down, settling his back against the thick trunk of a red gum. His stomach lurched as he slumped, head in hands.

Rusty returned within the hour, followed by a farmhand leading a couple of bullocks pulling a dray piled high with fences.

'We leave sheep here... good spot,' he said. 'Owner, Mr Preece, give fencing and shepherd. We go back help Boss.'

'If any help is still needed,' Jos commented wearily.

'They gave me boots,' said Rusty, a brief smile flitting across his face.

'We'll have you in a jacket and cravat next,' quipped Jos.

Leaving Clyde and Muna with the shepherd, Jos and Rusty turned towards home. The flames were now out of sight, lost in a pall of smoke maybe fifty miles distant. With shoulders slumped, faces and bodies streaked with sweat and black powder, they picked their way in silence through a carpet of ash. Jos was thankful for Rusty's unerring navigational instincts which now steered them through the changed and bewildering landscape. He could barely raise his head when they splashed through the silt and mud of the creek opposite Toomara, unable to face the inevitable destruction.

'House stand!' shouted Rusty. 'Look, Jos, house stand!'

A gust of wind blew ash in circles and covered them with grey dust. Rubbing his eyes, Jos studied the scene. A lone building, ringed with smoke-blackened tree trunks and charred outbuildings, stood like a beacon amidst the ravaged landscape on the highest point of the station. The homestead, and almost certainly the family, had survived. Jos sucked in his breath with relief as the front door flew open, and Flora came running out to meet them.

'You're both safe, thank God.' Weeping, she threw her arms around them. 'This is just unbelievable, we expected the worst.'

'So did I,' Jos confided, with a telling glance at Rusty.

Flora's eyes strayed to the direction from which they had come, a troubled expression on her face. 'What happened to the dogs?'

'They're safe, and the sheep too... thanks to Rusty,' said Jos. 'He sensed the danger from the first puff of smoke, and moved them south. It was the right thing to do. They're on the Preeces' station, about five miles from here; fenced on their land on the other side of the creek. They lent us a shepherd to guard them, and he kept the dogs to save their feet until we can get back.'

Flora shook her head. 'It's a miracle – even the stock has survived. Donald will be so relieved. He's out on the station looking for you both at this very moment.' She lifted her apron to wipe her face, leaving black streaks across her cheeks.

'How did you cope here?' Jos asked.

Flora sank wearily onto a flat-topped rock, once a feature of her flower bed. 'We filled every receptacle and soaked every towel and blanket we possessed with water. Donald and Angus patrolled the station until the last minute, clearing debris off the roof and away from the buildings, and soaking the ground with water. The smoke was so frightening; we could barely see our own feet.' She sat abstractedly rubbing her hands up and down her thighs. 'We grabbed the children and all clung together as the inferno approached, and then, thank God, watched it move on. It was over in a few minutes, but at the time the roar and the heat just overwhelmed us.'

'And you've lost the shearing shed and the outbuildings,' said Jos, gazing around.

'I'm afraid so, and your hut has gone. Just before the blaze struck we sent Angus to collect your belongings; but it was too late. He picked up an armful of clothes, your fiddle, and then had to run. You'll find them in the back lobby.'

'Did he pick up my travelling bag... from under the bed?'

'Not that he said. Was there anything important in it?'

The colour drained from Jos's face. 'A few things I'd brought from home... my savings since arriving here.'

A look of dismay spread across Flora's face. 'Oh Jos, I'm so sorry. We didn't have time to think.' She took his hands in hers. 'We should've taken more care.'

Jos turned away. He needed time to regain his composure. 'You're all safe, that's what really matters,' he managed to mumble before striding off to inspect the remains of his hut. Lying on the ground were the ends of a few charred timbers and a blackened tin plate and mug. Where his bed had stood, a heap of charcoal and the remnants of a burnt blanket. He kicked and kicked at the pile in frustration but there were no fragments of his bag to be found; not a coin, a pewter button or piece of scorched leather. Every penny he had squirreled away over the last two years had gone. Consumed with anger, he thumped his fists on the unforgiving earth and shouted obscenities. Tomorrow he would have a confrontation with Angus.

That night he slept in the homestead with the family, and once again, under cover of darkness, he slipped out with a spade. He knew the exact location of his buried packet. He dug down a foot and unearthed the stones. The package was unharmed.

The following morning Angus had gone walkabout.

A few days later the rains came. A new generation of green shoots broke through, and within weeks the land returned to green pasture. Autumn melted into winter and the routine of the station was re-established. Only Donald seemed unable to pick himself up. Twenty years older than his wife, his walk was less sprightly, his shoulders permanently drooped. He seemed unable to rise above the losses he had sustained and the abuse of the trust he had placed in Angus.

Jos continued to live with the family until the spring of 1842 when the system of assignees came to an end, and he was granted his freedom. He had served just two and a half years. The Stewarts wanted to retain his services as an employee, but he needed to earn money fast if he was to set up on his own in Australia. Through Donald's recommendation, he secured a job as a land surveyor, and spent six months charting virgin territory near the red centre. The expedition was arduous but successful, and on completion he was paid handsomely. He returned to the Stewarts and sent a long letter home to Westmorland detailing his plans for their future.

In February 1843, six months after Jos had penned the letter to Hannah and Edward, he lay on his bunk, listening to the breakers crashing on the red cliffs of Sydney harbour. Beyond an angry sea boiled, and a journey of many weeks lay ahead.

Jos was at last on his way home, a free man, literate and with money in his pocket. Flora had straightened his collar and clung to him in a way he found unsettling. The girls had pleaded with him not to leave, but he did not look back. He had a duty to those at home.

Chapter 30

March 1838

Following Jos's trial, and the night spent with Hannah at Highburn, Tom returned home to Ravendale. This time he barely noticed the landscape as he tramped on. The dispiriting outcome of Jos's hearing, Edward's anger and Hannah's muted reaction to her husband's deportation weighed heavily on his mind.

It was barely eight months since his last visit, but the decline in his parents' physical wellbeing was disturbingly apparent. His father, once straight of back, was now bent as a wind-beaten mountain ash. His mother's breathing laboured from years spent cooking over an open fire. It was Robert, his youngest brother, who now held everything together at the farm

'Fetch us a whisky, son,' said James. 'It's what we rely on these days t'dull the aches.'

Tom poured them each a draught and took his place by the hearth, quickly settling back into the familial setting. The dogs lay prostrate, their noses resting on their paws, eyes and ears alert. His father puffed on his pipe and his mother looked relaxed, her hands folded across her spotless apron. He was full of admiration at how she had maintained her standards.

'How did the trial go?' asked James.

Both hard of hearing, his father and mother watched his face intently as he described every detail of the proceedings. At the conclusion of his story they shook their heads as though in disbelief, but both held their counsel.

'And how are ee getting along in Halesden?' Mam wanted to know.

Tom decided not to add to their worries by telling them he had lost the job George had secured for him, or of his emerging political interests. Instead he described all the wonderful technological innovations. The gas lighting, the steam-powered water mills, the railway which carried the raw cotton from the Liverpool docks to Manchester and the finished goods from Manchester to London. Both parents, now octogenarians, shook their heads again, but this time with smiles of wonder on their faces.

'Where's Rob?' Tom asked.

'Ee'll be back soon. Ee's bin over to the market at Shap with some butter yer mam made. Ee'll have t'be teking one of those steam trains you've been telling us aboot when we're gone. There's no living for him here.'

'No company either,' lamented Peggy, picking up a sock she had been knitting. 'There's only Richard Green from Naddle still around from the days when you were a youngster.'

'And Hannah, but without her husband,' Tom added.

'Aye.' They continued to discuss old friends and past times until a gentle rhythmic snore signified James had fallen asleep. Peggy put down her needles and rocked herself gently.

'I think mebbe we've stirred up sad memories,' she said.

Tom dropped to his knees beside her chair and took an arthritic, veined hand in his own. 'I was thinking about Lucy – she was the most gifted of us all. What might she have achieved if she'd lived?'

They reminisced over the day of Lucy's funeral, and Tom described Peggy's sophisticated sister who had turned up so unexpectedly at the graveside.

'Being so close by, it was a shame she didn't have time to visit you here,' he said. 'D'you ever hear from her?'

'Nah, like us she's getting on in years, and lives her life differently from the way we do here. I think Jonathon had a letter from her some while back.'

They sat in companionable silence, listening to the wind thundering in the chimney and watching the occasional flame flickering amongst the embers.

'I could've been a better brother to Lucy,' Tom blurted out. The temptation to confess his shameful secret almost overwhelmed him, but Mam tightened her grip on his hand, and he thought better of it.

'Don't ee have any misgivings about yer sister, son. She loved ee as much as you loved her, right up until the day she died.' She gave him a guarded smile, such that he wondered if there was anything insightful behind his mother's comment. He wanted to question her further, but her head had fallen on her chest. Now the only sound to fill the room was of her soft breathing in rhythm with that of her husband.

Tom sat immobile for some time, her words of comfort having caught him off guard. When he finally pulled himself together he adjusted her rug, kissed the thinning white hair on the top of her head, and crept out of the room.

That night, beneath the comforting cobwebbed rafters, he slipped into a contented dream. He was seated by the force with Jos and Lucy; hypnotised by the balmy sun and pounding water; seduced by the words of a poet and inspired by the thought of a fulfilling future. The next morning he returned to Clattonbury to formally join the Chartist movement.

Chapter 31

The mills closed at midday on Saturdays. With time for recreation, the farmers' wives trundled into Halesden with their baskets and handcarts, and set up stalls in the market square to sell their wares: eggs, butter, homemade bread, honey and vegetables. Drink flowed at the taverns and street entertainers proliferated.

In the centre of the activities Tom now took his place on the back of a farm cart, shoulder to shoulder with Sean Kelly and the Chartist activists. These weekly gatherings quickly became a rallying point for disaffected artisans and mill workers, and an additional entertainment for the single young men who sauntered around, parading their finery for the benefit of the unattached girls.

'Call 'em in, David,' said Sean. Betha's eldest son blew a series of blasts on a hunting horn, and gradually folks could be seen wandering up from the side streets or turning their attention away from the market sellers.

Alexander Postlethwaite, a shoemaker and Methodist lay preacher, was the first to pick up the loudhailer. As if proselytising from the pulpit he whipped up fervour with extracts from the *Northern Star*. 'We contribute nine million pounds annually in taxes to maintain a church from which most of us dissent. The Archbishop of Canterbury is paid fifty-two pounds a day and yet the poor have to maintain their families on tuppence per head a day.'

Each quote was followed by a resounding cheer from the supporters and a quick blast from David's horn.

Tom followed. He had mastered the skill of engaging with his audience back in the little church in Newton Rigg. His eyes roved round the crowd; those drifting at the back, those pushing and aggressive at the front – he made contact with them all. Always conscious that their main target was to enlist the support of those who already had the vote, he moderated his language to appeal to those who loitered on the edge.

'Friends, remember ours is a moral movement. We represent the thousands who toil from dawn to dusk in tropical temperatures in the factories; the law-abiding citizens who have made this country the success it is today.' He paused. 'We pay our taxes, but do we have a say in how our money is spent? No! We obey the laws of the land, but do we have any influence over the making of these laws? No! All we ask is that every man, every father of future generations, should have a voice in the way our country is run.' He paused again, waiting for the applause to die down.

'And my friends, remember: once we get the vote – and we will – we must exercise our right conscientiously. Here education is the key.' He raised his hand in a rallying gesture. 'Sign on at the Mechanics' Institute; attend the evening classes being run by the free churches in this town; visit the library; read the national papers; send your children to a Sunday school. We must be ready for this social revolution; we must show we are capable of using our vote responsibly.'

'What does it matter tha' we canna read?' a voice called out from the crowd. 'We can hear all we need to know.'

'I thought ee were supposed to be deaf, Nobby Wright!' another heckler shouted back.

Tom pressed on. 'You make my point well, brother. Think how much better it will be if you can make up your own mind rather than having to depend on what other folks tell you.'

Like heckling jackdaws, the good-natured banter continued until Sean drew the meeting to a close with a final impassioned plea, to sign up and contribute to the cause. The speakers clambered down from the cart and a three-piece band of troubadours jumped up in their place to take advantage of the temporary platform. For the rest of the afternoon the market square throbbed with the sound of music.

The Saturday gatherings were just part of a much wider campaign, including regular torchlight rallies in the nearby hills. These theatrical presentations, with their rousing speeches by visiting lecturers, drew from a larger catchment area and were a great opportunity to spread the message and gather signatures for the petition. By July 1829 a million and a quarter names had been collected nationally and were presented to Parliament.

The petition was soundly rejected by the Whig government.

'Do not give up hope,' Tom and Sean now urged the Saturday crowds. 'We always knew we were in for a long haul. This petition was just the first step – next time we will triple the numbers. Westminster won't be able to ignore us when so many are battling for emancipation. This is what we are owed.'

During the next two years the campaigners worked towards consolidation to establish a sound, countrywide organisation. The *Northern Star*, the main source of communication, became a national daily soon outselling

The Times. Meanwhile Sean and Tom joined those working at the coalface, maintaining momentum amongst the rank and file with regular rallies and meetings.

Tom was bedding down the fire when there was a tentative tap at his cottage door.

'Come in,' he called without turning his head. It was not unusual for Luke, or one of his parishioners to drop by in the evening. His heart missed a beat as, quietly closing the door behind her, stood Betha, her dog at her side.

'What brings you here?' He took her hands in his, and studied her face. 'I'm pleased to see you of course, but I suspect there must be some trouble at home.' He shifted a pile of books and papers from the one spare chair. It's a chilly night; I'll make us a hot drink.'

'Yer right of course, it's Sean. I've seized the opportunity to come over while he's away. He's on yet another march, to the Potteries this time, and has taken David with him. I'm so worried the same will happen to them as happened to Arthur.'

Tom nodded, encouraging her to go on.

'As you know, Sean wields considerable power in the Trade Union movement and on the Chartist network. He's becoming increasingly hot-headed and he's influencing David. With all the cheers and applause he gets at the meetings the boy thinks he's a hero. David's still so young and impressionable.' She paused, as if to rally her thoughts. 'And that's not all. I've another worry. Elias Bennett has become a disciple of Sean's, but I suspect his motives. He's only concerned with causing trouble. I try to keep him away from our house as much as possible because of Molly, but Sean doesn't know the background as to why she lives with us.'

Tom handed her a mug of hot milk and she sat warming

her hands on the smooth glaze before adding, 'I'm here to ask you to have a word with him. He doesn't listen to me,' she ended wearily.

The night grew dark and Betha seemed in no hurry to leave. They discussed her home life, the depressed state of the economy and its bearing on the Chartist cause. Tom was impressed by her knowledge of the movement and was not surprised when she asked, 'Why d'you always direct your message to the "brothers"? You must realise you and Sean have quite a following amongst the local women too.'

'And we're glad of it, Betha – but now is not the time for expansion. We need to take small steps and be prepared for a long campaign. Votes for men is all we dare hope for at present; anything more would be asking too much of our supporters in Westminster.' He leant forwarded and patted her arm. 'Gender equality will come later, but in the meantime we need everyone's help.'

They sat in silence as the flicker of a flame cast shadows across the whitewashed walls, and the church clock struck the hour.

'Have you heard anything from Arthur?' Tom hoped his voice sounded casual.

'No, not for months. I'm worried something may have happened to him – or he's found another woman... I'm not sure which would be worse.'

Tom laid his hand briefly on her knee, quickly withdrawing it to fondle her dog. 'I'm sure there's no cause for concern, Betha. If he'd been taken ill, or worse, someone would have got a message back to you. And remember, the ratio of men to women in Australia is so high the chance of him finding another female companion is remote.'

'But you don't know him,' she burst out unexpectedly.

'He's always been attractive to women. I can't trust him to be faithful.' She raised her hand and touched Tom's cheek. 'He has your charm, you see.'

Tom froze. In the distance, coming from the direction of the church, the shriek of a tawny owl penetrated the silence. He steadied his voice. 'It's a late hour to be visiting, Betha. I must accompany you home.'

She jumped up from her seat. 'I'm sorry, Tom, I didn't realise.' For the first time that evening her bright eyes twinkled. 'I'm not here to destroy your reputation.'

'I know,' he said, reaching for his jacket. 'I'll walk back with you.'

'Nah, I won't hear of it,' she insisted. 'You've more important things to be doing. I have the dog and there's plenty of moonlight.' She slipped on her clogs and stepped out into the deserted street.

'Goodnight, lass.' Stars sparkled above as Tom stood shivering at the door, listening until her footfall had finally faded away.

A depression swept across the whole of the industrial midlands and north during the winter of 1842, and the future looked bleak as families suffered unrelenting hardship. In London echoes of the French Revolution preoccupied the government, and locally magistrates were terrified of armed rebellion. To quell the rising hysteria nocturnal open-air meetings were banned by Royal Proclamation, and the military dispatched from the south-east to areas of possible confrontation. In tandem with this growing discontent the Chartist movement was gathering momentum as a second national petition of three million or more signatures was nearing its target.

There were raised voices, and the air was dense with tobacco smoke when Tom stepped into the Old Bull inn one Friday evening. Above the bar a banner caught his attention: *All labour to cease until the People's Charter becomes the law of the land.* He shouldered his way through the throng and sat down in the chimney nook between Amos Smith, the apothecary, and Albert Irvine, an ironmonger. Sean was standing at the bar and perched next to him, on a stool, sat Elias Bennett.

Elias's face was red and bloated as he banged his fist on the counter. 'I 'aven't brought 'ome more than a pound a week for two months now. 'Ow am I supposed to feed my wife and kids on that? I say strike – show the buggers what we're made of. Plugs are being drawn on machinery across the country; we must do the same.'

Tom caught Sean's eye, and noted his troubled expression.

'What d'you say, Tom?' Sean raised his voice. 'You've seen the new banners.'

Tom hesitated. He knew most of those present were in sympathy with the Chartist objectives, but the issues were becoming muddled. He now worried that the longstanding political aims they had worked hard to achieve might be jeopardised by anger over cuts in wages and loss of jobs.

'I know times are hard for you all,' he said, 'but we've come this far, and have made tremendous strides. It's only another couple of weeks until we present our petition. Let's hold fire until we hear the outcome.'

Elias resumed his fist-shaking rant. 'What does a parson know aboot our lives, or any of the snooty shopkeepers in this town? We could starve to death for all they care.' Nearly slipping off his stool as he remonstrated, he glared threateningly in the direction of the nook. 'I say withhold your custom from any tradesmen who haven't signed the petition – read out their names at the next town meeting. We need to shame the bastards!'

'Yer right, Elias. Get at 'em through their pockets,' another voice joined in.

Elias's eyes travelled menacingly round the room. 'And we might need one of these.' He paused for effect before drawing a dagger from its sheath. Its blade gleamed in the dull light.

Amos and Albert exchanged glances, and without a word got up and pushed their way out of the inn, leaving Tom isolated on the bench. Anxious to take some heat out of the dispute, he stood up and cleared his throat.

'Think carefully, friends. The whole country acknowledges the Chartists are a force to be reckoned with; without the need for violence. Be proud of our campaign – we've collected three and a half million signatures in the last couple of years – a third of the adult population of Great Britain have pledged their support. That has to be enough to trigger a debate. Listen to what Sean has to tell us about the plans for presenting the petition. I can assure you all, this time Westminster will to be taken by storm.'

Elias stumbled back against the bar, and the inn quietened as Sean mounted the step behind him and explained the preparations for the demonstration.

'The lists of signatures you have all been collecting are being displayed on a continuous roll of paper. Once joined together they will stretch for six miles – further than from here to Oswaldtwistle!' A gasp concertinaed through the room. 'This roll will be attached to a massive wooden frame, on the sides of which will be listed the six points of the charter.' Sean's voice surged with excitement as he continued. 'Our supporters will gather at Lincoln's

Inn Fields in the early morning of Monday, May 2nd. Led by a brass band, they will escort the petition through the streets of central London. I'm telling you, brothers – Londoners will never have seen anything to compare with the parade that has been planned. A hundred thousand marchers are expected, with mounted escorts carrying Chartist banners.'

The walls of the Old Bull shook with the ovation that followed.

Chapter 32

At the end of April a letter from Robert summoned Tom home for the funeral of their father. It could not have come at a worse time. It would mean being in Westmorland when the petition was presented. Despite his outward show of confidence at the meeting in the Old Bull, he was not optimistic that Parliament was ready for such a challenge. Rationally he knew the pace of constitutional change could not be forced, but what the response would be from the campaigners in Halesden if this litany of disappointment continued, he hardly dared to imagine. And how would Sean react?

After the burial at Shap the family returned to Ravendale to determine the future of the farm. James's will was outdated. Many of the assets he had allocated no longer existed and the farm as a business was no longer sustainable. It was agreed Peggy should go to live permanently with Elizabeth, and Robert should sort out the sale of the stock, equipment, house and buildings. The tenanted land would then be returned to the Lowthers.

The brothers and sisters bid each other goodbye with an air of finality, to return to their scattered homes. Tom set off alone via Highburn, lamenting that he would soon have no compelling reason to return to the dale.

'I was hoping you'd call by,' said Hannah as though it was a regular occurrence. 'I've received a letter from Jos. I'd like ee t'read it to me.' She handed over a wrapper with a broken seal, the ink smudged by rain or seawater.

'Shouldn't you wait until Edward gets back? He can read it to you.'

'Ee's away until late tonight. I canna wait that long.'

'But it's addressed to both of you,' said Tom, unconvinced.

Hannah seemed agitated as she grabbed the letter back. 'Yer'll see, ee's drawn a map on the back page. I need t'know why. I know I can trust you to be discreet, and I'd appreciate a bit of advice before I 'ave to discuss it with my son.'

Tom relented, and drew several sheets of paper out of the homemade envelope. Having scanned the first couple of paragraphs he marvelled at the neat hand and educated tone of the missive. Jos had come a long way since leaving England.

After the formalities of asking about the family the true purpose of the letter became clear.

I have been granted my freedom early and can now plan for our future. To raise capital I've worked for six months in the bush with a surveying team, mapping out plots of land for sale to settlers. We had no contact with the outside world so I was unable to write and tell you of my whereabouts.

It was a gruelling experience as the weather was unbearably hot. Each day we set off before sunrise with our instruments and packs. The sweat ran constantly into our eyes while flies buzzed in clouds round our heads – at times I thought I was going insane. Water always defined our route, and at sunset we would settle by a creek where tree ferns and callobs would bring cool relief. It is after sunset when the bush comes to life. Cicadas sing loudly until dawn and nocturnal animals slide, prowl or jump silently about.

From our Aboriginal helpers I learnt to navigate by the stars, which will be a really useful skill. It was a well-paid job so I've put aside a fair sum of money.

What this venture has confirmed in my mind is that the opportunities for sheep farming are excellent, particularly for those of us with experience who can also deal with the seasonal variations in weather. The land is cheap. The natives do not understand ownership in the way we do so this leaves the way clear for the European settlers to squat ever further into their territory. Where I have been assigned for the last few years is as good a place as any. Everywhere is covered with gum trees so the landscape can look monotonous. But the underlying terrain is hilly, not unlike the eastern fells.

I am due an allocation of land so have saved every penny to apply for a licence, and peg out a claim. We will need to clear it for pasture, erect a paddock fence and buy some stock. Providing I lease a run close to Donald Stewart, the boss at my old station, he has promised work until we build up a flock. Both Edward and I will be able to hire out our skills at shearing and lambing time until we get established. We will have to build our own home, a bark house to begin with – we could call it Low Toomara.

The sunsets in the bush are remarkable, and this is the time when the kangaroos come out to forage. It is a vision of the three of us, sitting in the evenings on our veranda, looking out across our land, dotted with our sheep, which has kept me going for the last three years. No foxes here; but the dingoes are equally destructive!

The plan below shows the area where I think we might settle. Mr Stewart's station is to the north and east.

I sincerely hope you will both want to share this dream.

The letter finished with the promise of a visit home, once he had set aside enough money for the journey.

'Jos seems to be making plans for a good life for you all out there,' said Tom in a noncommittal tone as he returned the letter to the envelope, and handed it back.

Hannah sat quietly; rocking her chair and staring down at her broken nails and calloused hands. Appreciating she needed time to assimilate the contents of her husband's letter, Tom wandered over to a small oak table in front of the window. Here a wooden carving of a golden eagle was displayed. He carefully picked it up to examine – a ten-inch wingspan, and talons outstretched as though about to alight on its nest.

'Where did this come from?' he exclaimed in amazement. 'The proportions and the detail are so true to life, and it gleams like the lectern at Carlisle Cathedral.'

'Aye, it's lovely,' agreed Hannah. 'Jos spent two winters carving it for us. If he wasn't out with the flock he was whittling away here by the fire. Ee was obsessed; it was as though he was driven by some deep need, shaving a bit 'ere, sanding a sharp edge there, showing Edward how it was done. Ee handed it over to Edward the day he was taken to court – a keepsake, ee said... or maybe it was an omen.' She sighed. 'I keep it well polished.'

'I can see that,' said Tom, smiling at her. He ran his

finger along the length of a wing. 'The surface is so smooth, the colour so warm. 'Did he carve it from memory?'

'I don't think so, but I doubt ee modelled it on a church lectern,' she laughed. 'I found him one day studying a piece of paper. Ee was so absorbed I crept up behind him. I was interested to see what he was doing. Ee shouted at me to go away… it was odd. I'd rarely seen him so angry, and certainly not with me. There were words on the paper, and I did catch a glimpse of a drawing at the bottom. Goodness knows where ee got it from… mebbe Simeon, or stole it most likely.' She shrugged her shoulders.

'And now he's writing you perfect letters,' said Tom. 'You must both be so proud of him.'

'Aye, we are. I keep all his letters in this box. Ee carved it for me after Edward was born. Jos was always good with his hands.' She laid the latest missive neatly on top and replaced the lid. 'Life threw us together. I accept that, and ee does too.' She picked up the box and set it down next to the eagle. 'Jos knows his duty, ee does that.' She gently stroked the bird's head. 'I know I was never anything special to him. I think it was your sister that won his heart and he was never able to let go – but we rubbed along just fine. Now I've got a lot t'think aboot. Will you come with me, down t'the church?'

Tom perched next to Hannah on the roughhewn bench under the sycamore tree, staring ahead to the ring of mountains enclosing the dale. Eventually Hannah spoke.

'I'm glad it's going so well for Jos but I'm not going to be able to join him. How could I leave all this?'

'You never were one for change.' Tom patted her hand. 'So often I've turned over in my mind whether I did the right thing that day in court. If I'd confirmed Jos's story

I'd have done wrong in the eyes of God and my position in life... but maybe it was something more personal and less admirable that drove me.' He gave her a sidelong glance. 'I've certainly had misgivings. Jacob Armstrong and his boys gained nothing but a moral victory. You lost your husband and breadwinner, Edward lost his father and Jos his liberty. How was that of any help to anyone? It was all down to me, and it needn't have happened.'

'D'you still have regrets?' Hannah asked.

'Since reading that letter I'm not sure I do. It seems I may have inadvertently opened a door... and Jos, to his credit, has picked up the challenge. He now has the promise of a full, rewarding life. Something he never anticipated when we were youngsters.'

'Aye, and perhaps Edward too,' Hannah mused.

'Mebbe, he's young, who knows what choices he'll make?'

Hannah elbowed Tom as a field mouse scuttled through the grass and disappeared in a clump of golden celandines. 'So long as I've a roof over my head I can manage here. I wouldn't want t'hold Edward back if he wished to join his da.'

'But won't you be lonely?' asked Tom. 'You realise once our farm is sold up I'll no longer have a reason to return to Ravendale.'

'I know that,' she replied, her expression unreadable. 'Now tell me about Luke, Agnes and the girls. How have they adapted to living in a town?'

Happy with this change in direction of the conversation, Tom continued animatedly. 'They're doing really well, and the whole family is helping out at the school. Luke can see real prospects for Anne and Rebecca. They're both smart girls and should be able to establish independent careers for

267

themselves until they get married. That's something they would never have achieved here.' He nodded his head. 'It's been a good move for them all.'

Hannah jumped up from the bench. 'I canna sit around here gossiping,' she said. 'I must get back to get Edward's tea, ee should be home soon… and you need t'be getting on your way.' Without another word, or backward glance, she marched off.

Tom watched her swaying gait until she disappeared behind a clump of trees. He felt guilty for his lack of sympathy for Hannah's dilemma, but once again her passivity had frustrated him. He threw his bag over his shoulder and set off for Shap to catch the evening coach south and, more urgently, to learn the outcome of the petition.

In the King's Arms he found back issues of *The Times*, left by travellers passing through. He found a quiet corner to scan the news of the presentation of the Charter. He read how the tail of an orderly procession was still at Oxford Circus when the head arrived at the Houses of Parliament. He read about the amazing spectacle when the floor of the Commons was obscured by a sea of white paper when the petition had to be dismantled. He read how Thomas Duncombe had championed the petition and asked leave to present it to the House. He read how the clerk to the House had delivered the petition, and how the demands cited ranged beyond the original six points of the charter.

Finally he turned to the Friday edition. Here he discovered the hearing had taken less than an hour; the six points of the Charter had not been debated and despite all their efforts the movement had achieved nothing in bringing together the workers and those who held power over them. Their national petition had once again been comprehensively thrown out by both the Whigs and the Tories. Deeply disheartened, Tom began to question whether making the petition the focal point of their campaigning had been misguided.

On the way back he loitered a few hours in Burnley, wandering the streets and gauging the mood of the locals. He skulked in the shadows, listening to the conversations on the street corners where the unemployed gathered. In the back streets he found pikes, cutlasses and bayonets were being openly traded. In front of the town hall a half-demented man screamed in rage.

'We canna live like this, not another day, we're being left to rot – we must fight the bastards, bring 'em to their knees.' Beside him a middle-aged woman, in stained and ragged clothes, clutched the hands of two barefoot children.

Filled with foreboding Tom made straight for Halesden, and the Lewises' cottage. A cold, damp mist was swirling round when he finally reached their gate and tapped on the door. Never had he seen Betha so distressed as when she jumped to her feet to greet him.

'Tom, I thought we were going to win through, you said we would… how can this have happened after all the time and effort Sean's put into the campaign?' She thumped her knuckles into his chest in sheer frustration before it turned to tears. He held her close, her shuddering body pressed hard against his.

'So where is Sean?' he asked once her rage was spent.

'Away at yet another meeting – up on Enfield Moor this time. I wouldn't let David go, it could easily get out of hand and lead to violence.' Tom acknowledged her son sitting sulkily at the table.

'He should be home before too long,' she said wearily.

An angry shout from the street announced the arrival of

Betha's brother. He staggered in, clothes dripping muddy water. 'I stumbled into a bog up on the moor,' he raged. 'It's foul out there and I couldn't see what was ahead. It was quite a struggle to even pull myself out.'

'Come and dry out by the fire,' said Betha soothingly. She pulled the felt hat from his head, and helped him off with his boots, handing them to David to empty outside. Tom stayed in the background while she unbuttoned Sean's shirt, pulled off his trousers, and took a towel to dry his naked body.

'How did it go?' she asked as she rubbed his shoulders and arms to restore the circulation.

Sean's words tumbled over each other through chattering teeth. 'Elias is such a firebrand. I was floundering, and I admit I was scared. I needed you, Tom.' He grabbed the towel from Betha and began scrubbing at his legs.

'The passion was there, just like at that first meeting on Kersal Moor, but this time the mood was dark, the language incendiary. The crowd were so hostile, crying out for action. You can understand why when so many were begging food from those around them.' He ruefully rubbed the red marks on his neck and chest. 'The weather didn't help, with clouds so low you could only see for twenty yards… and the midges biting.' He looked directly at Tom for the first time. 'D'you remember the slogan we all chanted – back in '39? It was the same up on the moor, but this time the words had changed and the tone was aggressive. "Peacefully if we may, forcibly if we must."' He gripped his hands together and his shoulders shook involuntarily. 'It proved such a powerful echo rising out of the gloom; the mantra keeps swimming in my head. I think maybe they are right. The time for revolution has come.'

'No, Sean!' Tom tried to reason with him. 'Not

everyone is fighting the same cause. The whole situation is a rats' nest, spreading out of control. I fully understand the dire circumstances so many are suffering, but the employers have their hands tied; they have empty order books and their businesses are at a standstill. You must see our campaign for social and political reform is being hijacked by the more immediate problems relating to the downturn in trade.' Tom was aware that his voice was becoming heated. 'We're in danger of losing all the goodwill we've built up over the last five years, Sean. We must keep faith with the more enlightened voters in the town.'

'Yer not listening, Tom,' Sean shouted back angrily. 'The men want more, and they want it now. They're screaming for a national strike, and if they encounter opposition, to meet force with force. I'm telling you, Elias has already drawn up plans to arm our supporters.'

'And I'm warning you, Sean.' Tom waded in, thumping his fist on the table. 'That'll fan hostilities and could lead you all into serious trouble. Think about David, think about Sam... and think about your sister.' He grabbed his hat from the peg behind the door and marched out.

Chapter 33

Because of its isolated location Clattonbury was sheltered from the national unrest, and weathering the economic downturn well. The union representative negotiated with Andrew and his partners a package of reduced hours, with a proportional reduction in remuneration for the women and young people. Every worker was still taking home a wage, and some even appreciated having more time to spend with their families. Tom and Luke played their part by extending the evening adult education classes and the activities of the Sunday school, creating the sense of community they had experienced in their own childhood.

The summer of 1842 was unusually dry, and the unbroken days of hot weather were welcomed by the youngsters who played and swam in the cool waters of the river. However, this drop in rainfall was a cause for concern at the mill when, for the first time in several years, they had to resort to steam power.

'You realise what this means,' Tom confided to Luke. 'We are as vulnerable as the rest to attack, should any militants come this way.'

Tom called in at the manager's office to discuss the situation, but was nonplussed when an ebullient Andrew slapped him on the back. 'Good news, Tom – I've just received a big order from France, so full-time employment again.'

Tom sucked in his breath through his teeth. 'I'm really pleased to hear that, Andrew, but I have to say the timing is not great. When I was in town yesterday the workers were hatching plans for mass marches, in favour of a national strike. I think it's time we explained to everyone in the village exactly what's going on in Halesden, Blackburn and the rest of the country.'

Andrew sank back down on his chair. 'How's that for instant deflation?' he said wryly. He busied himself piling the leather-bound ledgers on his desk before addressing the problem. 'I know you're right, Tom,' he said finally. 'I've detected a lack of direction from the national movement, which has left the local activists making their own decisions. And I've been aware the public mood is turning ugly. I'll call a meeting for Saturday morning when our employees report to the office to pay their rents.'

When the community gathered together in the compound for the meeting Tom spoke first, and at length.

'To conclude, any call for a national withdrawal of labour should be aimed at forcing the government to recognise the injustice in the way we are governed by Westminster. A strike should not set the mill workers against their masters, and should not involve violence.' He stepped aside for Andrew.

'Friends, as you know I am wholly in favour of a wider franchise, but now is a difficult time for me to support a walkout. I have received, this very week, a sizeable order from France. Successful completion of this contract will pay all your wages until Candlemas. I don't wish to influence you one way or the other but I do need your co-operation if we are to keep to the schedule and complete on

273

time. When you return home to consider your options ask yourselves, will a strike really be a demonstration on behalf of Chartism?'

By August the threat of a general strike, stretching from the Staffordshire coalfields to Scotland, was becoming a reality. Everywhere the local authorities were fearful of an eruption of violence, and extra constables were hurriedly recruited in Halesden.

Ill at ease, Sean now stood with Elias on the makeshift platform to shout above the general babble in the market square. Hordes now attended these Saturday meetings, and the once-friendly banter had given way to malicious accusations.

Tom had distanced himself from the campaign since their tense confrontation after the lost petition, and this was of great regret to Sean. They had been close friends and allies since the start of the protest movement, and he relied on Tom's steady hand.

Sean stepped to the front of the cart to address the crowd. 'Our next step, brothers and sisters, is a national turnout, and we will remain on strike until the Charter becomes law.' Rousing cheers drowned out his subsequent words.

Lingering beyond the stalls of vegetables and gingerbread, Sean spied Tom. He lifted the hailer in his direction. 'What d'you say, Reverend Shaw, will you join us in our struggle? We need everyone's support.' He watched Tom hesitate for a long moment, then, with relief, weave his way through the throng towards the farm cart.

'I appreciate this could be the greatest show of industrial strength ever witnessed in this country,' Tom shouted up at the stage. 'But remember our motto: peace, law and order. The Chartists are known for the discipline of their campaign and that's the way we will win through. We must *not* resort to physical violence.' His voice was practically drowned out by booing hecklers as he continued. 'It will endanger all the goodwill we have so painstakingly built up. We cannot hope for success without the patronage of those in Parliament who can intervene on our behalf.' He raised his voice to a roar. 'D'you really want the last five years of hard-fought campaigning to have been wasted? You have my support, but only if it's a peaceful demonstration.'

Elias seized the loudhailer from Sean, a wild look in his eye. 'Don't listen to that blaggard,' he said, shaking his fist in Tom's direction. 'Everywhere the army is being mustered, we'll 'ave no chance if we don't fight back. What does a man of God know of the lives the rest of us have to live? Whatever ee claims, ee's still one of them, an ignorant middle-class pig.'

A few volatile voices shouted in agreement and an egg splattered on Tom's shoulder. Sean wrestled the hailer back from Elias.

'You're right to remind us, Reverend Shaw. We are not here to destroy property or harm others. Our message is simple: to withdraw our labour, and encourage others to do the same until our demands are met.' He paused to assess the reaction of his audience, who now shuffled uneasily, muttering among themselves. Adopting a tactic he had seen Tom use many times to calm a crowd, he spread his hands, palms down in a wide, dramatic gesture.

'Quiet, please; I must have your attention. I have some important information to pass on.' Gradually a hush settled, until even the clopping of a horse's hooves could be heard fading into the distance.

'Friends, listen well. In the next few days we will be

given the date when our first march will take place. Once the message reaches this town a bell-ringer will tour the streets asking you to assemble here at dawn the following day.' Sean paused to shake the loudhailer. 'We will join the procession as it passes through Halesden, closing every factory in our path. Men, women and children will walk together in a show of unity.' He paused to let the enormity of what he was saying sink in before raising his voice. 'There'll be ten thousand of us assembled in Burnley by midday... and not a single mill in operation!'

'And make sure you bring yer pikes and clubs with you,' Elias bellowed above the uproar. 'Daggers and muskets too if you 'ave them.'

The crowd erupted, and with a sinking heart Sean watched Tom turn his back and walk away.

Chapter 34

17th August 1842

'Luk, sir, luk beyond the turnpike road – you can see the church spires, and the factory chimneys!' The children scrambled towards the schoolroom windows and stood on tiptoe. The pall of smoke that habitually hung like a shroud over the towns on still days had drifted away. The distant view was bright and sharp.

'You're right, lad,' said Luke. 'The air is as clear as on a sunny day in the hills. I must let them know down in the village. He turned to his wife. 'Agnes, take charge while I go and find Mr Gasson and Mr Shaw.' He grabbed his hat and headed off at a run towards Long Mill. Mopping his forehead with his handkerchief, he knocked firmly on the door of the site office, and walked straight in. Here he found both Andrew and Tom in discussion with one of the machine engineers.

'Quick! Come outside. The sky is free of smoke from here to Accrington. 'Come and look for yourselves.'

Andrew shaded his eyes from the sun. 'They've done it, they've damn well done it – the marchers have closed down all the factories in their path.'

Unable to disguise the dismay in his voice, Luke asked, 'D'you think they'll be coming this way? We're a long way off the direct route to Burnley.'

'Aye, but they've got everything well organised,' Tom replied through gritted teeth. 'The plan was for small contingents to peel off so every mill and factory is included. The aim is to collect thousands of supporters before the final entry to Burnley. They're not going to pass us by.'

Luke saw the colour drain from Andrew's face as he paced about.

'How do we handle this, Tom? It could put all our employees' livelihoods in jeopardy.'

'Let your workers know what's happening and then carry on as usual until they arrive… and keep the gates open as a sign of co-operation. I cannot think of any other way. Luke and I will be at your side when they arrive. If you offer support for this one-day turnout we may get away without any damage to the machinery.'

Within the hour a pulsating, hypnotic beat of drums could be heard approaching. Responding, as if drawn by the bagpipes leading a Highland army, the villagers, old men, pregnant women and grandmothers clutching the hands of pre-school children, drifted down the side streets and gathered in front of the mill. As the throbbing grew closer they were joined by the factory workers, who tumbled out of the mill and formed a tight-knit group behind their master.

Once the procession rounded the final bend it was apparent the march was about forty strong. At the head half a dozen women, their camisoles pulled off their shoulders and skirts hitched up because of the heat, were singing a Chartist hymn. Behind the men, brandishing their weapons, were flanked by constables bearing truncheons.

'Luk at the banners… and Jesus, luk at the points on those pikes,' a young woman standing behind Luke cried out in alarm. Luke's heartbeat quickened. He had never shared Tom's political commitment and did not have his physique.

He was content with his niche as a good teacher, improving the life chances of the youngsters in his care, and any ambitions he had were for his daughters. He recognised a small number of the supporters, but most were strangers. Listening to the coarse comments and rough accents he suspected some were railway navvies, perhaps being paid by those who either supported the Anti-Corn Law League, or weren't averse to the closing down of mills when they had no orders.

Their leader, who pushed through to the front as they approached the gates, was no stranger. It was Elias Bennett. At his shoulder loomed a solidly built red-bearded fellow, with a Cornish accent. The shouting and cursing from the followers made it clear there was already liquor taken and they were spoiling for a fight.

Tom walked calmly towards the mob, as though approaching a herd of frightened animals whose reaction he couldn't predict.

'Bugger off, you! We're 'ere to speak to the ventriloquist.' Elias raised his voice amid laughter. 'To demand he turns off the power to the looms, and lets 'is workers join our march to Burnley.'

Andrew Gasson stepped forward to join Tom. 'Good day, my friends.' His voice was strong and authoritative. 'I am fully committed to the cause you are demonstrating on behalf, and will willingly close down for today in support of the Charter. Those of our employees who wish to join you do so with my blessing... but I cannot promise anything beyond that.'

'That ain't good enough,' grumbled a voice in the crowd. 'You tell 'em, Elias.' Elias pulled a flask from inside his jacket, took a long swig and passed it to his companion.

'D'you realise in Manchester children are starving 'cause their fathers and mothers have no work? Show some compassion.' He hawked and spat on the ground in front of Andrew.

'I'm fully aware of their plight, but a long strike will not help their situation.'

The brutish Cornishman strode forward and seized the lapels on Andrew's jacket, a gnawing hatred in his eyes. 'We 'aven't time to waste with yer talking.'

'You show 'im, Davy,' a scrawny young woman with festering sores on her arms called over his shoulder. 'We're right behind yer.'

The throng began grumbling among the ranks and an agitated cry came from the rear. 'Charge thro' the gates… charge thro' the gates.' A constable raised his truncheon in Davy's direction – but changed his mind and dropped his arm.

'Elias, think, man!' Tom shouted above the hubbub. 'No one here wants to raise a fight with our master. We respect him and he's offered his support. It's our political leaders we have a quarrel with, not our employers… and force is not the way.'

'Who's this damn fellow?' slurred Davy, releasing his grip on Andrew and staring menacingly at Tom. 'Why should we listen to 'im?'

Luke looked hard into the face of the speaker with the dilated pupils; there was something familiar about him. 'It's Tom Shaw. He's been a leading activist for the Chartist cause in Halesden for several years… and he's our priest,' Luke said.

'Ah, God's puppet,' Davy mocked, standing with hands on hips waiting for a reaction. 'Your offer's not good enough, Reverend. We need the support of every man for as long as it takes. I lost a brother at Peterloo – bayoneted by the military. They don't care about us.'

Elias pointed his pike in Tom's direction. 'We 'ear tell there are two thousand soldiers out on the streets of Manchester and unknown numbers in Burnley. That's why we're armed – to fight back. You're a coward, Tom Shaw.'

Luke watched Tom clench his fists before looking questioningly at Andrew.

'This rabble is fired by emotion and fuelled with alcohol,' Andrew whispered. 'If you offer to go with them you may be able to exercise some control.'

Tom frowned. 'I'll join you on your march,' he spoke up, 'and I'm sure some of our friends here will too. But first let me fetch my jacket.'

He turned his back on the mob, and as he did so the cry went up once more. 'Charge thro' the gates!'

The swarm of men and women lunged forward, wielding their weapons indiscriminately. Tom threw an arm round Andrew to pull him away from the onslaught, but as he did so was struck a vicious blow on the side of his head by Davy. He stumbled across a low stone wall and fell awkwardly to the ground, blood pulsing from a deep gash above his ear. Luke dropped to his knees and pressed his necktie to his head to staunch the flow. The incendiary language of the belligerent mob assaulted his ears as they swept through the factory like a team of road cleaners, wrenching the plugs from the engines as they went. Tom's leg stuck out at an unnatural angle and Luke feared the worst.

Their mission accomplished, Davy, as a last gesture, threw a lighted taper under a shed where rubbish and oiled rags were stored. Flames shot skywards, and served as a signal to the children, who had been kept in safety at the school by Agnes, to come charging down the hill. The whole community clustered together like frightened sheep, as the marchers went whooping and laughing on their way.

281

Chapter 35

Sick with fear, Betha brushed down her dusty skirt and leant against a wall. The streets around were uneasily quiet; yet the shouting, swearing and pistol shots still rang in her ears. The square was littered with abandoned banners, broken glass, loose stones and general detritus. Young Sam sat, head in hands, on the steps of the town hall and a moan came from a nearby doorway. Betha kicked at a child's boot in frustration. It slid across the blood-spattered cobbles. She shook her head in disbelief at how the day had ended.

Escorted by Sean and her two sons, Betha had left Halesden in a grey dawn.

Her enthusiasm had risen with the sun as Sean, waving a Chartist banner, led the procession through lines of clapping onlookers to join the main parade on the turnpike road. When they passed Riding Mill the chimney was smokeless and the gates firmly closed. The same applied to each factory they passed on their way out of town. There were no confrontations, and Betha could not help but feel proud of her brother. She found herself walking in step with a sprightly young lass in a forget-me-not blue dress, who told her she was in service at Inglestone Manor, the residence of Mr Hargreaves.

'It 'appens t'be my day off,' the girl said. 'I only get one a month but I just couldn't miss this opportunity.' Her eyes shone. 'I've nivver been out of Halesden before. There'll be 'ell to pay if the master ever finds out.' She laughed merrily.

'I admire your spirit,' said Betha, 'but take care travelling on your own. Have you made plans for getting home?'

'I've two brothers up ahead,' she responded cheerfully. 'They'll look after me.'

At each crossroad they mingled with columns coming from other quarters, and Betha took time to study those around her. Ragged children clutched the hands and skirts of their parents. Shabbily dressed women stooped to pick up stones from the side of the road, storing them in their aprons. Young boys strode out, swaying their banners, voices raised with excitement. Men flaunted pikes embedded with files; their rowdy, drunken behaviour leading to personal skirmishes breaking out in the ranks.

On reaching the outskirts of Burnley drums rolled in time with the tramping feet, and the marchers broke into song. The procession slowed almost to a standstill as they filtered towards the town centre and a wild-eyed girl hurled a stone at a shop window. On hearing the shattering of glass others joined in and the special constables retaliated with their truncheons. Soon the women were pelting the constables with stones.

'I'll forge ahead,' said Sean. David wants to come with me, but Sam will be safer staying with you.'

'Tek care,' Betha called after them anxiously. 'Don't get mixed up in any violence.' Feeling the pressure of the human tide from behind she found it difficult to breathe, and in the stifling midday heat the stench of unwashed bodies was repellent. She linked her arm with Sam's and manoeuvred them both to the perimeter of the square where, mingling with the crowd, a detachment of the Lancaster Yeomanry circled, bayonets at the ready. Down a side street she spied horses, mounted by the militia, prancing restlessly. All the while her eyes searched anxiously for a sight of Tom.

The first of the Chartist leaders mounted the steps of the town hall, and standing on a makeshift dais, raised his hand for silence. Betha caught his first words.

'Comrades, we are no longer prepared to be treated as slaves…' From then on his voice was drowned out by bursts of cheering. A movement above drew her eye to an overhanging balcony which looked down on the square. Here three soldiers stood to attention; muskets cocked. One, brandishing a loudhailer, put it to his mouth and, shouting over the speakers below, read the Riot Act. Betha could sense the hostility disseminating through the crowd as, crushed together, they stood their ground and retaliated by chanting Chartist slogans and singing protest songs.

Shots cracked above the heads of the masses, and an army of police and foot soldiers battled their way through to the town hall steps. Here they seized the ringleaders, and those standing nearby. The mob surged forward in an attempt to release their comrades, and confusion reigned when a hail of missiles were directed towards the militia. Standing on tiptoe Betha caught sight of Sean being manhandled towards a waiting coach.

The ensuing fracas was brought to an abrupt standstill when a clatter of trotting hooves burst forth from the side streets. Men and women gathered the children in their arms and pulled each other by the hand as the cavalry stampeded through, grabbing banners and mowing down anyone in their path. All she could hear was the thump of retreating feet as the crowd withdrew, like a retreating wave sucking all within its path.

The smell of gunpowder wafted in the air, and she

witnessed a horse rear its front legs, kicking out at a young woman who toppled to the ground. A man nearby dragged her away, blood spurting from her mouth; it was the girl in the blue dress. She clambered onto a low wall and craned her neck above the fleeing crowd, frantically searching for a sight of David or Tom. How long she had stood there, bewildered and frightened, she didn't know; but now she found herself alone.

'Time to go home, missy.' An elderly, moustached constable put out his hand to help her down. 'What a disastrous day.' He shook his head. 'Are you far from home?'

Betha looked at him blankly. 'What's happened to the speakers, the Chartists, the ones standing on the steps?' she stammered.

'Bad news, missy, they've been taken into custody. I fear it could be the end for some of them. Not the outcome they deserve in my view. Did you perhaps know any of them?'

'Aye.' She stumbled over to her son and tapped him on the back. 'Time to go home, Sam.'

It was the early hours of the morning when Betha, boots in hand, reached Tom's door. Sam limped at her side. Receiving no answer to her knock she lifted the latch, and stumbled into the shadowy interior.

'They've arrested our Sean and David is missing,' she blurted out. 'They say it could be the death penalty for the leaders.' She burst into a paroxysm of hot tears as she collapsed in a heap on the floor, next to the bed.

Tom pulled himself up to a sitting position, and reached out to touch her. 'Betha, I'm so sorry. Tell me what happened. What went wrong?'

'Everything went bloody wrong. Before the meeting even started the marchers were spoiling for a fight, firing missiles, shouting abuse.' She sniffed, wiping her nose on her sleeve. 'Once we arrived in town the police and troops were everywhere in far greater numbers than anyone expected; there must have been hundreds gathered in the square and side streets. The demonstration had barely started when they read the Riot Act. It was when we stood firm, refusing to disperse and go home, that the military retaliated. First there were shots over our heads; then the cavalry charged.' She paused for breath and drew her legs up under her chin.

'I was so scared. I saw Sean with some of the other leaders being carted away – then the horses stampeded. I saw a young girl from Halesden being kicked in the face by one frightened stallion. I'd been talking to her earlier on the march – such a pretty, innocent young thing now covered in blood.' The memory revitalised her anger as she raged. 'Damn you, Tom Shaw, why weren't you there?' She beat her fists on the bedcover. 'We needed your support. I expected better of you… and Sam here says you're a traitor.'

'From what you've just told me I could have done nothing,' Tom said.

'You were always good in a fight. If you'd been there you could have lowered the temperature, brought some calm to the situation. You'd have known what to do,' she added accusingly.

Tom shook his head. 'I could have done nothing,' he repeated calmly before asking, 'How did you manage get back here alone?'

'We just kept walking – on and on. Good Lord, where's Sam?' In her irate state she had temporarily forgotten his existence.

'Curled up asleep, over in the corner.' Tom pointed, a hint of amusement in his voice.

'We overtook several groups sheltering in barns. Some were nursing their wounds; some waiting for their strength to return; some just hoping their hangovers would pass. Most of the injuries we saw were superficial, but it's rumoured there'd been deaths at the hands of the military. It was all so frightening.' She sighed deeply. Finally her swollen eyes adjusted to the dim light and she focused on Tom. His head was swathed in bloodstained bandages.

'Tom, what's happened t'you? What did you do to your head?' She was horror-struck to see Tom swing his splinted leg over the side of the bed and begin to explain.

'I knew as soon as the marchers arrived here it wasn't really Chartist-led. Elias Bennett was at the head and accompanied by an aggressive element: a Cornishman called Davy Pascoe, whom Luke thought he recognised, and navvies from other areas... not our regular supporters. We volunteered to join them on the march, but they stormed through the gates and this fellow Davy took me off guard. He landed a punch, I lost my balance and fell over a wall, breaking my leg. I'm not as agile as I was when I first came to Lancashire,' he added ruefully. 'I could do nowt to help after that.'

Betha was mortified. 'Oh Tom, I didn't stop to think... to look. I didn't even notice you'd been hurt, I was so bound up with my own problems. I'm so sorry.'

'I'm sorry too,' Tom replied, 'and desperately so if Sean and possibly David have ended up in custody.'

'Does this mean we've failed?' Betha asked. 'Will this be the end of the campaign?'

'It's much too early to say. We've been fighting a just cause, no one can deny that, but a different long-term strategy is needed.'

Betha laid her head on the red-stained pillow beside Tom. He placed an arm across her limp body, and soothed her as though she was a child until she relaxed. It was the tenderest of moments, lying motionless beside him in the peace and quiet of his cottage. Within minutes she had sunk into a deep, dreamless sleep.

Chapter 36

Different versions of the events in Burnley circulated; some obviously exaggerated, none that could be confirmed. Similar confrontations had taken place throughout the industrial heartland, and all had been brought under control by the authorities. Tom had no contact with Betha's family, but a message reached him through the Chartist grapevine that David had found his way home unharmed. Within a couple of weeks Sean, and the other leaders from the district, were released on bail.

After the turbulent summer the government speedily re-established order throughout the country, and if their jobs still existed the workers drifted back to the mills. A week of heavy rain sluiced out the pools and filled the river so Long Mill, no longer dependent on steam, was once again working at full capacity to complete the French order. September brought an abundant harvest, leading to a drop in the price of bread and relieving much of the poverty. By October enthusiasm for the strike had worn itself out.

An unexpected visitor hailed Tom as he perched stiffly on the stone bench outside his cottage. It was David. Overjoyed to at last have contact with the Lewis family, he ushered him to sit down.

'Mam asked me to call by if I had an opportunity,' said

David. 'To let you know she hasn't been able to come over, or make contact, because Father has come home.'

The news struck Tom like a hammer blow. He managed to keep his voice light, concentrating on asking appropriate questions. 'And how is your father?'

'Ee's in a bad way, sick and very bitter. Ee's making Mam's life a misery.'

'What's he been doing these last few years? He must have earned his freedom long ago.'

'He took on his allocation of land in Australia and tried to make a go of farming, but lost all the money he had saved for his passage home when the creek dried up. He didn't have the skills needed for the outdoor life, and was too ashamed to let us know. It was his local church that eventually paid for him to return.'

'That must've been a bitter blow for him,' Tom said, 'and hard for your mother to deal with someone so dejected. Perhaps Sean can get him interested in the Chartist cause? I remember the rector at Halesden saying he was an educated man.'

'I doubt if anything would interest him,' David sighed. 'Anyway, the campaign in Halesden has come to a standstill and Sean is talking about going back home to Belfast.'

'Would it help if I paid you all a visit?' asked Tom. 'Andrew could give me a lift when he next goes into town.'

'Nah,' David said with emphasis. 'Mam specifically asked me to tell you to keep away.'

Winter set in. Tom continued conscientiously with his duties, but no longer able to make the journey to Halesden on foot, had been forced to abandon his political interests. His greatest sadness was losing contact with Betha, Sean and the boys. He had cleared the air with

Betha, but was unsure what bitter feelings might still rankle within Sean.

Unable to shake off the sense of futility and disappointment which now bore down on him, his mind kept returning to Jos. The letter he had read out to Hannah was so full of optimism and drive. For perhaps the first time in his life he put himself in Jos's shoes and recognised the frustration and jealousy he must have experienced as a young man, unable to foresee a change in his future. Education had raised Tom above his childhood friend, but an old longing was returning for the simple life they had shared, where he could smell the earth and live in harmony with the seasons. When a letter arrived from Edward, informing his Uncle Tom that the long-serving curate at Ravendale had died and there was a vacancy waiting to be filled, Tom began to question where his future lay. The salary was poor, but to return to his old haunts, support the rural community, and inspire the few children remaining in the dale was a strong draw. He submitted a written application. No interview was necessary; there was no competition for the post. In due course he was approved by Lord Lowther and appointed by the bishop as the perpetual curate of the tiny dale parish.

Betha arrived early for Tom's final service at Clattonbury, and found a seat, partly hidden by a pillar, near the front. David and Sam had escorted her but she had been unable to persuade Sean to join them.

'You get off. I'll mind Arthur for the day. Say goodbye to Tom for me, thank him and wish him all the best for the future.'

She appreciated the offer, but suspected the true reason was that he felt unable to face his friend and political ally after the anguish of the march, and disappointment of the last few months.

She looked about with interest. It was the first time she had set foot in this church with its plain walls and wooden floor. With no moulding on the supporting pillars, no elaborate tracery on the font and no stained glass windows, it was in stark contrast to the old church at Halesden. Her heart pounded as Tom stepped up to the pulpit. His hair was thinning at the temples and the lines between nose and mouth were now deeply etched, but he was still a handsome man. She listened intently as he reworked the same text from Psalm 121 that he had taken on his first Sunday in Halesden, more than a decade earlier. Words had been his currency then, and he used them well today as he recounted his experiences during his time in Lancashire; the highlights, the disappointments, his admiration for the Chartists and love for his parishioners. He contrasted the geographical influences on his life; the peace of the mountains and dales against the invigorating challenges of the industrial landscape. Her eyes never left his face.

'Finally,' he said, 'I wish to show how happiness is within the grasp of us all. Rather than another quote from the Bible, good book that it is, I give you the closing lines of one of William Wordsworth's odes. I hope the words will speak to you as they always have to me.

> *'To me the meanest flower that blows can give*
> *Thoughts that do often lie too deep for tears.'*[10]

His eyes drifted round the congregation, where every seat and square foot of standing room was taken. Was it her imagination or was he seeking her out?

Andrew Gasson stepped forward after the final prayer

and presented Tom with a gift from the community, a miniature home communion set. She observed the wondering smile on his face as he lifted the lid on the velvet-lined presentation box to reveal an engraved silver chalice, paten and wine ewer. She knew he would never have owned anything so fine before. She also understood it would be a well-used gift in the scattered community to which he was returning.

A soft covering of snow had fallen whilst they were in church, and temporarily smoothed and hushed the landscape. Stepping out into the crisp air she could not face the pain of a final goodbye so stood at a distance, under the dry shade of an old yew tree, to wait and watch.

Tom shook first Sam's and then David's hand, and embarked on a lengthy conversation before embracing them both.

'What did he say?' she asked her sons when they joined her. 'Did he ask about me?'

'He told us to keep the flame burning. He is relying on us to continue Sean's work for emancipation, as one day in our lifetime we will get the vote… and he asked us to take special care of you.'

She turned her head away and dabbed her cheek with the back of her hand.

The worshippers slowly melted away, but Betha refused to move until she saw Tom take Agnes's arm and limp down the hill, accompanied by Luke and his daughters. He did not look back.

Chapter 37

Leaning heavily on his stick, Tom looked down from the stony pathway onto the farmhouse sheltering at the head of the valley. Hot and weary from the trudge across the Shap fells, he perched on a broken wall and took a deep breath of bracing mountain air. A friendly breeze fanned his face.

Time after time in the cotton towns he had sat in choking smoke and squalor by the bed of a dying parishioner. Together they had recalled the clarity of the air and allure of the rural lives they had once led. Now, overwhelmed with memories of the halcyon days of his own childhood, he could recall every intimate detail of the homestead and barns spread below. The porch had been limewashed by the new owner, but he could still smell the dung in the yard, imagine starched white aprons flapping on the washing line, hear a sweet voice singing in the dairy and feel the smooth stones in the yard beneath his feet. But the cluster of buildings maintained their indifference. He was a stranger. Tom knew he would visit again, probably many times because it was within his small parish, but Ravendale Head was no longer home.

He retraced his steps to the tiny church where the vicarage, now uninhabitable because of frequent floods, was used as a cow byre. He paused again and looked upwards – what remained unchanged was the skyline, the fells and mountains piling range upon range. They still offered the continuity he craved.

'Tom! Tom Shaw!'

Tom looked about. A distinctive whistle, the welcome siren call they had used to contact each other as boys echoed up the valley, and a figure emerged between the hedges of starburst hawthorn bounding the path.

'Welcome home,' Richard Green called out. 'Did ee have a gud journey?'

'Aye, I picked up the coach at Lancaster. It arrived early so I cut across country without bothering to stop off in Shap.'

'So ee haven't heard the news?'

'What news? I've spoken to no one until now.'

'Jos Teasdale turned up yesterday – quite unexpectedly.'

Tom steadied himself against the wall as his face drained of colour. 'Have you seen him?'

'Aye, ee looks fit and prosperous. He's come home to take Hannah and Edward back to Australia.'

Tom set down his bag and wiped the cold sweat from his brow with his sleeve. 'I'd hoped to stay temporarily at Highburn,' he said. 'I'll need to make alternative arrangements.'

'No room at the inn, eh!' Richard laughed. 'Ee can stay with us. Our youngest lad is trying his luck in Kendal so you can have his bed.'

A distant figure could be seen approaching Richard's farm. It was early for a social call. The large felt hat suggested someone from foreign parts, and as he drew nearer Tom couldn't fail to recognise the easy gait. When the visitor rounded the last bend he stepped out onto the road to meet Jos on neutral territory. They shook hands with the formality of two lawyers at their first encounter. Despite their years spent in the wider world, they were still held in check by the strong northern trait of withholding emotion when an issue ran deep.

Jos's sunburnt face exhibited a confidence and worldliness as he took the initiative. 'Let's go for a stroll and catch up on the years,' he said, with the hint of an unfamiliar twang. Tom nodded and picked up his stick. Without further exchange they slipped into an easy rhythm, drawn like migratory birds towards the ascent dominated by Harter Fell.

Tom broke the silence. 'It seems strange to be walking here without dogs playing at our heels. I must find a collie as soon as I can. D'you remember Nell and Remy?'

'How could I forget? The best companions we boys ever had.' Both faces softened into smiles as they shared a lifetime of unspoken thoughts.

'I think it's time we stopped buggerin' aboot,' Tom chuckled. 'Tell me everything I need to know about Australia.'

As the story unfolded the floodgates opened. Jos recounted his experiences of the tedious, claustrophobic journey, the desolate landscape, the overbearing heat, the prehistoric wildlife, the Aboriginal people and the terror of the bush fires.

'But it's a country which holds great promise for the future,' he said with enthusiasm. 'Virgin land beyond the settlements is cheap, and if you choose well it will support sheep. That's what I plan to do: buy a run and rear sheep, just like I did here; but this time I'm confident I'll make a good living.'

'You're going to need capital to get set up. And who'll buy your fleeces?' Tom asked.

'You're right. Most of the wool is shipped back to Europe so you only get paid once a year, and that could be a problem. I propose to breed wethers, that I can sell on immediately to those wanting to increase the size of their flocks. It will be hard physically, but will generate the working capital I need.'

'I've read that gold has been discovered in South Australia. Isn't that a temptation?'

'No!' Jos shook his head decisively. If gold fever takes hold it'll be like California – too many brigands. Australia is still a lawless country. I won't bore you with my own experience, but I have unfinished business in that respect when I get back.'

'Don't jeopardise your future again, Jos.'

'No fear of that.' He grinned. 'I've well and truly learnt my lesson.'

Their gaze was drawn skywards as a lone raven sailed overhead.

'You do realise I had to tell the truth at your trial,' said Tom, anxious to clear the air.

Jos took some time to respond, a look of concentration etched on his face as though he were anxious to choose the right words.

'I was angry and full of hate at the time – with everyone, and you in particular. Life seemed so unfair.' He ran his fingers through his hair in the characteristic comforting way he had had as a youngster.' But I realise it's the best thing that could ever have happened to me and I thank ee for it… now!' He grinned.

By the time they reached the tarn where they swam as boys, they were as comfortable with each other as they had been as youngsters. They settled side by side on a low rock and pitched loose stones into the silent pool, causing a pied wagtail to flutter off in alarm. Tom twisted the ring on his finger; the ring his mam had given him at the time of his ordination; the ring which had drawn him back like one of the shackled hawks on the Lowther Estate.

'It was the memory of peaceful places like this I returned to whenever life was getting me down in Lancashire,' he said wistfully.

'Not always so peaceful,' Jos reminded him. 'Half the Highburn flock once perished in these waters!'

Tom remained silent, unsure of Jos's response to the memory of that fateful night.

'Now just a ripple on the tarn… so much has changed since those days,' Jos continued before exhaling deeply. 'This place, the people… you and I. D'you know, Tom, the only woman who has stayed in my head over the years was your Lucy.' Just for a moment his voice faltered. 'And I did wrong by her.'

Tom bit his lower lip. 'So did I,' he blurted out.

Jos's eyes widened and a sudden breeze ruffled the surface of the black waters. 'The night of the bathing party… after the clip?'

'Aye.'

A gentle wave skated over the mossy stones on the shoreline. 'It seems she cast a spell over both of us,' Tom said ruefully.

'We canna wash away our past, but it's Lucy I'll thank for my future.' Jos's voice dropped. 'There's something I must confess to you, Tom. After Lucy died I felt so desolate and ignored I stole her writings from your da's barn where she told me she kept them. I wanted something to connect with her, to remember her by, and I was the only one who knew of their hiding place. I took them with me all the way to Australia in the lining of my fiddle case. On the outward passage there was an Irish chaplain, a good man. He helped those of us keen to improve our chances in the New World and I spent my days learning to read and write. I wanted to be able to read for myself the poems you used to recite to us, and I wanted to write like Lucy. By the time we reached Port Jackson I was literate.'

Tom sat quietly, not wishing to disrupt his flow.

'Lucy sustained me during that long sea passage. I know I raised her to the status of an angel in my dreams – her voice; her gentle, confident manner. At times she felt so real I thought she must still be alive.' He glanced up at Tom from beneath lowered lids, as if seeking a reaction. 'But I like to think I've followed her example, and she's changed my way of looking at the world.'

'We were surprised to have found so few transcripts after she died,' Tom said, 'but I'm glad you did what you did, really glad. Lucy couldn't have wished for a better legacy.'

Their moment of introspection was shattered by a rumbling blast from the nearby quarry. They laughed together as the birds took cover and lambs scampered in all directions seeking the protection of their mothers.

'Nowt changes round here,' said Jos with a shake of his head.

There was something else Tom needed to know. He focused on keeping his voice casual. 'Your Hannah would've been a wonderful mother to a large family. I've often wondered why you didn't have more children.'

'She wasn't keen,' Jos replied matter-of-factly. 'I felt I'd done enough harm and I didn't want to push her. I knew Hannah had always wanted you, but as my options were limited I was content to be second best. But thank you for giving me a wonderful son!'

'So Edward is my boy?' Tom struggled to keep his voice calm.

'Aye. I assumed you'd guessed. You always had a special bond with the lad. But I loved him too… as much as if he'd been my natural son.' He sprung to his feet. 'Now I'm off to see if I can spot any eagles. Edward tells me there are still several pairs over towards High Street.'

'I'd like to come with you,' said Tom, 'but this old leg won't let me walk far these days.'

'I was going to ask about that,' said Jos, 'when the time was right.'

'Now is as good as any. Sit back down and I'll tell you my story.' Tom narrated the tale of his years spent serving the cotton towns, his skirmishes with his employers in Halesden, his admiration for his employer at Clattonbury and his deep regret over the lost Chartist cause.

'That must've been a big disappointment.' Jos touched Tom's shoulder briefly. 'It's a longstanding injustice that has to be addressed sometime soon or there'll be serious trouble. At least you can take credit for helping to sow the seed.' He offered a hand to help Tom to his feet. 'Now I need to lay a few ghosts.'

Resting against a convenient rock Tom watched Jos stride away into the distance, his vigour symbolic of his future. His thoughts turned to Hannah; the conceiving and birth of Edward and the night following Jos's trial. Undemanding, God-fearing Hannah, who had made her wishes clear all those years ago. Slowly her plan was beginning to unravel.

Kneeling at the entrance to Hugh's Cave, Jos laid his cheek on the cool earth. The aromatic smell of damp peat and ling was a haunting reminder of forgotten emotions. Having been exiled for so many years he found the power of the location overwhelming. A trace of stale woodsmoke assaulted his nostrils as he unwrapped the oilskin packet. With trembling hands he lifted the journal and loose sheets of paper which had accompanied him to the other side of the world. He cast an eye over every page; each poem faithfully copied out by Lucy. The sketch of the eagle he had so faithfully reproduced; executed by Lucy. He hadn't lost her; in his head she would always be part of his life.

He searched the rock where he had carved their initials. Scraping away the lichen with his thumbnail, he found they were still there – he had done a good job. Maybe they would still be there in a hundred years, a symbol of what might have been.

Overcome with self-pity he sat motionless, staring down at his hands and reliving the long-buried incident that had taken place in this cave so many years before. From beyond the mountains, two large winged birds approached. Tears danced before Jos's eyes as the eagles swooped and displayed before turning in unison towards the coast, the last rays of sun on their gleaming backs; free spirits setting off into the sunset. He identified with their motivation. He knew exactly where his future lay.

Darkness had descended by the time he reached the lake, and Hannah and Edward were settled by a glowing fire when he arrived home. Hannah's fingers were busy as ever with a part-crocheted blanket, while Edward whittled away at a piece of wood cut from the crab apple tree which grew by the gate. Jos went into the scullery to remove his boots and wash his hands before joining his family. Restless to get started on their new life, he quickly turned the idle chat into a discussion on their future in Australia.

'You do understand, I've paid for a return passage?' Jos looked uneasily from his wife to his son; then turned back to Hannah for her response. Her calm but firm reply left him in no doubt that she would not be joining him.

'I'm sorry, Jos,' she said. 'I'm just not brave enough.'

He leant across and laid his hand on hers, not willing to challenge the internal strength he knew she possessed. 'I understand,' he said. 'Once I'm established I'll send money to make life easier for you here, and if ever you change your mind I'll come back and collect you.'

'Thank ee,' she responded in a shaky voice.

'And how about you, son?'

Edward looked questioningly towards his mother. 'Mam won't be able to manage here without me.'

'Of course I can.' She smiled encouragingly. 'God has given me everything I want here: good neighbours, the church... and Tom is back, ee'll luk after me. What I want for you, son, is a future and prospects. I know I'll miss sharing your successes and troubles but if ee write regularly, and tell us every detail of yer new life, I'll be proud and happy.'

Jos watched Edward blink to hold back the tears.

'Then I'd like to take my chance with Da.'

On the day the Teasdales were to leave for the New World a small band of well-wishers gathered at the crossroads. Tom was standing a little apart from the others when Jos approached.

'I'm pleased you'll be lodging with Hannah,' he said kindly. 'You'll be able to keep us all in touch by letter.' He fumbled in his coat pocket and pulled out a parcel. 'Here, Tom, this is yours now.'

302

'What is it?'

'You gave me your son, now I have something to give you... or rather to give back.'

Gripping the package, Tom began to peel back the worn cover, fold by fold. 'Lucy's commonplace book?'

'Aye, Wordsworth's poems have served me well. I've kept just the one. The slip of paper you gave me after her funeral.' Jos patted his chest. 'It'll remind me of everything I've left behind.'

'She'd have been so proud of how you've turned your life round, Jos.'

'Trust me, old friend, she'd have been proud of both of us.' He gripped Tom's shoulders. 'Brothers?'

'Aye, and this time we've changed the ending.'

Edward lingered until Jos had moved on before saying his last farewell to his Uncle Tom. Keeping his eyes firmly on the ground, he mumbled, 'Goodbye Da, look after Mam and the farm for us.'

For the second time Tom shook his head in amazement. Edward knew. He wondered if he had been told or just worked it out for himself. He took his son's strong hands in his own.

'Remember lad, who you are and what you make of your life will be based on what you learned from your da, here in this dale. You had the pick of teachers and I wish you both the best of luck.'

Tom followed Edward's eyes as he took a last searching look towards Highburn. There was no sign of his mother. He knew their last goodbye would have been said in the privacy of their home, and this he understood. He was comforted to know that Edward had Jos's steady hand to guide him.

The farewell party screwed up their eyes as the silhouettes grew smaller and smaller before disappearing around a bend in the track. As the little group turned away to their scattered homes two young deer leapt across the path ahead of them.

'Did ee see that?' called out Richard in delight. 'They must be sheltering up in the forest. What do ee think, Tom? Have ee any plans for tonight?'

Tom responded with an enigmatic smile.

Hannah, unable to settle to her routine tasks, was pacing round her vegetable patch when Tom returned.

'What's this?' she asked as she went to hang up his jacket.

'Just a few papers Jos gave me for safekeeping – documents he travelled with on his voyage out on the convict ship.'

Hannah pulled her shawl taut across her chest against the draught. 'Anything official will be better in your care,' she said innocently.

Chapter 38

Buttercups drifted across the meadows, pink pinnacles of foxgloves swayed in the gentle breeze, and skylarks swooped and sang overhead as Tom ambled up the Nan Bield track to meet his brother. Jonathon, now in his sixties, was still a fit man, holding the living at Troutbeck and the headmastership at the grammar school in Ambleside. His visit to Ravendale was to support Tom at his first service back in the dale.

Catching sight of him in the distance Tom hollered a greeting, then waited on the grassy bank alongside the cascading falls where they chatted about the weather, and Jonathan's journey.

'You may not have heard,' said Tom. 'Jos has been home and is taking Edward back to Australia with him. Hannah has chosen to stay here in the dale.'

'I did hear,' his brother replied. 'You'll miss Edward.'

'Aye, but I'm glad he's eager for adventure, and making the best of the opportunities life offers.' He laid down his stick and lowered himself onto the soft, springy turf. 'It's hard to believe now, but it was at this very spot that Jos, Lucy and I made all our plans when we were young. I used to read to them from the poetry book you lent me – then Lucy taught herself to read and write by copying them out.'

'Did she? I didn't know that. Our sister would have made her mark in the world if she'd lived.'

Tom broke off a piece of grass to chew. 'I think Lucy was the only woman I've ever really loved… and that was in vain,' he added hastily.

'You do know she wasn't really our sister?' said Jonathon.

The words hit Tom like a boulder pitching down the mountainside. 'Nay, nobody ever said that.' He waited, heart thumping, for further explanation.

'It was a closely guarded secret, not easy to achieve round here.' Jonathon smiled. 'Lucy was Mam's niece – the daughter of Aunt Mary who went to London with the Lowthers.'

'The refined woman, who turned up unexpectedly at the funeral?'

'Aye, that's the one.'

'Did you know who she really was then?'

'No, though I thought it a coincidence that she should happen to be in Shap on that particular day. Father disclosed her true parentage when we were discussing his will – around the time you went off to Lancashire. I assumed you'd been told as well. Apparently it all fell into place because Mam lost a baby within days of Lucy's birth. Lucy was brought back to Ravendale, and the family closed ranks. No mention was ever made of her origins again.'

'Did Lucy know?'

'I doubt it.'

'Did Da ever say who her father was?'

'He said it was someone from the literary community Mary had met at one of the London coffeehouses. I had the impression she had a reputation for being somewhat rebellious when she was a young girl. Whoever he was he paid over a tidy sum for Lucy's upkeep, or so Father said.'

'If only I'd known.'

'Why, would it have made any difference?

Tom focused his eyes on a beetle, scurrying past a nest of ants. 'It would have helped me understand things better,' he said.

Jonathon pulled out his clay pipe and tapped it on the ground. 'After Father died I received a letter from Aunt Mary, asking me to keep her informed of how her sister and family were faring. I think she retained an interest because she didn't have children by her husband. He was twenty-five years her senior.' Jonathon paused, as if not sure whether to continue. 'She mentioned that she had unexpectedly received a letter from Lucy, just a week before she died, in which she'd asked Mary to recommend her for a situation in London.' Jonathon shrugged.

'So Lucy was planning to run away to London on her own?' Tom could scarce believe it.

'It seems so. You know the ring Mam handed over when you were ordained? That was intended for Lucy when she reached twenty-one. Mam had the blacksmith enlarge it for you. It was the only keepsake from her father.'

'It's inscribed with the letter M.' Tom tugged at the ring. 'I wonder who "M" was?'

'Or could it have been a W?' Jonathon said in a casual voice.

Tom spat on his finger and twisted the gold band, but it had been there so long he was unable to slide it over his knuckle. The brothers sat, lost in their own thoughts, until Jonathon asked, 'D'you think you've made the right decision, coming back here?'

Tom knew his future was precarious, dependent on a

small stipend and what he could earn from the seventeen acres of fellside land which went with the living. 'I realise I'm clinging on to a way of life that's almost gone, but I've lost my energy for the urban environment. For as long as I live I'll never forget my arrival in Halesden, and the initial impression the town made on me.' He laughed at the memory. 'And things didn't improve: unhealthy conditions, conflict between the classes. Little time for banter, laughter or important things like wrestling and hunting! Education can separate you from the place you come from.'

'From what Luke has told me, you did an exceptional job for the community in Halesden and Clattonbury,' said Jonathon. 'That's something solid to take comfort from.'

'Mebbe, but I failed in my political mission when Chartism collapsed… and I lost close friends in the process.' Tom pulled a flask of whisky from his pocket and offered it to his brother. As the alcohol took effect his mood became more reflective.

'Jonathon, you've been a priest for forty years now. How confident are you there's life after death?'

His brother took time before replying. 'I'm inclined to agree with Tom Paine: *We only die when we fail to take root in others*. Perhaps that's all we can say with certainty… that's our eternal life.'

Tom laughed heartily, and with a sense of relief. 'So you too are a religious sceptic. Maybe growing up here has made us both pragmatic.' Cloud shadows raced across the fells and the solitary bleating of a lamb could be heard calling for its mother in the quiet of the late afternoon. 'This is the spirituality I understand,' said Tom. 'From now on this is my hallowed place.'

'But will living back here be enough, Tom? You flourished in a more challenging environment.'

'Hannah's crippling lack of ambition used to frustrate me... now she's shown me it's the sense of community that binds us. I look forward, with humility, to being the accepted leader here; no questions asked. I won't have to explain or justify the words of the Apostle's Creed or the teachings of the Old Testament; these are just part of the rituals that provide permanence and comfort. I'll leave the real adventuring to the next generation of Shaws,' he added with an inward glow of pride as he took another nip from the flask. 'Just look at these, brother.' He turned over his hands, displaying the palms to Jonathon. 'I need to hone my practical skills so I have the hands of a worker again. Now that would be something worthwhile.'

Tom kissed Hannah's cheek as he slipped out of their bed and dressed for the Sunday service. He walked purposefully down the lane and turned the key in the church door. It was chilly; he would need to get a fire going. He slipped on the frayed cream vestment which had belonged to his predecessor and hung on a nail behind the pulpit. Finally he tolled the single bell.

Slowly a few men and women could be seen coming down the path from the slate quarry, from across the beck and over the moorland. The little church would be full. Tom had returned to his own people where the church still had a hold on their hearts and minds, and he was free in a way no townsman could ever be.

'Priest Shaw, can ye pray for rain? My crops are shrivelling,' called out old Willie, the shepherd from High Gills.

Tom settled his eyes on the old man for a moment or two. 'It's no use praying for rain, old fella, while t'wind's in this quarter. Let's sing a hymn instead.'

Credits: Poems by William Wordsworth

1. *The Convict*
2. *Michael*
3. *Michael*
4. *The Brothers*
5. *Strange Fits of Passion Have I Known* (Lucy poem)
6. *Composed upon Westminster Bridge*
7. *To a Skylark*
8. *She Dwelt Among the Untrodden Ways* (Lucy poem)
9. *The Brothers*
10. *Intimations of Immortality from Recollections of Early Childhood*